READERS

'The per

☆☆☆☆☆

'Reading *The Baby Dragon Bakery* felt like curling up
with a warm pastry and a fuzzy blanket.'

☆☆☆☆☆

'Utterly enchanting! *The Baby Dragon Bakery* is a treat.
Sweet, cozy, and brimming with magic.'

☆☆☆☆☆

'The perfect book to cozy up with in front of the window
while it's raining with a cup of coffee.'

☆☆☆☆☆

'A cute cozy read that you won't want to put down!'

☆☆☆☆☆

'This series has my whole heart. I just loved everything about it.'

☆☆☆☆☆

'The connection between the characters is unmissable.'

☆☆☆☆☆

'I classify this as a sorbet of a romance. A little palate cleansing,
low stakes, feel-good, sweet characters, and sometimes
you just need something like this.'

☆☆☆☆☆

'Going into this I knew I would love it, but I didn't expect to be kicking
my little feet and squealing at how adorable this was throughout!'

☆☆☆☆☆

'An absolutely scrumptious tale of love, friendship and believing in
yourself and true love. And of course, lots of little dragons and the
odd, baby griffin and chimera!'

☆☆☆☆☆

'The characters and the world are so well-developed
I cannot wait to see what's next.'

☆☆☆☆☆

'The chemistry is electric. I loved seeing all the characters again and the gorgeous dragons. The cutest series ever!'

☆☆☆☆☆

'I definitely enjoyed getting lost in this world again, so if you like a cozy, romance, with some sweet dragons along for the ride, this one is for you!'

☆☆☆☆☆

'With its charming characters, magical world, and irresistible romance, *The Baby Dragon Bakery* is an absolute must-read for fans of the friends-to-lovers trope and cozy fantasy.'

☆☆☆☆☆

'I absolutely loved this book from start to finish, the minute I started reading it I just couldn't stop!'

☆☆☆☆☆

'A cozy series which will have you smiling throughout.'

☆☆☆☆☆

'This is a beautiful story of insecurities, friendship, love and finding your destined person. I enjoyed the journey so much.'

☆☆☆☆☆

'A true comfort read.'

☆☆☆☆☆

'A wonderful read!'

☆☆☆☆☆

'I love being part of The Baby Dragon Club!'

☆☆☆☆☆

'I absolutely loved this book.'

☆☆☆☆☆

'Such a cozy read.'

☆☆☆☆☆

'I loved this!'

☆☆☆☆☆

A. T. Qureshi is a Pakistani, Muslim American who adores words. She is the award-winning author under the name Aamna Qureshi of YA fantasy novel, *The Lady or the Lion* and its sequel, and the adult novel *If I Loved You Less*.

Aamna grew up on Long Island, New York, in a very loud household, surrounded by English (for school), Urdu (for conversation), and Punjabi (for emotion). Much of her childhood was spent being grounded for reading past her bed-time, writing stories in the backs of her notebooks, and being scolded by teachers for passing chapters under the tables. Through her writing, she wishes to inspire a love for the beautiful country and rich culture that informed much of her identity.

When she's not writing, she loves to travel to new places where she can explore different cultures or to Pakistan where she can revitalize her roots. She also loves baking complicated desserts, drinking fancy teas and coffees, watching sappy rom-coms, and going for walks about the estate (her backyard). She currently lives in New York.

**By the same author:**

Young Adult:
*The Lady or the Lion*
*The Man or the Monster*
*When a Brown Girl Flees*
*My Big, Fat, Desi Wedding*
*A Witch's Guide to Love and Poison*

Adult:
*If I Loved You Less*
*The Baby Dragon Cafe*

# The BABY DRAGON BAKERY

A. T. QURESHI

avon.

Published by AVON
A division of HarperCollins*Publishers* Ltd
1 London Bridge Street
London SE1 9GF

www.harpercollins.co.uk

HarperCollins*Publishers*
Macken House, 39/40 Mayor Street Upper
Dublin 1, D01 C9W8, Ireland

A Paperback Original 2025
25 26 27 28 29 LBC 9 8 7 6 5
Copyright © Aamna Qureshi 2025

Aamna Qureshi asserts the moral right to
be identified as the author of this work.

A catalogue record for this book is available from the British Library.

ISBN: 978-0-00-874293-5

This novel is entirely a work of fiction. The names, characters and incidents portrayed
in it are the work of the author's imagination. Any resemblance to actual persons,
living or dead, events or localities is entirely coincidental.

Set in Birka by HarperCollins*Publishers* India

Printed and bound in the United States

All rights reserved. No part of this publication may be reproduced,
stored in a retrieval system, or transmitted, in any form or by any means,
electronic, mechanical, photocopying, recording or otherwise,
without the prior written permission of the publishers.

Without limiting the author's and publisher's exclusive rights, any unauthorised
use of this publication to train generative artificial intelligence (AI) technologies is
expressly prohibited. HarperCollins also exercise their rights under Article 4(3)
of the Digital Single Market Directive 2019/790 and expressly reserve this
publication from the text and data mining exception.

For Justine,
my partner in crime.

# CHAPTER 1

It was a crisp evening at the end of September, and autumn was just beginning. The leaves had started to change color, lush greenery giving way to shades of red and orange and yellow. The air was brisk, the humidity of summer replaced with a slight chill in the night. The breeze smelled warm and earthy, like wood and amber. Black-scaled dragons flew in the air above the glittering party at the Sterling Estate, their eyes shining like purple jewels.

Lavinia Williams wrapped her arms around herself, taking in the revelry as she sat on the side of the dance floor. Her feet ached from dancing for the last few hours at the home of her good friend Genevieve Sterling but, more relevantly, she was here for the engagement party of her other good friend, Saphira Margala, who had recently become engaged to Genevieve's brother, Aiden.

The party was outside, taking advantage of the stunning estate and this perfect in-between weather, not too summer-hot nor too wintry-cold. String lights twinkled above the dance floor and the outdoor tables, while more tables were set up under canopied tents lit with glowing lanterns. A live string quartet played music, while waiters walked around with fizzing flutes of champagne, handing drinks to the remaining guests dressed in their very finest gowns and suits.

Lavinia was beyond happy to be at one of her best friend's engagement parties. Ever since Saphira and Aiden had gotten together last spring, Lavinia had watched as her already bright best friend grew more and more radiant, lit from within with a joy that was incomparable.

Here the happy couple was now, joining the few people left on the dance floor. The party was nearly over, and mostly everyone had gone. It was very late in the night, or very early in the morning—Lavinia had lost track of time.

On the dance floor, Aiden reached for Saphira's hand. He had been in an expertly tailored suit earlier, but had since shucked off the jacket and tie. The top few buttons of his white dress shirt were undone, the sleeves rolled up. As for Saphira, her hair had been up in a complicated updo, but it was half down now.

The massive engagement ring on her left hand sparkled. It was a gorgeous basalt stone surrounded with diamonds, set on a gold band; Lavinia loved the gold accent. She admired the six gold bangles jingling on Saphira's right arm as Aiden lifted her hand and twirled her.

Saphira held up the end of her white silk dress, twirling on her bare tiptoes. She would wear purple at the wedding that June, for the basalta dragons that she and Aiden were claimed by, hence the white now.

As Saphira's bridesmaid, Lavinia had been given the rundown on the Drakkon family customs in which Saphira would partake. Saphira and Aiden's baby dragon, Sparky, flew overhead, playing with the other Sterling dragons, the adult dragons letting the babies fly around them.

The happy couple sang to each other as they danced, their eyes locked, smiles wide on both their faces. Once, Lavinia had thought Aiden to be awkward and stoic, and while he was still more the strong and silent type around everyone else, with Saphira, he was as dazzling as her, two stars shining in the night sky, sparkling together.

There could have been a hurricane or a tornado and neither would have noticed, they were so entranced with one another. Then Aiden sang the lyrics wrong, and Saphira threw her head back with open-mouthed laughter. Aiden gathered her into his arms, kissing her neck, and Lavinia's chest felt tight.

She had to look away from Aiden and Saphira, the scene was so intimate. It felt intrusive to watch, and while she was overjoyed that her friend had found such a fairy-tale love, the scene made her ache. She yearned for a love like theirs—for a love like the one she had witnessed her own parents share her entire life.

Lavinia had always looked up to her parents, basking in the warmth of their beautiful relationship, the way they loved each other. She adored her mother, especially, and wanted to be just like her.

Her mother, Beena, had met Garrett, her future husband, the winter after she had turned twenty-four, and now Lavinia was fast approaching that same time, with winter just around the corner. A frisson of stress shot through her, making her feel agitated.

Then a man approached her, a drink in each hand, and Lavinia felt flustered for altogether different reasons.

"Here you go." Theo Noon handed Lavinia a crystal goblet, and she gratefully accepted the chilled drink. Theo was Lavinia's best friend, and had been since they were children. They were both twenty-four now, much changed from the eight-year-olds they had been when they had first met. Where in the past they had run through garden sprinklers in the summer together, now they attended engagement parties. Scenarios might have changed, but one thing remained: he was always her partner in crime, always by her side.

Theo was tall with wavy brown hair, which at its worst made him look like a mop but at its best, like tonight, fell into perfect curls that she wanted to wrap every one of her fingers around. He was wearing dress pants and a navy-blue button-up dress shirt, the sleeves of which—this late into the party—were rolled up.

Lavinia hardly ever saw him in formal wear, and he looked especially handsome tonight. She found it difficult to look away.

She had always thought him handsome, in a distant, objective way. Then, a few months ago, things suddenly stopped feeling objective and started feeling very, very personal. She didn't even know when it had happened, her developing feelings for her best friend but, after denying it to herself for some time, she found she could no longer pretend; there was no escaping what she felt.

The problem was that she didn't know how he felt. Sometimes she was so sure he felt a similar way, but then sometimes she couldn't tell at all. To make matters worse, there was no one whose second opinion she could seek.

She hadn't discussed it with anyone. Theo was her best

friend, which meant that he was the first person she told anything, but of course, she couldn't talk to *him* about it, and it felt wrong to discuss something with anybody else and not with him, and so she had been quiet.

"What is this?" Lavinia asked, shifting her attention to her drink. It was garnished with a cinnamon stick, and she took a sip as he sat down beside her. The liquid was cold and refreshing as it went down her throat, the flavor strong and surprising.

"An apple ginger fizz," he said, taking a sip from his own glass.

"Oooh. Fancy."

"And fun."

"My favorite combination," Lavinia said. Theo snorted.

"Your favorite combination is more like *chaos* and fun."

She waved her free hand. "Same thing."

They sat and watched the dance floor for a moment, both enjoying the general splendor.

"It's nice to see Saphira," Theo said. "I feel like it's been a while, even though it's probably only been a little over a week."

"I feel the same," Lavinia agreed.

There was a time when Lavinia would see Saphira almost every day, as she worked at Saphira's business, the Baby Dragon Cafe. Theo would also be a frequent visitor. He had a job at the Rolling Pin Bakery, which supplied Saphira's cafe, and would come by every few days to drop off bakery deliveries.

But now that Lavinia had just started her second year of vet school—where she studied mythical animals such as dragons, griffins, chimeras, and phoenixes—she didn't get the chance to see Saphira as much. She only worked at the Baby Dragon once a week, now, because she didn't have any other time with classes and her internship at the Animal Hospital.

Because the cafe was doing so well, Saphira had hired a lot more staff and wasn't there as much either; she oversaw things as the business's owner and manager, but spent less time with her boots on the ground.

"I kinda miss how things used to be," Lavinia said. Though it was fantastic that the cafe was doing so well and that she was in vet school, it had been fun to work with one of her closest friends, even when the busy routine had made her perpetually tired.

"I kinda miss it, too," Theo agreed. "Early morning deliveries were hell everywhere else, but I loved swinging by the Baby Dragon and seeing you and Saph and the little draggos." He smiled. "The free drinks weren't bad, either."

"God, I could go for a coffee," Lavinia said.

Theo elbowed her. "It's, like, four a.m. You don't need a coffee, you need sleep."

She ignored his comment, instead lamenting dramatically. "Now everyone's growing up and getting *old*," Lavinia said. "I mean Saphira is *engaged*."

Saphira was twenty-seven, and Aiden was twenty-nine, nearly thirty, but *still*. At the age of twenty-four, Lavinia felt that none of her friends should have been taking such adult steps.

Now that Saphira was engaged, she had officially moved out of her apartment on Main Street and into Aiden's cottage. For the past year, they had been back and forth between each other's places, but Saphira had moved out of her apartment entirely now. It made sense for her to move into Aiden's place, as the cottage was bigger, and his garden had space for their baby dragon, Sparky, who was turning two in October. Dragons matured after age two and continued developing until age five, at which point they were used for riding.

Lavinia was happy for her friend, but there was no denying that everything was different now, and it would only continue to grow more and more so as time went on. She knew she had two options: she could either resist it or embrace it.

She was attempting the latter, to be excited about all these new changes, but it was difficult. There were things to be positive about, but everything shifting in new and strange ways made her eye twitch.

"Come on," Theo said, finishing off his drink. He set his goblet down.

"Where?" she asked, doing the same. Theo shrugged, giving her a smile. He stood, offering her his hand, and she took it. She didn't need any plans when she was with Theo; they always managed to enjoy their time together, and they had done so since they were kids, spending hours and hours in each other's company at her house. When Lavinia looked back on those days now, she could never quite remember what they had done to keep themselves entertained, but she knew they had never tired of each other.

As they grew older, the hours were more often spent in talking, and they would discuss every single thought or emotion they were having, and when they ran out of even those, they would find other things to talk about. Sometimes, Theo would explain the entire plot of whatever fantasy show he was watching, detailing every storyline and character, the deviations being made from the books and lore. Other times,

Lavinia would inform him about the drama going on in her extended family, and describe what her distant cousins and aunts were getting up to.

It didn't matter how much time they spent together, if they felt like chatting, there was always something to talk about. When they were tired, they didn't need to talk; they could sit listening to music or in companionable silence.

Now, they walked around the outskirts of the party. The music changed from an upbeat dance tune to something slow and soft. Couples began slow-dancing, a romantic aura seeping into the environment. Lavinia shivered, biting her lower lip.

They continued walking, down a path under glowing string lights, until the music grew quiet. They were off to the side, alone, away from the party, its noises fading into the background. From here, they had a gorgeous view of the rolling hills and the mountains in the distance. It was a clear night, and the sky was studded with thousands of stars, twinkling and shining. It was where their home—Starshine Valley—got its name from.

Theo whistled. "Look at that view."

"It's stunning," she said. She loved their hometown, the comfort and familiarity of it.

They sat down, content to admire the landscape. The night felt cooler now, away from the dance floor and the lanterns. When a sudden breeze ruffled the trees, Lavinia squealed, huddling closer to her best friend.

"I told you to bring a sweater," Theo laughed.

"You know, instead of being a know-it-all, the gentlemanly thing to do would be to offer me your jacket," Lavinia told him pointedly.

"I left it behind," Theo replied, showing her his empty arms. "Come on—it isn't that cold."

"Do you see what I am wearing?"

She was wearing a corset midi dress made of maroon satin, and the thin fabric was doing nothing to ward off the night's chill. She was short and curvy, and while in her teens she had been insecure about her weight, now it was something she embraced. She loved to choose clothing that accentuated and flattered her body shape.

Theo looked down at her outfit, and as his eyes traveled back up to her face, his gaze snagged on the bare skin of her collar and shoulders, courtesy of the strapless dress. Lavinia's straight dark brown hair was held back with a stylish headband so there was nothing to obstruct her decolletage.

He clenched his jaw, and heat coursed through her.

With some apparent difficulty, Theo looked up. He rapidly blinked.

"Right," he said, clearing his throat. "Should I go grab my jacket, then?"

"No, that's okay," she said, voice high. He looked away, turning his gaze to the stars in the sky.

Lavinia's heart pounded. *Was she imagining it?* Moments like this, she thought that maybe, just maybe, he was as attracted to her as she was to him.

"Look," Theo said, pointing up at the stars. "Doesn't that look like a bow and arrow?"

"Where?" Lavinia asked. She shifted her focus to the sky, trying to see. "I can't see it."

"Right there," Theo pointed. She put her face beside his to see what he was seeing, but she couldn't make out the shape.

She pouted. "I don't see it!"

Theo laughed. "Look," he said, taking her hand. He brought her finger to the sky and drew along the stars, making the shape of a bow and arrow. Finally, she saw it.

"See?" he asked, turning his face to hers just as she turned to him, and then, they were mere inches apart.

The crooked grin tilting his lips froze, the mirth in his expression giving way to something else, something deeper. She took in a shuddering breath, inhaling the warm scent of his cologne.

His brown eyes darkened. Right then, she thought that he did feel the same way as she did. While she had known of her feelings for a few months now, she had never acted on them, too afraid to ruin the equilibrium between them, but maybe it was time. If Lavinia wanted to find love by the winter—the way her mother had—this was her perfect chance.

Her heart pounded with both trepidation and anticipation, fear and courage mixing together. His lips parted. They were so close she felt the heat of his body just beside hers, the breath exhaling from his lips. Desire spread through her, and courage overtook fear.

She drew closer, holding her breath. He inched toward her, and she felt the warmth of his body. Emotion spiked through her, too complex to comprehend, but it didn't matter, he was going to kiss her, she could see it on his face, feel the intention in his body.

She closed her eyes, heart soaring. She pursed her lips, drawing closer.

Suddenly, she felt cold air.

## CHAPTER 2

Lavinia opened her eyes and saw that Theo had jumped a foot back, no longer near her. It was like being doused by a bucket of ice water. He was avoiding looking at her. Horror at herself gripped her with frozen fingers.

"It's getting late," Theo finally said, and she was astounded by how normal his voice sounded. Lavinia herself was trembling, throat thick. "Do you want to head out?"

"Mhm," she managed to squeak out. Theo stood, turning toward her. He offered her his hand, but she did not take it. Her hands were shaking, and she didn't want him to see. She stood on her own, regret chilling through her. All the warmth from a moment ago was long, long gone.

As she followed Theo back to the party, staying a step behind him, she shook her head, mentally smacking herself. She could be so delusional. Of course he wasn't going to kiss her. God, she was so stupid.

Lavinia felt like her head was made of stone, it felt so heavy. Through a haze, she followed Theo to where Aiden and Saphira were on the side of the dance floor, sharing a glass of champagne.

"No, don't tell me you're leaving already!" Saphira said, pouting. She tossed her dark hair back over her shoulder, and Lavinia took a deep breath, giving her friend a brave smile.

"Unfortunately," Lavinia said. Usually, she would tease, or say something clever, but her brain was hardly working, still processing what had just happened.

"Thanks so much for coming," Aiden said, giving them both a warm smile.

"Congratulations again," Theo said, shaking Aiden's hand while Saphira gave Lavinia a hug. Lavinia reciprocated the hug quickly, not wanting to hold on for fear of letting her emotions overtake her. She could not be messy at her friend's engagement party; Saphira would worry and fuss, and that was the last thing Lavinia wanted.

When Lavinia pulled away from Saphira, she gave Aiden a hug as Theo kissed Saphira's cheek. Saphira glanced between Theo and Lavinia, her eyebrows crinkling slightly. As she was about to open her mouth, Lavinia heard someone call Aiden's name. They all said their goodbyes, but Saphira looked over her shoulder one last time as she was whisked away.

"I love you!" Saphira called, blowing a kiss. "See you soon!"

Lavinia went to say goodbye to Genevieve then, who was dancing with her grandfather, a jovial old man with snow-white hair. After they hugged, Genevieve gave Lavinia a curious glance, looking closely.

"You okay?" Genevieve asked, holding Lavinia's arm.

"Yeah, just tired." Lavinia forced a smile, then blew Ginny a kiss before heading to the valet, who brought round Theo's car. Lavinia got in, and once the door shut, she was enveloped in stifling silence as Theo drove her home. She felt as if she was underwater, with no sight of the surface to break.

It wasn't a long drive, but to Lavinia the ride seemed endless. She kept opening her mouth and shutting it. For the first time in her life, she couldn't think of anything to say to her best friend. The car suddenly felt small and cramped, the space oppressive. Tears welled in her eyes and she rapidly blinked them away, chewing on the inside of her lower lip.

She had been rejected. He did not feel the same as she did, not at all.

There was nothing wrong with that, she knew there wasn't. It wasn't his fault, and there was nothing she could do about it, and it was fine, really it was—but what wasn't fine was how awkward things were now between them.

She couldn't mess up her friendship with Theo. She wouldn't.

When Theo pulled up in front of her house, she tried her best to act normal.

"Thanks," she said, but the word sounded mechanical even to her own ears. She inwardly winced. "Um. Well, bye."

Theo was quiet for a moment, his knee bouncing. But then he looked up at her, giving her his usual smile.

"See ya," he said. She couldn't bear to look at him.

Lavinia got out of the car, her high heels in her hands, and ran barefoot to the door of her home. Closing the door softly behind her as she let herself in, she released a long breath, feeling nauseous. The house was quiet, her parents and little brother asleep.

Tiptoeing up the stairs, Lavinia maneuvered through the dark until she reached her room. She flipped on the lights and shut the door. Her heels fell to the floor with a resounding thud, and once they did, Lavinia's knees felt weak. She walked to her bed and collapsed face-down onto her pillows, wanting to cry.

She had been rejected by boys in the past, but no matter her experience with the emotion, it always hurt in a way that was so personal and shattering. Deep down, she always knew things happened for the best, but that didn't stop the reality from hurting.

And now Theo was just another one of those boys, which felt impossible to understand. He was Theo, he was *her* Theo.

She rolled off her stomach until she was lying flat, staring up at the ceiling as she took deep, deep breaths, listening to the sound of air entering and leaving her lungs. It was difficult to digest how wrong she had been, but that wasn't new either.

She could be so delusional when she liked someone; it was horrifyingly embarrassing.

But she had to face reality now. Lavinia sat up, slapping her cheeks to keep the tears at bay. She would not cry over this. She would forge forward, just like she always did.

Lavinia got off her bed and unzipped her dress, grabbing a nightshirt and throwing it on. She pulled her straight hair back into a ponytail, reaching for the scrunchie she had put in her clutch, but it wasn't there.

She went over to her vanity, grabbing another one from the drawer, meeting her gaze head-on as she looked in the mirror.

This was fine. She was fine.

In the mirror, her face broke. Anxiety spiked through her with a thousand needles. All these months she had nursed her feelings for Theo, thinking that eventually he would feel the same, that things would work out between them, and she would get her happily ever after.

But now? Things had decidedly *not* worked out, and such a miscalculation brought her dangerously close to her deadline. She had always thought she would follow her mother's path: excel in undergraduate school (check!), then find the love of her life in the winter after her twenty-fourth birthday, and get married after graduate school. In her mind, because Lavinia wanted a love like her parents', she needed to follow a similar timeline.

Her head pounded, and she rubbed her temples.

"That's enough," she chided herself. She couldn't think about this any further tonight; she needed some sleep before she could come up with a game plan to try and salvage some dignity from this calamity.

She went to the bathroom, washing off her makeup and getting ready for bed. When she came back to her room, she grabbed the lip balm from the top of her vanity, where it was laid out with all her makeup from when she had been getting ready.

As she did, she spotted a dark bottle of cologne.

Theo's.

He must have forgotten it; he had come over after work to get ready there before they headed over to the engagement party together.

Lavinia's fingers itched as she held the bottle. A dangerous shiver ran through her. She knew she should give it back, but she pulled the cap off, then sprayed.

Mist filled the air and she inhaled the scent of sandalwood, feeling warm. Lavinia closed her eyes. He usually smelled like this, except mixed in with the scent of dough and sugar, all warm and sweet.

Surrounded by the scent, Lavinia felt as if he was there, his body just beside hers, like that moment under the stars, his hand in hers. They were best friends; they grew up together, of course they had touched a million times before, but that moment had felt different—and the memory of how wrong she had been brought tears to her eyes. Her lower lip trembled.

Lavinia opened her drawer, putting Theo's cologne away. She wouldn't give it back. Instead, she hid it away, then shut the drawer with a snap.

She would do the same with her feelings. She would bury them.

It was time to grow up.

# CHAPTER 3

Theo Noon was at the Rolling Pin Bakery, restocking the display shelves.

The Rolling Pin had been his place of employment for more than two years, ever since he had graduated university, and the task was one he had done thousands of times before. Working mechanically, he listened to the familiar voice of his boss, Suki, in the background. She was currently on the phone, managing an order.

As Theo added butterscotch blondies and dirty chai cupcakes to the shelves, inhaling the scent of brown sugar and cinnamon, his gaze strayed to the large windows at the front of the bakery. From there, he saw out onto Main Street, the heart of their slice of Starshine Valley.

People walked along the street in light jackets, a few with their pet baby dragons. Crinkled leaves crunched beneath the pedestrians' feet as even more leaves fell from the sky, the trees along the wide sidewalks showcasing different shades of burgundy, rust, and mustard.

Ordinarily, it was a sight Theo would enjoy, but today,

he hardly had the brain space to appreciate anything. After finishing up with the display shelves, he went back to the kitchen, where his colleagues were all hard at work at their stations, some lathering frosting onto lemon loaves while others scored bread.

He went to his station and rolled up the sleeves of his flannel shirt, then washed his hands before he started working on making dough for more donuts. When the dough was ready, he floured his surface and began kneading.

Usually, kneading was calming for him—the smell of fresh dough, the pillowy feel of it in his hands, the bounce and stretch. But he had been fidgeting all day and, as he kneaded now, he lost himself in a train of thought.

Theo had been replaying what had happened last night in his head on a loop all day; now he revisited it again for what must have been at least the tenth time this hour.

The engagement party had been a beautiful event for Saphira and Aiden, both of whom he had gotten closer to in the last year. Theo had been overjoyed to see them so happy; he and Lavinia had been having fun all night—dancing, eating delicious food, and spending time in each other's company.

He always had fun with Lavinia. She was his favorite person in the whole world by far, without a question.

Then something had happened later in the night, when they'd been sitting under the stars, in the quiet, just the two of them. That was nothing new; it was often just the two of them, in their own world.

But she'd said something about what she was wearing, and he'd noticed how stunning she was, though there was nothing new about that either; she always looked gorgeous to

Theo. However, last night, her in that dress, the two of them under the stars, he'd forgotten she was his best friend. All he could think about was what a beautiful woman she had become.

He'd tried to distract himself by making shapes out of stars, but that had just made it worse. As he'd held her hand to point out the shape of a bow and arrow, it was as if the bow from the stars had sent an arrow leaping from the sky and straight through his chest. He had leaned in, before he'd realized what he was doing. When he'd opened his eyes, Lavinia had been leaning in, too, her eyes closed.

Was she really about to kiss him? Or had he imagined it?

Either way, there was no imagining how he'd reacted. He had freaked out.

Theo groaned inwardly now at the memory; it was as if he had short-circuited. But how else was he supposed to react? Lavinia was his best friend. Sure, she was a girl, and he knew that boy–girl friendships could be quite complicated sometimes . . . for others, though it never had been for them.

He had never allowed himself to think of Lavinia in that way.

For one thing, his romantic entanglements in the past had always ended badly; he had decided he wasn't cut out for relationships. All the times he had tried to form a connection— in high school, or in his early university years—he had failed spectacularly, so he had finally stopped trying. It wasn't that he didn't *want* to be in a steady relationship, it was that he realized he was just not cut out for it.

Which was why he had never considered Lavinia romantically. Anytime a glimmer of romantic feelings for her rose up within him, he promptly buried it away. Nothing was more important to him than their friendship.

But if she, somehow, someway, could think of him that way—perhaps it was time he allowed himself to think of her in that way as well.

If he let himself, what could he feel?

Then came the second matter. She couldn't think of him in that light; it wasn't possible. She was a hopeless romantic at heart, and yearned for a grand, sweeping love story. She did not simply want to fall in love, she wanted a *great* love. She thought about things like invisible strings and destiny being written in the stars and fateful encounters.

She deserved someone swoon-worthy who could make all those dreams come true. Someone much better than him, for sure—a prince from a fairy tale, or a knight in shining armor, or one of those fancy titled lords from the period dramas her mom liked watching.

Theo wasn't any of those things.

He was just a guy. Like, *literally*, just some guy.

With a sigh, Theo finished up the donut dough, then covered it with a tea towel to let it proof. He washed his hands, listening to the rush of the water as Suki entered the kitchen. While the rest of them wore simple beige aprons with their names embroidered over the left breast, Suki's apron was sage-green with little white flowers embroidered around her name. She was a petite woman, with black hair styled in a pixie cut.

"Theo, if you're finished, can you man the front?" she asked.

"Of course." He nodded, drying his hands.

"Thanks." She walked up to the sink to wash her hands

and, as she did, she looked at his face closely. "Everything okay? You look a little stressed."

"Yeah, just a little tired," he said, trying to give her a smile. "It was Saphira's engagement party last night, so we got back late."

"Oh, yes, you told me about that!" Suki looked excited. "Do you have any pictures? I want to see how handsome you look."

Some of the tension left Theo's shoulders, and he pulled out his phone from his back pocket. Suki was his boss, but he was fond of her in the way literature lovers were fond of their English teachers: with respect and reverence. Not only was she an exceptional baker, but she was an exceptional person.

Two years ago, she had given him a chance when she had no reason to. He hadn't trained at culinary school; he had a business degree and had only done a few culinary courses. And not only that, but she had allowed him to bake his own fusion desserts for the Baby Dragon Cafe, trusting him not to sully her good name as everyone knew the Baby Dragon sourced their baked items from the Rolling Pin.

"Oh, you look wonderful!" Suki exclaimed, zooming in on the photos. She zoomed out; it was a picture of him and Lavinia, and the sight of her in that satin dress made heat flush through him once more. "Lavinia looks gorgeous, as well."

"Thanks, Suki," he said. She handed him back his phone, and he stuck it in his front pocket. She gave him a fond smile as he headed out of the kitchen toward the front of the bakery.

The day was almost over, but soon there would be a rush of people picking up things for the evening. Theo's eyes strayed to the shelves and shelves of croissants, buns, loaves of bread, pastries, donuts, and more sweets—the sight of which used to make him so excited, but lately made him feel so . . . uninterested.

He still came to work every day, but it wasn't with the same enthusiasm he used to. The only thing he really looked forward to was baking the desi-fusion desserts he made biweekly for Saphira's Baby Dragon Cafe, which stood a few shops down on Main Street. A needle of guilt pricked him then, and he glanced over his shoulder in the direction of the kitchen, to Suki.

Theo rolled his shoulders, pushing away his thoughts. He was probably just in a funk; that's what Lavinia had said when he'd spoken to her about it a few days ago.

He was sure he would feel passionate about the Rolling Pin again. He had to. He couldn't disappoint Suki.

Since it was quiet out front, Theo reached into his front pocket to check his phone for the time. As he did, he felt something else. Theo pulled out the soft fabric and recognized it immediately: Lavinia's scrunchie.

She was always leaving her stuff at his place or in his car or in his sweatshirts, and he was long used to it. Yesterday had been no different. She had left the scrunchie in his car, and he'd put it in his pocket this morning to give to her whenever he saw her.

He would pop over to the Baby Dragon once he was finished at the Rolling Pin; she was working there today.

Theo held the scrunchie in his hand; as he did, he caught the faint scent of her shampoo, which smelled like coffee. She always smelled like coffee and caramel, from either working in the cafe or from drinking too much of it, strong and sweet. It was a familiar, comforting scent for him, like the scent of dough.

The front door dinged, and Theo's gaze snapped up as he quickly pocketed the scrunchie. And good thing, too, for the person who had entered the bakery was always so perceptive.

"Hiya, Saph," Theo said, smiling at Saphira. She was wearing a dress with singe marks on the hem, and he knew the damage must surely have been caused by the mischievous baby dragons at her cafe.

"Hey, Theo, how's it going?" Saphira asked, coming up to the counter. She was practically floating.

"Same old," Theo replied with a shrug. "What's it like being officially engaged?"

Saphira smiled. "Well, Aiden did propose a few months ago, and the party was mostly just a formality for his family, but *officially* officially—it is as fun as it was yesterday, and every day before." She giggled. She was so giddy it made Theo's heart warm.

"What can I get you?" he asked. "And where's Spark?"

She was hardly ever without Sparky, her baby dragon. Sparky was a basalta dragon. He had originally belonged to Aiden, who was hopeless with dragons, so Aiden had hired Saphira to train Sparky. The two had promptly fallen in love and now shared custody.

Saphira pouted. "My golu-molu is waiting outside," she said. "He's getting big, so I'm trying to train him not to come into the little shops with me anymore."

The bakery was more of a grab-and-go place than somewhere to sit and linger—unlike the Baby Dragon Cafe—and as such was pretty small; not big enough for any pets larger than newborns under four months.

"Big?" Theo repeated, shocked. "I remember when he was

tiny enough to fit in your lap!" Sparky had been a mischievous baby, but he was so cute, he could get away with anything.

"He's turning *two* in October!"

"That is wild. Time flies." It was the sort of thing adults said, and he'd never understood it as a kid, but more and more, he was realizing how true it was. He'd been at the Rolling Pin for over two years now, but it didn't feel as if he had accomplished much. Twenty-four used to seem like such a grown age, but now that he was here, he felt the same as he always had, which scared him.

"I know! *Anyway*. I am here for some focaccia," Saphira said, looking at the bread selection. "The one with the most vegetables, please. I'm supposed to be making dinner tonight. I'm going to pretend I made this, and Aiden is going to be so impressed with me he'll fall in love all over again."

Theo laughed as he pulled a pan-sized piece of focaccia off the shelf. "Do you really think Aiden will believe you made this?" he asked. He knew Saphira wasn't much of a cook, and every time he had eaten with Aiden and Saphira, it was always Aiden who cooked.

"Hush you," Saphira said, holding up a hand. "I'll distract him if he asks any questions." She wiggled her eyebrows, and Theo cringed.

"That's TMI, thank you very much," he said. He considered Saphira like an older sister. Actually, since she was here—perhaps he should ask Saphira for her opinion?

"Hey, I was wondering," Theo said, as he put the focaccia into a bread bag. "Has Lavinia mentioned being interested in anyone to you?"

Saphira gave him a funny look, surprised. She considered

his words carefully, and for a second he thought she would say yes. Anticipation pulsed through him. He paused in ringing her order up, giving her his full attention, not wanting to miss a word.

"You're the first one she talks to about anything, Theo," Saphira said. "I'm sure you would know before me."

He felt disappointed by that—but then he wondered why, exactly. Saphira watched him closely as he cleared his throat and handed over her focaccia and change.

"I just saw her at the cafe," Saphira said. "She did seem a little off, but she didn't say anything to me, even when I asked." She nibbled on her lower lip as she glanced at Theo. "She's your best friend. If there's something you want to ask her, just ask her."

"You're right," Theo said. He was being silly. It was Lavinia! They talked about anything and everything, sometimes to the point of knowing *too* much about each other (she had explained the particulars of a decidual cast to him once and he was still low-key traumatized).

He could talk to her about this, of course he could.

He smiled. "Thanks, Saph."

"No problem." She blew him a kiss, then was on her way.

The door dinged as she exited, and he watched as she went over to where Sparky was tied to a lamp post, where the baby dragon had been waiting patiently while Saphira was in the Rolling Pin. Sparky had grown up; he was the size of a small horse now, and he would keep maturing and growing until he reached age five, when he'd be bigger than even the biggest horse.

It was jarring to see Sparky so big—Theo felt as if he'd

blinked and Sparky had doubled in size! It seemed like only yesterday that Sparky had been small enough to fit in Saphira's arms, his little paws pressed against Saphira's cheeks. While the dragon was still adorable now, he was less chaotic, which was perhaps a good thing.

Saphira gave Sparky a kiss, and he licked her hand, then they were on their way. Theo genuinely loved seeing how happy Saphira was, the way she practically bounced and glowed. They had gotten closer in the past year, now that she had more time off from the cafe to relax. Theo and Lavinia had often hung out with Saphira and Aiden, and it was always fun.

Lavinia always got this wistful expression on her face when she looked at Saphira and Aiden. Theo knew it was because she yearned for a love like that, one that would make her shine as bright as the stars.

His stomach sank. He doubted *he* was the one who could give her that, but still—he wanted to at least talk to her.

He rarely ever had a thought without discussing it with Lavinia. No matter how small or inconsequential, or stupid or silly—he told her everything. It was how he lived his life; she was the air he breathed.

There was no way he couldn't talk to her about last night. At the same time, he was scared. He didn't want things to change between them.

Last night had gotten weird on the car ride back to her place, when he was dropping her home. It wasn't that they couldn't sit without talking; they often spent time in comfortable silence together. But yesterday felt different in a way that it had never been between them, and he hadn't known what to do. He *still* didn't know what to do.

Lavinia was the one constant in his life; he couldn't ruin that. He wouldn't.

He sighed, rubbing a hand over his tired eyes. He would talk to her and see how she felt, then go from there. This was all new to him, which meant that he didn't know how *he* felt yet, either, though he suspected it was something obvious he just couldn't put his finger on yet. Either way, he wanted to know how Lavinia felt.

He wanted them to be in sync, the way they always were.

# CHAPTER 4

Day One of burying her feelings was going exceptionally well for Lavinia.

She was still smarting from last night's humiliation, so the memory of that alone was enough to convince her to let go of any romantic feelings she might have in favor of preserving her friendship. That was the most important thing, she reasoned.

The rejection still stung, and the pain of all those hopes dashed was a bitter ache, but as long as she didn't think about it for more than half a second, she would be fine.

She *was* fine. She was always fine. Lavinia could tell when certain thoughts were leading down a spiral staircase, and she always closed the door on those thoughts before she fell and fell.

She needed to go onwards and upwards, which meant she needed to move on. She could be so delusional sometimes, and it was not healthy—it was childish and silly. She was twenty-four, so she needed to be a serious person now or she would just keep getting her heart stomped on again and again.

It wasn't Theo's fault, she knew that. It was her own, for

letting herself get carried away imagining that just because she liked him, he would like her too. Whenever she liked anyone, she daydreamed about the ways it could play out like a perfect fairy tale, all the scenes bright and beautiful and perfect.

But life wasn't a romance movie. The sooner she accepted that, the better.

She was at the Baby Dragon Cafe today, where she had worked since it opened almost two years ago. Because of her vet studies, she only worked here once a week now, on Saturdays. It was a good day to come in because the cafe was so busy. Lots of people came in and out: teenage couples on first dates, young parents with their little kids, and old women who sat knitting together. Lavinia loved seeing and chatting to all the different customers, especially when they brought in their baby dragons—red, blue, white, or black.

The cafe had high ceilings, with big, open windows, from which Lavinia could watch people walking down Main Street. There was a large fireplace surrounded with bookshelves and lounge chairs. Vases of flowers and candles decorated each of the tables, which were surrounded by wooden farm chairs. There were also some Mughal touches in the artwork hanging on the walls, a nod to Saphira's heritage, which Lavinia shared as well on her mother's side.

Lavinia was at the counter now, tending to the drink orders, while other staff handled the kitchen and the garden out back. She finished up the order, then went to drop it off at a table by the stone wall, where a middle-aged woman was sitting reading a book. A blue-scaled azura dragon was nestled comfortably in a bed by its owner's feet, its paws playing with the fringe at the end of the woman's skirt.

"Here's that flat white for you and some karela juice for your dragon," Lavinia said, placing the coffee on the table and the steel bowl by the dragon on the floor. The azura sniffed the air and immediately lit up, leaving the fringe to happily lick up the green juice from the bowl. Warmth spread through Lavinia's chest, and she petted the baby dragon's scaled head.

"Thank you!" The woman smiled, and Lavinia returned the gesture, her smile remaining as she returned to the counter. The Baby Dragon Cafe was one of Lavinia's favorite places in the world. She had seen this place come to life, and it was all thanks to Saphira's hard work.

She thought of the little garneta baby dragon waiting for her at home. Her mother was watching the dragon for her best friend Famke, who had hatched her dragon egg in June, only to be involved in a severe car accident in July. Her leg had been broken in two places and would take five months to heal, so Beena had offered to take care of her baby dragon, Biter, while Famke recovered.

When Lavinia had a spare moment in the afternoon, she made herself a hot butter pecan latte in a to-go cup, which was easy to carry around. The cup was decorated with the cafe's logo: a mug with dragon wings. She loved the cafe's fall menu and all the fall flavors. With her coffee, she snagged a meethi tikki from the display shelves, the fried cookie sweet and crisp. Theo had made them, and while they weren't a fusion recipe, they were perfect as is.

He brought in fusion recipes for the cafe twice a week, and they were always scrumptious. While Theo had baked the cookies, he had originally learned the recipe from Lavinia's mother, Beena.

Theo and Lavinia had grown up eating these cookies, and the taste was comforting and homey. Which didn't exactly help with the whole Theo Situation that Lavinia was currently grappling with. With a pout, she put her cookie aside, just as a customer came up to the counter.

"I need coffee stat," Genevieve said, collapsing onto a barstool. She rested her head on her arms; her ink-black hair was tied up in a simple twist, revealing all the features on her makeup-free face as she yawned. "I just woke up."

Lavinia laughed, happy to see her friend. "It's two in the afternoon."

"What about it? Grandad was the last one off the dance floor, and I was his dance partner."

"Your grandad seriously has more energy than any old man I know," Lavinia replied as she pulled an espresso shot for a latte. Genevieve wasn't picky with her coffee order, and Lavinia knew what she liked.

"And way more than any old man rightly should," Genevieve added, taking the latte as Lavinia slid it her way. She took a sip, humming to herself. "Yum. What is it?"

"A spiced turmeric latte with an extra shot," she replied. "Should wake you up."

"Mm, it is."

She sat up straight, sliding her tote bag off her shoulder. It was black leather, which went with her outfit of black trousers and a maroon sweater. Her style was simple and the opposite of fussy, though clearly expensive. Lavinia was impressed with how put-together Genevieve was, despite their late night, but then again, Lavinia had never seen Genevieve frazzled, the way Lavinia herself often was.

Genevieve grabbed a notebook out of her tote bag, setting it on the table next to her latte. Her expression soured. "I have to study," she lamented. She was in her final year of university studying Dragon History.

While she didn't yet have a dragon of her own, she would receive a basalta egg to hatch when she turned twenty-one in December. Members of Drakkon families—those who owned and rode dragons—could hatch their dragon eggs at any age, but knowing Genevieve, she would hatch hers on her twenty-first birthday, the very earliest she was allowed to. She had been waiting to have a dragon of her own ever since she was a teenager.

Lavinia was happy her friend's time would soon come. Lavinia loved dragons the way she loved all animals, which was what made veterinary school so fulfilling, though the coursework was no easy undertaking.

"Ugh," Lavinia sighed. She did not want to think about the studying she needed to do, nor the homework that would be waiting for her when she returned home after work tonight.

"Ohmygod," Genevieve asked, suddenly remembering something. She set her notebook aside. "Did you see Oliver's girlfriend last night?"

Lavinia gasped. "Ollie has a girlfriend? Since when?" she asked, referencing Genevieve's cousin, who was in his mid-twenties but looked like a teenager and was hilariously ridiculous.

Genevieve started telling Lavinia all about it, and they soon became busy discussing last night, how wonderful it had been. A little while later, Lavinia's coworker Calahan Goode popped over. He was tall and well-built, with dark skin and short hair in tight curls. He was good-looking—more than once, Lavinia had seen customers of the cafe checking him out, which didn't surprise her in the least. In addition to being handsome, he was kind.

Case in point: he slid a plate in front of Lavinia. On it was a sandwich. "Sorry to interrupt, ladies," he said, eyes warm. "I just noticed you hadn't eaten anything, Lav, so wanted to give you this."

"Gosh, I didn't even realize," she replied, holding a hand over her heart. "Thanks, Cal, you're a lifesaver."

He gave her an easy smile, then disappeared back into the kitchen. Once he was gone, Genevieve started giggling.

Lavinia gave her a stern look. "Come on." Genevieve had this theory that Calahan had a crush on Lavinia, but Lavinia had never noticed anything of the sort. "He's just *nice*!"

"Since when are men just *nice*?"

"Men are nice to you all the time!" It was true; boys everywhere were always falling over themselves trying to get Genevieve's attention—not that she ever gave it to them.

"And ten times out of ten it's because they want to sleep with me!"

"Well, that's because you're you," Lavinia said. The Sterling women had this effect; she had seen it happen with Genevieve's cousin, Emmeline, too. Emmeline was older and supermodel gorgeous, and while Genevieve couldn't care less about strangers' attention, Emmeline enjoyed flirting and was happy to have fun.

"He is soooo into you," Genevieve teased.

"Stop it."

Ginny pouted. "You are so boring! You haven't dated anyone in forever—you need to spice things up. Do it for the plot!"

Lavinia snorted. She took advice from Ginny with a grain of salt because Ginny could be known to spice things up a bit too much. It was true she didn't care for the attention of random guys, but that didn't mean she didn't have her flings. Lavinia could hardly keep track of all of her friend's situations.

Genevieve was looking for someone who was her match, someone who challenged her. She was such an exceptional woman that it was hard to find such a person, but she didn't seem bothered by such tediousness. Whereas Lavinia was downright *exhausted* by all the failed romances of her life—the way hope and excitement always slowly but surely gave way to rejection and heartbreak. She would rise from the ashes like a phoenix, ready to start again, and now she was getting tired of it.

She didn't know how much more she could take, and she was running out of time. She had three months before her deadline. If she didn't find love by the winter, she never would.

Which reminded her of last night with Theo. Pain sliced through her.

She was fine, she reminded herself. She was always fine, even if it hurt. She kept her chin up and kept hoping—even if she was afraid that one day she would get knocked down and she wouldn't have the strength to pick herself up again.

Lavinia didn't believe she was that picky. She just wanted someone to genuinely like her. Was that so hard? Was it?

Apparently, yes.

She had dated or liked many guys, and it always ended up the same: with her either dumped or rejected. The confounding part of it was that guys always liked her in the beginning—she was a likable person!—but then, once the novelty wore off, they got tired of her. There was something about her that made her easy to like but not enough to commit to.

With a sigh, Lavinia took a bite out of the sandwich Calahan had brought her. Genevieve watched, dark eyes intense.

"This tastes really good," Lavinia admitted. There was nothing bread couldn't remedy.

"And it doesn't even have any tomatoes in it," Genevieve pointed out, brows raised. "You hate raw tomatoes."

Lavinia narrowed her eyes at Ginny. She usually brushed her friend off about Calahan, but today the gears in her mind were turning a little bit. Maybe it was time to pay attention.

Especially since she was on a time crunch. For the past few months, she hadn't even worried about such a thing. Because she had feelings for Theo, and thought he might feel the same, there had been nothing to fret over. She believed she already had her person.

But now, she most evidently did *not* have her own person.

Which meant she needed to find love more proactively.

Her gaze strayed over to Calahan, to where he was reaching up into a nook to pet an opala baby dragon. The white-scaled creature cooed, leaning into Calahan's touch. Gorgeous, kind, attentive, good with animals . . .

Now that she had resolved *not* to think about Theo, she realized what a great catch Calahan was.

"The gears are turning," Lavinia told her friend. Genevieve gave her a triumphant smile.

They continued talking, but eventually Genevieve realized no studying was going to be done as long as she was in the cafe with Lavinia, so she finished up her coffee and headed off. Left alone to continue her work, Lavinia began paying closer attention to Calahan.

The way he popped over every little while to check in on her, to ask her if she needed any help, and the easy smiles he offered her. She was beginning to see him in a new light.

Of course, it helped that he was incredibly handsome. He had that bookish look going for him, eyes behind thin-rimmed glasses. He was wearing a sweater vest, for god's sake!

And he was clever, she knew that already. He was also uncomplicated. Most importantly, it did seem as if he liked her—arguably, the most important thing.

*Hmm.*

Later in the day, things slowed down quite a bit. The cafe was less busy, just a few tables of seated patrons. A peaceful hum settled over the Baby Dragon, and even the usually mischievous dragons were relaxed, comfortable in the arms of their owners or asleep in little beds.

There were no orders to be made, nothing to do. Lavinia drummed her fingers against the bar, contemplating a fourth coffee just to have something warm to hold and sip on, but she knew she would be bouncing off the walls if she had more caffeine.

Then, Calahan came up to her at the bar, working around her as he took out a mug and tea bag.

"What are you having?" Lavinia asked, turning to face him. He showed the tea bag label: jasmine green tea. "Oooh. Is it good? I've never had it."

"I like it," he replied, pouring boiling water over the tea bag in his mug. He set it aside, letting it steep. "I try not to have too much caffeine on the weekend since I already have way too much during the week."

How responsible of him. She also had way too much caffeine during the week, but that didn't stop her on the weekend. The way she saw it, she deserved a treat for making it through the week, and flavored lattes were the perfect fit.

"I doubt you're having as much as your students," she replied. Since there was nothing to do at the moment, it was fine to have a little chat.

"Probably not," he said, dimples making an appearance in his cheeks. He tossed the tea bag then added honey into his mug. Another responsible choice.

"How's the old PhD going?" she asked as he stirred the spoon. He was studying Folklore and Mythology, and had been for as long as she'd known him. "How many years do you have left, anyway? I feel like you've been doing that forever."

He took a sip of his tea. "Trust me, it feels like that to me, too." He smiled. "I have another two years, then I'll be free."

"Will you though?" she asked, tone teasing. "Aren't you going to be a professor?"

"That is the plan, which, yes, fair point, then I won't be free." He laughed. "I'll be teaching more classes and grading even more papers."

He didn't seem to be stressed by the prospect. Actually, she realized that she never saw him tense or burdened. He had a serene energy, and being around him made Lavinia feel calm, as well.

Maybe that could be good for her. She could be hyper and too loud. Maybe it was time to find someone mature and steady—to grow up and stop believing in fairy tales.

(It was just so hard *not* to believe when she saw the evidence of storybook romance right in front of her! Most recently, in Saphira and Aiden, but originally, in her parents. But perhaps love like that was rare—not meant for her.)

"I'm already a teacher's assistant in a few lectures this semester, and I thought the workload would be tedious, but actually I'm really enjoying it," Calahan continued. "I know a lot of students these days are lazy and don't really care about what the professor's teaching—a lot of them really only take the class to cover a general credit—but then there are some students who are passionate, who are interested, and they ask such good questions. It's just nice that the love for learning isn't entirely dead." He stopped, a little sheepish. "Sorry, went on a bit of a rant there."

"No, it's nice to hear you talk about it!"

"How's your school going?" He pushed back his glasses. "You're in your second year now, right?"

"Yup," she replied, leaning against the counter. "I also have two years left, but luckily this is my last didactic year, and then we begin rotations shadowing different vets for the last two years, which will be exciting. I'm lucky that I intern at the Animal Hospital, so I get to have some experience already."

"Do you know yet what you want to specialize in?" he asked, taking another sip of tea. "You get to choose an animal, right?"

"Yes, I can choose from dragons, chimeras, phoenixes, and griffins, or I can do pediatrics and cover all the species, which is what I primarily do at the Animal Hospital right now with Dr. Quan. I really like it! So for now, I'm thinking of that."

Starshine Valley was large and divided into different sections: the dragons enjoyed the hills around the valley, while the chimeras preferred to be down by the lake; the griffins lived in the dense forests, and the phoenixes built their nests up high in the mountains. Though each species had their own part of the valley, all baby animals came to the Animal Hospital on Main Street.

"That's so great," he said. "You're gonna be amazing at it."

"Aw, thank you." Lavinia beamed. She really hoped she would be. She loved all animals, but the babies in particular held a special place in her heart.

A large part of that was thanks to Sparky—he was impossible not to love! It was special, too, to see the way Saphira and Aiden had bonded with the baby, how the three of them were their own little family. Lavinia knew how important the baby animals were to their owners, and it would be wonderful if she could help the animals who were ill and preserve that bond.

It was nice talking to him. She had, of course, talked to him loads of times before, but this was the first time she had noticed just how lovely it was. Were those butterflies fluttering in her stomach?

Then, she heard someone clear their throat, and she remembered they were in fact at work. She turned, and her eyes widened as she realized who it was.

"Theo!" She jolted. His wavy hair was tousled from the wind, curling against the nape of his neck above his flannel shirt. She hadn't even noticed when he'd gotten there. Her heartbeat quickened, and she grew hyper-alert.

"Hey, Theo," Calahan said, lifting his free hand in a wave.

"Hey."

"See ya," Calahan said, touching Lavinia's elbow as he

walked past her and headed back to the kitchen. Theo made a face.

"Everything okay?" she asked, confused.

He blinked. "Uh. Yeah."

They both stood in silence then. It was awkward, painfully so, and she hated this. She needed to get over her feelings for him *immediately*; there was no use holding onto the idea of them, an idea that would never happen.

Theo looked at her carefully, as if he wanted to say something but didn't know how. Her thoughts spiraled to the worst, embarrassment making her skin heat. He must have been considering how to let her down easily, and mortification shot through her at just the thought. She did not think she would recover from such a confrontation.

Thoughts frantically jumped around her mind until an idea broke through, surely inspired by Genevieve and her chaotic advice. But there was no time to lose. Theo opened his mouth to speak.

"Theo, I need to tell you something," Lavinia quickly said, nerves buzzing through her. His eyes went wide with surprise.

"What is it?" he asked.

Lavinia looked over her shoulder, though no one was around. Even so, she leaned over the counter. He did the same, until they were eye-level with one another, their faces inches apart.

She gazed up into his eyes, which were a perfect chocolate brown, framed by criminally long lashes. She inhaled the scent of dough from his skin, momentarily distracted. Her chest ached.

"I wanted to talk to you, too," Theo said, his throat moving as he swallowed. His face was white and he looked . . . nervous. Anxious. She knew that look; it was the look he got before he had to bring up something uncomfortable.

He was going to bring up last night. He was going to reject her again.

She needed to take control of this situation, *fast*.

"I like Calahan," she blurted out.

Theo's mouth jutted open. He blinked. "Oh?"

"Yeah. I have for a bit now." (*A bit* being five minutes.) "And I don't know what to do!"

He stood utterly still, unmoving. Slowly, his eyebrows furrowed, first with confusion, then with a deeper emotion as his lips turned down into a frown.

He looked upset.

*Oh god.* He was probably upset because she said she had liked Calahan for a bit and she was only telling him now. She always told him everything the moment it happened.

"I'm sorry I didn't tell you sooner," she said, tucking her hair behind her ears.

He moved back, snapping his mouth shut. He worked his jaw, eyebrows still crinkled. He was very quiet, and she could see his mind working as he processed this information.

Then, strangely, his hand went to his front pocket, as if to pull something out. She saw the imprint of his hand curl into a fist, but when he removed it from his pocket, his hand was empty.

Theo took a deep breath, a determined expression on his face. "So. What's the plan?"

Now it was Lavinia's turn to go quiet. Her eye twitched.

It was their usual line, whenever one of them liked someone

in the past; they always helped the other figure out how to get together. But it had been some time since Lavinia had liked someone and told Theo about it—she hadn't realized that if she told him she liked Calahan, this would be his response.

But of course it would be. He was her best friend. She was so stupid! She hadn't considered what a precarious situation this would become.

She felt like throwing up, but that might have been due to the three coffees she'd had today.

It was too late to turn back now.

And that was how Lavinia found herself enlisting the help of her best friend (who she had feelings for) to help her get with someone else (to get over aforementioned feelings).

Which wouldn't be complicated. Or messy. And that wasn't a bad idea.

Not at all.

# CHAPTER 5

Lavinia had found a way to push off Theo's question yesterday at the cafe, but today was Sunday, her day off from all work, internships, and school. It was also Sunday, the day Theo came over to her house. The bakery was busy in the morning, but he usually came by for an early dinner, as the Williamses had a late brunch on Sundays.

After sleeping in, she had joined her family for breakfast. Sundays were for the elite combination of fried eggs, shami kebabs made of spicy minced meat and lentils, and parathas, the flatbread's dough lathered in ghee until it was practically fried.

The meal was paired with mango juice, then followed with biscuits and elaichi chai, which she was now lazily drinking in the living room, shafts of sunlight pouring in through the wide windows. Her stomach was full as she sat with her parents and little brother, Alfie, who was eleven.

The baby dragon, Biter, was asleep in her bassinet, which was a special dragon bassinet made of stones. Biter was nestled in a pile of blankets, her red scales shimmering in the sunlight.

Her little chest rose and fell as she slept soundly, the sound of her breathing soft.

Biter was three months old, which meant she spent most of her time asleep. Lavinia knew all about taking care of babies from her experience at the Animal Hospital and her classes, and at this age, baby dragons weren't high maintenance at all, so long as they were fed (special formula in bottles) and kept warm (hence the blankets). Famke had provided everything the Williamses would need to look after Biter until Famke recovered in December.

"Alfie, don't bother her," Lavinia scolded, as her little brother went to touch Biter's red head.

"I'm not!" Alfie protested. "I just want to pet her."

"Be gentle," Beena ordered. "If you wake her up—well, you know where she gets her name from."

While the little dragon only had her deciduous—or baby—teeth, her bites could still be painful when she wanted them to be. Lavinia watched as Alfie gently patted Biter's red scales. The little dragon hummed in her sleep, nestling deeper in her blankets.

"She's so warm," Alfie said, smiling to himself. His face was the picture of contentment.

The house was slightly chilly, but sitting in the sun, Lavinia was warm, too. Her legs were over Beena's lap, and Beena rested her teacup on Lavinia's knee. Lavinia bit into a buttery biscuit, taking a sip of chai.

Lavinia had never moved out, and a big part of that was because she loved her family. They got along really well. She also didn't want to miss spending time with Alfie, who had grown up before her very eyes and who she adored. And now the added—though temporary—fun of Biter.

Another part of the appeal of staying home was evidenced by her full stomach. Her mother was a fantastic cook. Lavinia had picked up a few things from Beena, but she was always so busy with school and work that she hardly ever had time to spend in the kitchen with her mother. Beena's true prodigy was Theo.

Even now, Beena asked when Theo would be coming round. "I'm making murgh cholay for dinner," she said. The hearty spiced chicken chickpea dish was one of Theo's favorites.

Mention of Theo made her heart skip a beat.

"Umm," Lavinia said, trying to sound normal. "Whenever he's done with the bakery."

"You haven't spoken with him today?" Beena asked, confused.

"He's at work!" She tried not to sound defensive.

"Ask him when he's coming," Alfie said. He moved away from the bassinet and went to sit on the couch across from her, hugging their father's arm. Garrett had glasses and short brown hair. While Lavinia looked more like her father, Alfie looked more like their mother; he had darker hair and a deeper brown skin tone.

Alfie had already asked her a million times since he had woken up if Theo was coming, when he was coming, how long would he be coming for.

"He's coming! Relax!" Lavinia said. "I swear, you people care more about Theo than me, your own blood!" She tried to sound offended but couldn't quite manage it; Alfie was her little munchkin.

"Well, are *you* going to play football with me?" Alfie asked, eyebrows raised.

Lavinia sank deeper into the sofa. "No." She took a sip of chai. "And maybe grow another two feet before you can catch up to Theo."

She and Theo had been thirteen when Alfie was born and practically spent the next decade using him as their favorite toy, playing with him constantly. As such, Alfie practically hero-worshipped Theo, especially since Alfie didn't have an older brother.

An hour later, they were all in the same position in the living room and her family members' wishes came true as a knock sounded on the door. Alfie shot up.

"I'll get it!" he said, running out. Lavinia's pulse quickened, and she took a deep breath, ordering herself to calm down and act like a human being. A moment later, Theo entered, his arm slung around Alfie's shoulder.

"Hiya," he said. Garrett waved, and Theo walked over to hug Beena hello. She kissed his cheek as he bent over, and Lavinia kicked his stomach from where her legs were still over her mother's lap. "Oi, be nice to me," Theo said, deflecting. "I come bearing gifts." He threw a brown paper bag onto her lap. It was still warm, and the smell of bread wafted out.

Lavinia gasped with delight, pulling the fresh loaf of bread out. As Theo went to look at Biter, still asleep, she split the bread open, closing her eyes as she inhaled the heavenly scent.

"A work of art," she said, squeezing the bread. She watched it bounce back, then squeezed again. "I want a bed made out of this stuff."

Alfie bounced over to rip off a piece of the bread. "That sounds gross."

"No, that sounds *delicious*." She hopped off the couch and

threw an arm around Alfie's shoulder, leaning in close. Even though she was many years older, he was only an inch shorter than her. "Just imagine how soft it would be."

Alfie laughed at her theatrics.

"I can get behind a bread-bed," Theo agreed, playing along as he came over. He sat down on the couch. "Slice it open and tuck in like a piece of chicken."

Lavinia was grateful things weren't awkward between them, and she smiled as he continued. "Exactly! And if I got hungry, I could just take a bite out of the blanket. I wouldn't even need to get up."

"A two-in-one," Theo affirmed. "That's what we call an excellent business model."

Alfie giggled.

"You two are so silly," Beena said fondly.

Alfie settled down on the couch between Beena and Theo. "Alf! That was my seat!" Lavinia cried. Her little brother ignored her, already talking Theo's ear off about how he was the fastest kid in his class.

Lavinia went to the kitchen to get a plate for the bread and a knife for the butter Theo had brought with it. When she returned, Beena had migrated to the other couch, taking the opportunity to snuggle with her husband. Those two were ridiculous.

Lavinia went and joined them, much to her parents' chagrin. Beena cried out in protest as Lavinia wiggled in between the couple, forcing them apart.

"Please!" Lavinia said. "Not in front of the children!" She gestured to Alfie, and Garrett pinched her side. She squealed.

"Alright, pumpkin," he said with a laugh, moving over so

she was no longer sitting on top of them. She used to hate being called pumpkin because she felt like they were making fun of her for being so round, but now she was fond of the pet name. She loved pumpkins.

"Thank you, Dad," she said. "Just for that, you get the first piece of bread." She broke off a piece of the end and gave it to him, but he handed it to Beena, knowing she liked the ends of bread loaves.

Lavinia broke off hunks of the bread and threw pieces across the room to Theo and Alfie, who caught them easily.

"Tch, don't throw food," Beena scolded, slapping Lavinia's thigh.

"Ow!"

Lavinia gave her father a piece, then tore off a bit for herself before putting the rest on a plate that she balanced on her lap. The brown paper bag had a cube of butter in it as well, which had softened from the warmth of the loaf.

"The butter's fresh," Theo told her. Lavinia dipped her bread into it, smearing some across, then took a bite.

"Mmm." The butter definitely had illegal amounts of fat content in it, but it was so rich and creamy and delicious, with a sharp salty taste to it.

"Well done," Beena said, impressed. Then, they heard a little cry, and everyone's attention shifted to the bassinet. Biter crawled out of her blankets, rubbing her ruby eyes with her paws.

"She's awake!" Alfie cried, running over to her. Biter hissed as she adjusted to being awake. Theo walked over to the bassinet, as well, and Biter blinked up at him.

"She is too precious," he said, picking her up. She crawled up onto his shoulder, nestling her face against his neck before she proceeded to nibble on the collar of his flannel shirt. Her red tail hung down over his chest.

"Uh, I think she's hungry," Theo said, holding a hand up in case she felt unbalanced on his shoulder, which didn't seem likely. He had very broad shoulders, Lavinia noted despairingly. She frowned. Biter was not helping Lavinia's situation in the slightest.

"Just a second," Beena said, getting up. She came back a few moments later with a baby dragon bottle of formula, handing it to Theo, who sat down, detaching Biter from his shoulder and settling her in his arms as he fed her.

Alfie crowded Theo's side, watching with big eyes. Lavinia's heart squeezed painfully at the adorable scene. First her baby brother and now their baby dragon!

When Biter was finished with the bottle, she burped happily, and they all smiled. "I feel bad for Famke with her broken leg, but I'm so glad she's having you guys watch this little cutie instead of her family's dragon caretakers," Theo said. Most Drakkon families had dragon caretakers, the same way horse owners had stable hands.

"I wanted to help, and Famke knew just how much Alfie has begged for a pet over the years," Beena replied. "Besides, the caretakers see Biter during the week when Garrett and I are at work."

Sufficiently rested and fed, Biter was full of energy now, and she jumped from Theo's lap onto Alfie's, making Alfie laugh. Then, she crawled up Alfie's arm, jumping back down to the carpet, rolling around the soft floor. Baby dragons at this age were just learning to crawl and jump, their wings fluttering ever so slightly.

After an adequate time with everyone, Lavinia stood up, hitting Theo's shoulder where he was sitting on the floor.

"Come on," she said. "That's enough Theo time for you all, now we're going upstairs."

Things were back to normal between them, and she would keep them that way. After spending some time with her family, they usually hung out in her room.

She took Theo's hand, pulling him off the ground and practically going sprawling herself in the process.

"Can I come too?" Alfie asked, handing Biter a chew toy. Beena was in the kitchen, making dinner.

"Hmm," she pretended to think. "No!"

Alfie pouted, about to cry. She pinched his cheek. "Watch Biter with Daddy. We'll be back down for dinner, alright?"

"Then we can play football, too," Theo added.

"Promise?" Alfie asked, still pouting.

"Promise."

Alfie automatically lit up. He was such a fake crier. Theo laughed, ruffling Alfie's hair. Lavinia loved seeing Theo with Alfie, and there went her stupid heart, getting all gooey again. She needed to stop, so she mentally smacked herself.

She went up to her room, Theo following her, telling her how his day at the bakery was, relating some gossip about his coworkers, who were in some sort of love–hate relationship and who always had some moment that made for a good story.

They entered Lavinia's room, which was maximalist in style—things everywhere. There were so many different eras and trends that she had enjoyed, and there were many memories in every corner of the room: movie and concert and airplane tickets, receipts from special days, all collaged together on cork boards. Books and trinkets and dried flowers.

Then her schoolwork, notebooks and textbooks and papers and folders, stray pens and markers and highlighters. She had a monthly calendar on the wall, then a weekly calendar on her desk. Now that it was autumn, she'd pulled out all her fall scented candles, but that was about the only thing that had changed in this room. It had looked like this since she was a teen, just with more and more bits added on as she lived her life.

She pushed some clothes onto her desk chair and they both sat down on her bed, talking about regular things, about everything. As they talked, they both ended up lying down in opposite directions, her feet up on her headboard, his hanging off the bed.

She told him about the rest of her evening yesterday, how her mom was watching a Jane Austen adaptation with her dad and she and Alfie ended up watching as well, Biter comfortable in her lap. Afterward, Alfie had helped her bake brownies for dessert—and Theo was horrified to hear they had just made them from the box instead of from scratch.

They always told each other every single little detail or thing that happened or that they thought or felt. Well, almost everything. But it was close enough to feel like things were back to normal, and thank god for that. She had missed him.

Even just one weird day between them, and it had made her feel unsettled, but now that he was here, she was glad. It was like he was a part of her, and every time he was gone, there was an undeniable sense of something *missing*, but whenever he was with her again, everything felt right, how it was supposed to be.

Until her gaze strayed to her vanity, to the drawer in which she knew she had hidden away his cologne. She should just give it back to him, she knew that, but she was greedy. She couldn't—she didn't want to.

She couldn't have him, but she could have this part of him, to play pretend in the dark hours of night, when she was at her most vulnerable.

Lavinia shook those thoughts away, reminding herself of her deadline and the path that would lead to success: Calahan.

An idea popped into her head.

She sat up. "I need a makeover."

# CHAPTER 6

Lavinia watched as Theo's expression turned confused. He was still lying down, but he looked over at her with furrowed brows, his hair flopping. "Huh?"

"I need a makeover," she repeated.

"Don't be ridiculous," he said. "You don't."

"No I really do, it's a vital part of every rom-com montage, and it's how we're going to tackle Operation Calahan." One thing about Lavinia: once she had a plan in her mind, she needed to see it through.

She hadn't had a plan with Theo; the near-kiss at the engagement party had been a spur-of-the-moment decision. Another sign of just how wrong that entire situation and idea had been. She wouldn't make the same mistake with Calahan.

She had three months until her deadline. She would make a plan; she would be prepared. Everything would work out.

Theo's jaw clenched. "You do know all those stories are rotting out your brain, right? None of that shit's real."

Lavinia loved romance movies and he loved fantasy, so they always flip-flopped between the genres. Though he would never openly admit it, she knew that secretly a part of him liked those romance movies too even if he thought they were as far-fetched as his fantasy movies.

"Hush," she ordered. While she could be hopeful to a delusional extent, Theo could be realistic to a pessimistic extent. "Back to my earlier point: makeover." She jumped off her bed, landing on her feet, then went to her closet. He sat up, giving her a look.

"Back to *my* earlier point," he said. "You don't need one. You're gorgeous."

A riot of butterflies fluttered around her stomach. "Shut up," she said, trying to sound normal. "You're my best friend. You have to say that."

He frowned. "I still mean it."

She ignored him, throwing open her closet doors. She cleared her throat, then grabbed her hairbrush from her vanity.

"While her style can ordinarily be described as trendy and artsy, fun and fresh, we are now about to witness outfit combinations the world has never before seen from Lavinia Williams," Lavinia narrated, speaking into her hairbrush as if it was a microphone. "Brace yourself."

"Oh god," Theo lamented. "Please don't tell me this is going to be as bad as picking a graduation outfit." Lavinia had in fact spent six months curating the perfect graduation outfit for her university graduation, only for it to barely be visible under her gown, but that was not relevant at this moment.

"I'm hearing some background noise, we'll need to clear that up before rolling," she said, ignoring him. Theo flopped back onto the bed, making her mattress shake, and she rummaged around her closet, throwing clothes off hangers and out of shelves.

Lavinia had many pieces that were many years old but that she loved and didn't want to let go of, even if the sweaters from middle school had tiny holes or the jeans from high school had patches. She had headbands from high school, belts she wouldn't be caught dead wearing anymore, infinity scarves (which she would argue were still practical!), and printed palazzo pants.

Lavinia began trying on outfits while Theo was on his phone, not paying attention except for when she prompted him to take in the final look, at which point he gave her a thumbs-up or a thumbs-down.

She didn't have work at the cafe until Saturday, which would give her all week to marinate on a show-stopping outfit for the next time she saw Calahan. Though perhaps it was also time to plant a little seed. In high-waisted jeans and a cropped sweater, she grabbed her phone, taking a break from the makeover to search up "professor memes" on Instagram. She found an adequately funny one, then direct-messaged it to Calahan.

Was she being messy? A little chaotic? Possibly. But she was on a time crunch, and maybe this was the path that was best for her.

It was the end of September, and she needed to find the love of her life before the winter. The clock was ticking! Calahan was a perfect candidate. If they started dating in the next few weeks, she'd have plenty of time to suss whether or not he could be The One.

If he was, she would perfectly follow in her mother's timeline for *A Successful Life*. If he wasn't . . . well, Lavinia didn't want to think about that. Failure was not an option she ever entertained or planned for.

Theo sat up and gave her a suspicious glance, noticing she had stopped her frantic outfit changing and was instead focused on her phone. "Who are you texting?" he asked. For a moment, she thought about not telling him, but then she pushed past the feeling and said, "Calahan."

A flicker of change came across Theo's face, something like displeasure. He was probably still annoyed she hadn't told him about her feelings earlier. With a sigh, he lay down again.

Lavinia was a big believer in fate, and she jumped onto her bed, looking over him. "You know, maybe Calahan is who I'm supposed to be with," she said. "He's the first person Saphira hired after me, and he's also been there the longest out of everyone else."

Theo was skeptical. "You're reaching, Lav," he said. Avoiding her gaze, he played with the edge of her sweater sleeve from where her hand rested next to his torso.

"But what if I'm not?" she said.

"I really think you are, though."

"But *maybe* I'm not!"

He finally looked up at her, letting go of her sleeve. "Okay, well, then why haven't you ever noticed him before?" he countered. The answer was lying on her bed in front of her, but she couldn't tell him that.

Instead, she said: "Timing! Duh! It's always about timing. *Now*, the timing is right." She fluttered her hands in the air. "The stars are aligning."

"Can we please calm down?" he asked, exasperated. Theo

was not a believer. Lavinia frowned at him, then grabbed a pillow and hit him.

"Ow!" he cried, clutching his side. She got up and went back to her closet. With a groan, Theo put the pillow over his face.

"We're looking for a show-stopping ensemble," Lavinia narrated. She already knew that Calahan noticed her; she simply needed to amp things up. She also knew that she was cute; she just needed to find an outfit that would attract the attention she wanted.

She usually wore little tops with high-waisted bottoms, which helped to make her look a bit taller, since she was very short. On her feet, she wore heels or platform shoes to help with her height, as well. Overall, this always led to a cute outfit, but she wanted something that would immediately stand out.

Lavinia looked out the window, where the sky was a mix of burnt orange and red. Leaves swirled in the air, dancing. Inspired, she went back to her closet, looking for something suitably autumnal.

For fall, she loved miniskirts with heeled boots, or tweed shorts with platform loafers.

"I could do a little plaid moment, that would be fun," she said, rummaging around her closet.

There was no response from Theo.

"Theo!" she snapped, turning back.

"Huh?"

"Wouldn't a plaid moment be fun?"

"Super." His voice was dry. He was just being no fun today. She wondered why he was in a mood. He was fine when they were downstairs.

Was he bothered about all the energy she was spending on Calahan?

But no—why would he be bothered?

She left her closet and instead dug through her dresser drawers, trying to find a plaid skirt. Before she could, she found a black leather skirt from university she had completely forgotten about. She held it up.

This was cute! Lavinia tried it on, and it was a little tighter than she remembered. A bit shorter as well, actually, but it wouldn't look as promiscuous if she was wearing stockings. The skirt was one of her night-out pieces, but it served the purpose! Leather was very autumnal. Plus sexy. She was going for sexy.

Lavinia found a light gray sweater to go along with it, to make the outfit a bit more casual for work at the cafe. When she was done, she checked herself out in the full-length mirror, twisting this way and that.

Very nice! The leather was really working for her, perfectly accentuating her curves in the most flattering way. She did a little spin.

Lavinia turned around. "What do you think?" she asked.

Theo sat up with a sigh, taking in her look. When he did, his eyes immediately widened. His jaw slackened, and a moment later, he snapped his mouth shut. "Absolutely not."

"What?!" she cried, looking down. "Why?"

He didn't reply.

She frowned, hurt. "I don't look good?" she asked.

He clenched his jaw. "The opposite," he grumbled.

*Oh.* Her skin flushed at his tone, her pulse quickening. She felt shy for a moment. His eyes were dark.

But no, she must have been imagining it. When it came to her crushes, she never knew when to let go, to let a dead thing lie. She held on with gripped fingers until her clawed hands were cramping. She liked to think it was hope, but it was something more desperate and unruly, something ugly.

She was doing the same thing now, as she always did, and she needed to snap out of it. It would only break her own heart to hope when there was nothing to hope for, nothing at all.

There was no chance for her and Theo.

He had rejected her, after all.

# CHAPTER 7

Theo needed to *not* be weird, which was a decidedly difficult feat to accomplish when Lavinia looked like *that*. Fuck.

But it wasn't for him; none of this energy or time or attention was for him—it was for Calahan. Theo was irritated, though he had no right to be.

It wasn't that he was worried for Lavinia. Calahan wasn't a bad guy; he was pretty perfect, as far as guys went. He was kind, clever, fun to hang around. Not obnoxious or problematic at all. Theo had always gotten along with Calahan, but now there was something about him that Theo didn't like much, though he couldn't quite put his finger on it.

It didn't matter what he thought. Lavinia liked Calahan; she didn't like Theo. He must have imagined that almost-kiss at Saphira's engagement party.

He was so stupid.

Why would she like *him*? He was twenty-four years old with a useless business degree, working at a job that had once been his passion but he wasn't even sure he liked anymore.

Of course she didn't like him—she liked *Calahan*, who was

smart and accomplished and mature and well-adjusted and a real grown-up. He was going to be a professor!

Lavinia turned back to the full-length mirror, and the view of her in that skirt was even more torturous from the back. He had to look away.

"I think your usual is fine," Theo said, clearing his throat. "Anyway, you don't want to have to change yourself to attract someone's attention."

"Blah, blah, blah." She made talking motions with her hands, ignoring him.

She turned back to her closet, and he lay down, turning his attention to his phone while he heard her change. His pulse quickened, and he closed his eyes as he heard the slow unzipping of her skirt. A moment later, she threw her skirt at him. The leather slapped his face.

"What was that for?" he cried, throwing it off.

"No reason," she said sweetly. She continued trying on outfits while he stewed, his mood positively vile. Until she bounced over in an oversized hoodie and knit shorts. He sat up.

"I think this is the one," he said. She looked adorable, but only her regular amount of adorable. "Yup, this is perfect."

She gave him a funny look. "This is my look for dinner. As in, my mother just called us to come downstairs. Didn't you hear her?"

Oh. No, he had not heard Beena calling them. He had been far too distracted with brooding.

"Come on," Lavinia said.

They went down, heading to the kitchen, where it smelled divine. Lavinia pulled out the mats to set the table, and Theo grabbed the plates from the cupboard. Alfie was standing on a stool by the stove, stirring the pot, which was simmering on the lowest heat. Beena was on the other side of the stove, cooking rotis on a flat, wide pan. Biter was asleep in the bassinet once more, Garrett watching over her.

Theo went over to Alfie, peering over his head. "Wow, did you make dinner?" Theo asked, though he knew that obviously Alfie hadn't.

"Yup," Alfie said, playing along. The dish was murgh cholay: a spiced chicken and chickpea stew that could improve Theo's horrid mood.

"Theo, top it off with some coriander and ginger, will you?" Beena asked, rolling out the aata into a perfect circle. "I'm just making the last roti."

"Of course." Theo got fresh coriander from the fridge, washing, then finely chopping it. After that was done, he took out a knob of ginger, peeling and slicing it into thin, inch-long strips.

Alfie hopped off his stool to go watch Biter with Garrett. Lavinia finished setting the table, while Theo garnished the murgh cholay.

"It's ready!" Beena called. Theo brought the dish to the table while Beena brought the rotis.

They all sat together, digging in. The light and airy flatbread with the hearty curry was perfect, and both Theo's stomach and heart were full as he sat around the dinner table with the Williamses, everyone talking and laughing.

"So good, Mama," Lavinia said, licking her index finger.

"That's because I made it," Alfie interjected, fake-proud of himself. She kicked him under the table, and he laughed. Theo watched fondly.

He loved visiting the Williamses. He had been coming here since he was a kid, and it felt more like home than any other place in the world—not his parents' place, where he grew up; or even the apartment he'd been in since he graduated university and moved back to Starshine Valley—but here.

Beena and Garrett truly loved each other—anyone could tell—and that love was reflected in their home, in their children. Theo always felt safe, at peace. There was never anything to worry about. Even if he made mistakes, he knew that everyone would have a good sense of humor about it.

The older Theo got, the more he realized that a lot of adults simply didn't have a sense of humor about anything. They were so bogged down by life's problems and anxieties, and the stress and unhappiness just exuded from them.

It wasn't like that with Beena and Garrett; no matter how tiring or tragic their day at work, no matter what was going on, they were always finding a way to turn even upsetting things into funny stories, cracking jokes and laughing.

Theo had always admired that quality about their marriage. Since he was a kid, he imagined that whoever he eventually ended up marrying would be someone he could laugh with. It would be the very opposite of how he grew up, where he was afraid to breathe in the wrong way in case it set his parents off.

"How are things at the Rolling Pin?" Beena asked, pouring herself a glass of water.

"Good," Theo replied automatically, but then he paused, thinking about it further. "Actually, a bit monotonous, if I'm being honest. It doesn't feel like it used to. It's kind of boring?"

With a sigh, he wondered if adult life was just like that. He had been there since he graduated university, first as a lowly assistant and delivery boy, now as a junior baker. He had been working hard for that promotion for months, and he'd assumed that once he was promoted, things would be better.

But they weren't. Working at the Rolling Pin was becoming tedious, which was a frightening thought. Baking was supposed to be his passion. If he didn't love it anymore, what would he do? Who would he be?

"There's nothing wrong with having a good routine," Garrett said.

"Love a good routine," Lavinia agreed, munching on a cucumber.

"Nothing wrong with being settled, either," Garrett continued, pushing back his glasses. "But it shouldn't feel like a chore. Remember, in life, if you're largely discontented, it's usually time for something to change."

Theo made a thoughtful noise in response. Garrett was a prenatal genetic counselor. He ran genetic tests for couples who were trying to conceive, or had already conceived, to spot any risks the mother or baby might face. Beena was a nurse, and they both worked at the same hospital. It was where they had met.

Which was another instance of fate intervening, Lavinia would tell him, and Theo would counter that Beena and Garrett were both from Starshine Valley, and there weren't many hospitals here (two to be precise) so, statistically, it wasn't so momentous that they ended up working at the same hospital.

"But the fact that they had shifts at the *same* time and were on the same *floor* and had the same *lunch* room—it was fate!"

It was impossible to argue with her, and often, they agreed to disagree. In a way, he admired how hopeful she was, the positive outlook she had. It was a beautiful way to look at the world. He could be too pessimistic; he sometimes wished he had more wonder.

Perhaps he was simply being pessimistic about the Rolling Pin, now. Suki was the best boss anyone could ask for, and while he had gotten his undergraduate degree in business, baking was the only work he had ever been passionate about. He didn't need a change. He just needed to get out of whatever funk he was in.

After dinner, Theo went out back to play football with Alfie. There was a slight breeze, and he listened to the sound of the leaves rustling on the branches. Inhaling the crisp air, he kicked the ball around with Alfie, teaching him some tricks with his footwork. Theo had been playing since school.

Even now, he played with a bunch of other guys twice a week, and they had games with other teams. It wasn't anything intense, just for fun. When he was younger, football was always a way to get rid of restless energy, and he still enjoyed it. He played with Alfie for some time while Lavinia went up to her room to prepare her notes for her internship tomorrow and to get a head start on some of her assignments for the week.

Theo was fine; he was used to hanging out with her family members even when she wasn't there. Even though he wasn't related to them, he still felt like they were his own.

Alfie and Theo stayed outside until it got dark, then came in. The house was comfortably toasty. Theo rubbed his hands together to warm them. He hadn't realized how cold the evening had gotten.

"Alfie, wash up and go do your homework," Beena said from the living room, where Biter was cuddling in her lap, little face on Beena's forearm. Alfie pouted, but after a stern glance from his mother, he acquiesced and went. Theo joined Beena in the living room, and she gave him a smile, eyes glinting.

"Should we make something?" she asked.

He grinned. "Yes, please."

Pretty much everything he knew, he'd learned from her. And not just in regards to baking, either. She stood and set Biter in the bassinet with some chew toys. Theo helped her pull the bassinet toward the edge of the kitchen, where they could keep an eye on the baby dragon. Not that the little draggo would cause trouble; she seemed perfectly content with her toys.

Theo followed Beena into the kitchen, watching as she twisted her hair up and set it with a clip from the edge of her sweater.

"Seviyan?" she asked, opening the fridge. "I don't think I've taught you that, yet."

"You haven't," Theo confirmed, rolling up his sleeves. "But yes, let's."

The sweet dish was primarily made of vermicelli, milk, and heavy cream, and Beena grabbed the ingredients. She showed him the steps, teaching him with gentle patience. Theo paid close attention, jotting down the steps in a new note on his phone. First, they boiled the milk and the heavy cream, and after that bubbled, she lowered it to a simmer.

"That'll cook for a bit," she said. "And we have to keep stirring it so the bottom and edges don't burn."

"Got it."

"But while that's simmering, we are also going to toast the vermicelli," she said, pulling out a pan. She opened the vermicelli packet and broke the thin round spaghetti in halves so it would be easier to toast. She browned the vermicelli with cardamom pods, the fragrant smell filling the kitchen.

"And now we combine," she said, emptying the pan of vermicelli and cardamom pods into the milk mixture. She added in sugar, not following any exact measurements but cooking instinctively.

Theo stirred the pot, watching the mixture thicken until it reached what looked to be the right consistency. He held up the spoon, showing Beena as she stood beside him.

"It shouldn't be too thick, nor too thin," Beena instructed. "If it's too thick, it becomes like custard, and if it's too thin, it's just milky. We need it in the middle."

She stirred the pot, then ran her finger along the back of the spoon, tasting. She thought for a moment, then added in a touch more sugar, stirring again.

"Almost ready—time for the secret ingredient," she said with a wink. She grabbed some soft medjool dates from a jar, splitting three open to pull out the seeds. Then, she dropped them in. "You add them in at the end because you don't want them to cook or the seviyan to get too sweet and the date flavor overwhelms the dish. And always use medjool—ajwa are too hard."

"You don't want to make a paste or anything?" Theo asked, jotting down the notes.

Beena shook her head. "The flavor will get soaked into the milk, and whoever wants the dates will have to hunt for them."

She got two spoons, then handed one to him, and they tasted it straight from the pot. It was good: milky, sweet, and warm. Usually, whenever he'd had seviyan before, they were cold, so it was a bit strange to have them hot now.

"We'll let it sit overnight so it can chill," Beena said. She added more milk to the mixture, then stirred. "It thickens in the fridge, so I always add a bit more milk before throwing it in."

"Ah." He wrote that down while she put some seviyan into a box for him to take back to his place.

"Thank you," Theo said, taking the box. "Now I just need to think about how to make this into a fusion dessert for the cafe."

"You mean the Baby Dragon Bakery?" Beena teased. It was what she called his contributions to the Baby Dragon Cafe.

"Yes," he said, smiling. He recalled what she'd said about how, if it got too thick, it would be like a custard. He was struck with an idea. "What if I let it get thicker and use it as a filling for cream puffs?"

"Ooh. I've had your cream puffs, and they're divine. That sounds delicious!"

"When I try it, I'll let you know," he said. He had a little sketchbook at home that he drew new ideas into, and he could already imagine how this could look. His gaze strayed to the time on his phone. "For now, I best get going." It wasn't too late, but they all had early mornings.

"Okay, darling," Beena said. He swooped down to kiss Beena's cheek, catching a waft of the familiar powdery scent of her perfume.

On his way out, he popped his head into Garrett's office to say goodbye. Alfie was sitting on the floor, doing his homework, and Theo ruffled his hair.

He went up to say bye to Lavinia last. Her room was a mess of all the strewn clothes she had tried on: they hung off her bed and desk chair, different articles all over the floor. She had cleared some of them away to make space on her rug, where she was sitting cross-legged, her school things spread out.

Instrumental music played in the background, and he knew it was a playlist titled something bizarrely specific like "studying in an old library in the melancholic rain" or "you're living a quiet life in the countryside." Her hair was pulled up in a high ponytail, and she was wearing her reading glasses, focused on the textbook in front of her with a notebook in her lap.

Theo stood in the doorway a moment, watching her. His chest felt tight for some reason.

Then she glanced up, noticing him. The serious studying expression on her face melted away.

"Save meeee," she said, reaching for him. She was being dramatic, pretending to cry, and he laughed.

"Who told you to be so hard-working and go to vet school?" He leaned against the door frame, fondness warming through him. She made a face.

"When I'm rich and have a private island, you are so not invited," she said. "Then you'll be sorry. *Sorry*, I say!"

He snorted. "We made seviyan," he told her. "Have some sugar, it'll help your brain."

"Ooh, yum," she said. "I'll get some in a bit. I'm almost done with my notes."

"See ya," he said. She waved, and Theo headed out.

He drove back to his place, though he was in no rush to arrive any sooner. When he did make it back to his apartment, he opened the door to a quiet and still space. Theo flipped on the lights, a strange sinking feeling in his stomach. It felt like going back to school after a long holiday.

He always felt this way after coming back from the Williamses', but today he felt it more keenly. The largely empty apartment was such a stark contrast to their lively home full of love and laughter. And Lavinia. No matter how much time he spent with her, it never felt like enough.

With a sigh, Theo kicked off his shoes. He put the box of seviyan in the fridge, then went to his room. He should sleep soon; he always had to get to the Rolling Pin super early, and lately, he'd had difficulty getting up in the morning. He wasn't sure if it was because he wasn't getting enough sleep, or because he wasn't as enthusiastic about his work anymore.

Theo brushed his teeth and shucked off his clothes from the day. He slept in his boxers. When he got into bed, he put his phone to charge on his bedside table but tonight, as he did, he saw that he had missed a call from his mom.

He knew he should call her back. He hadn't spoken to his parents in a few weeks. He should probably visit them soon, as well. They still lived in Starshine Valley, in the same house he grew up in, and he visited them every other month or so, purely out of formality. On the other hand, he visited the Williamses almost weekly. If more than ten days went by without visiting Lavinia's home—without seeing her family—he felt an acute sense of something missing in his life.

It wasn't like that with his own parents. He would never be good enough for them, he knew, and he had made peace with that a long time ago. Even so, every time he went over there, there was some comment or some silently exchanged glance between his parents that made him upset.

No matter how old he got, it still hurt. He was still that unwanted kid inside.

It was worse that it still surprised him every time it hurt, because then he just felt stupid. He should have known the reality of his parents' relationship with him by now, but his stupid heart wouldn't accept it.

There was a part of him that believed that, like magic, one day he'd have what Lavinia had—parents who loved him, a healthy family, all of it. Nothing his parents could do now would undo the past, but if they were just nice, just once, he'd forget everything and be content.

They were never happy with him. Even though they didn't scream or hit him, they were so negative. And always disappointed. When they were disappointed, they either berated him or they released long, exhausted breaths, as if they didn't know how to get rid of him.

Funnily enough, at least his parents loved each other. He recalled when he was in school, after he'd gone up to his room, he'd hear them talking to each other, laughing. They sounded happy. He could creep out of his room, quietly standing in the hallway, listening. A few times, he even went down, under the guise of needing water from the kitchen. But the second they saw him, the laughter died, and with horror, he realized he was the problem.

Just him. Nothing else.

Even then, he never stopped trying and trying and trying to make them happy, as if one day they could be proud of him. They refused to send him to culinary school, saying he had to get a real degree, so he didn't go; he did a business degree and took culinary courses on the side. He didn't mind the business degree—he was good at it, so it didn't require much from him—but still, that didn't get him in their good graces, so finally after he graduated he gave up.

He started working at the Rolling Pin since that was what *he* wanted to do, and it was just confirmation for his parents that he had ended up as the disappointment they always knew he was. They thought he was wasting his time—wasting his life. They were never proud of him, and he had internalized that to a degree so deep, he could never feel proud of himself, either.

His eyes welled up with tears, and he brushed them away, swearing lightly to himself. He needed to not be such a baby and grow up already. People's parents were shitty. It wasn't anything groundbreaking.

Theo felt restless. He shouldn't have thought about all that. He got out of bed and began pacing around his apartment, making laps around the small space, navigating around furniture. He ran both hands through his hair, anxious energy pounding through him.

Theo touched two fingers to his wrist to press against his racing pulse but, instead, he felt Lavinia's scrunchie there. He didn't even remember slipping it on before getting into bed, but the sight of it was comforting. He slowed his pacing, looking down at the scrunchie. He should have given it back to her, but for some reason, he hadn't wanted to.

Theo stopped pacing and sat down on his couch, taking deep breaths, trying to push his parents from his mind. He knew if Lavinia could hear his thoughts now, she would scold him for being so harsh on himself. She was always trying to get him to see all that he'd accomplished, to feel proud of himself, but he never could. He would never feel good enough for himself, either.

It was different for her. She could rob a bank and her parents would be proud of her for pulling off such a complicated task.

They always looked for anything to be positive about, and Lavinia was like that too; she kept her chin up. Everyone in her family had love to spare, which was why Theo was always going over there. In his house, he felt like he had to beg for scraps.

The Williamses didn't mind him hanging around, neither before nor after Alfie was born. He remembered that her parents tried having another kid for years, and then finally Alfie was born—Lavinia always told him that she would have a baby brother or sister one day. She told him with such surety and excitement, which was something he had found astounding at the time.

His parents didn't want to have him, and when he was around nine, his mother, Amaya, had gotten pregnant again, and he remembered hearing his parents talk about it. He was so excited. Until, one day, she told him she wouldn't be having a baby anymore. He still remembered the way she had sunk into the couch, relaxed, as if she had dealt with something that was bothering her.

She had been stressed before then, he knew that, but he had been so happy at the thought of a sibling, he hadn't cared that Amaya seemed unhappy. He always thought that if he had a sibling, he could have a partner in crime—someone of his own.

He had been overjoyed when Beena got pregnant the next year, and he knew with certainty that she wouldn't terminate the pregnancy because Beena and Garrett had wanted another baby for years. Everyone was so excited; he could tell both of Lavinia's parents were happy, as if they were getting the greatest gift they could have wished for.

He always wondered what it might be like for children who were so purely *wanted*, and then he saw for himself when Alfie was born. Garrett and Beena loved each other so fully, and from that love, a child was born. Theo thought he might be envious, but he wasn't. He loved Alfie, too, and the Williamses all had love to spare. He spent even more time there, wishing he could just stay there forever.

Theo's family life was tumultuous, so he was always hiding out with Lavinia and her family. She had always been the one good thing in his life, the one constant. He had football and baking and other friends, but Lavinia was always his main source of happiness, the reason he stayed sane amidst everything else.

He took Lavinia's scrunchie off his wrist and went back to his room, sliding it into his bedside table's drawer. He needed to stop whatever thoughts or feelings were going on deep inside of him. Maybe he was simply getting mixed up, imagining that he had romantic feelings for Lavinia when he didn't.

And even if he did, it wouldn't matter, anyway. Lavinia wasn't interested, and he wouldn't jeopardize their friendship.

He couldn't.

# CHAPTER 8

Lavinia went to work at the Animal Hospital the next day. She had her internship three times a week and lectures every weekday. She had been interning there with Dr. Quan since last summer, and she loved it.

During that time, there had been other interns as well, but most of them stayed for a few months to get a little bit of pediatric experience before moving on to shadowing other vets in the field. Not Lavinia. She enjoyed pediatric work, and enjoyed staying in one place. She had built relationships with many of the patients and loved seeing them.

The Animal Hospital was where the babies were brought, while the grown animals received house calls. Lavinia liked dealing with the babies, and she hoped to eventually work at the Animal Hospital full-time, rather than do house calls. Hopefully, they would offer her a full-time job when she graduated from veterinary school.

She had different appointments and paperwork to do throughout the day, which kept her busy. Around midday, she had another appointment, one she was particularly looking forward to.

"Shall we?" Dr. Quan asked, standing by the door of their shared office. He was a slender man with thick black hair and a clean-shaven face.

Dr. Quan had been a pediatric veterinarian for over twenty years, and as such, he knew everything there was to know, his knowledge and experience vast. He was an excellent mentor to Lavinia, and just as wonderful with the magical animals, patient and gentle. Even the most chaotic babies tended to calm down around him.

"Yes," Lavinia said, taking off her glasses and setting aside the papers she had been reading through. She stood, following Dr. Quan toward the patient rooms down the hall. When they arrived at the correct room, Dr. Quan pulled the file from the folder hanging on the door. He entered, and Lavinia followed behind him. In the room, Saphira was waiting with Sparky.

The baby dragon lit up when he saw Lavinia, immediately coming over to rub his nose against her torso.

"Hi, Sparky," she said, scratching his scaled chin. He flapped his wings happily, and wind blew Saphira's hair back. The vet rooms were big enough for the biggest baby animals, so there was plenty of room for him here.

She recalled when he had come in for his first appointment last year to get shots—how little he had been. How quickly time passed; how quickly things changed!

Lavinia petted Sparky, then waved happily at Saphira. She refrained from hugging her friend, as that would be unprofessional, and she needed to be on her best behavior in front of Dr. Quan, as well as maintain some workplace standards of decorum for herself.

"Hello Saphira, hello Sparky," Dr. Quan said, giving them both a smile. "How are you both doing today?"

"We're doing well, thank you," Saphira replied brightly.

"Is there anything pressing I should know?" Dr. Quan asked. Saphira shook her head. "Wonderful." He turned to Lavinia. "Lavinia, why don't you begin?"

"Of course." Lavinia began the visit, running through the usual check-ups. She took Sparky's vitals and numbers, Dr. Quan watching. When she was done, she reviewed her notes, then turned back to Dr. Quan.

"Nothing out of the ordinary," she said. She turned to Saphira. "Everything looks great."

"Wonderful," Dr. Quan replied. "Lavinia, I think you can handle it from here."

Saying goodbye, Dr. Quan left, and Lavinia took over the rest of the visit.

"Everything is truly good, right?" Saphira asked, fiddling with the sleeve of her chunky cardigan. Gold bangles jingled on her arm. "Nothing to worry about at all?"

Lavinia laughed. Saphira could be a worrier, especially when it came to her baby. "Yes, our little munchkin is perfect," Lavinia reassured her, scratching Sparky's chin. He hummed, then licked her hand. "He's a basalta dragon, so he is a bit bigger than other baby dragons, but perfectly normal for his breed. He *is* a bit more mature, I would even say, but I am sure that's due to your expert training."

Saphira smiled, pleased, holding her left hand to her heart. Her massive engagement ring sparkled, the diamonds around the basalt stone catching the light.

Lavinia was sure Sparky's maturity also had to do with

the fact that the Sterlings had the cream of the crop when it came to their basalta dragon eggs. Aiden's father was on the Dragon Council as the basalta representative. There was one representative for each of the four breeds of dragons.

"Good," Saphira said, releasing a breath. She came over to Sparky's other side, and Sparky nuzzled against her side, sitting by her feet. Saphira absent-mindedly stroked Sparky's head. "I've discussed this with the Sterling caretakers, but I want your opinion as well," Saphira said, tucking a piece of hair behind her ear. "Do you think I can saddle Sparky? I was thinking after his second birthday next week."

Lavinia had a good idea of the answer, but she checked Sparky's records and charts anyway, just to be sure. "That will be fine, especially if it's only your weight that he's carrying with the saddle. Of course, when dragons are fully mature, they can carry two to three adults, plus dead weight like luggage, but you're not doing anything like that."

"No, no, definitely not," Saphira said "And yes, it'll just be my weight. He's eager for me to ride him, and I'm just as excited."

"And you've discussed it with the Sterling caretakers?" Lavinia asked. The caretakers would know more specific information regarding the egg Sparky came from and his family history.

"Yes, I did, and they also said it was okay," Saphira replied.

"Then I don't see any issues at all," Lavinia confirmed.

"Yay!" Saphira clapped, excited, and Sparky flapped his wings, catching onto her energy. He bounced, and the ground lightly shook. Luckily, the patient rooms were equipped for rowdy baby animals, so nothing fell over or broke. Lavinia laughed.

"Alright, alright, don't get too excited," Lavinia said, scratching under Sparky's chin. "We still have to give you your vaccine."

It was a yearly vaccination shot for Sparky's immune system. At the mention of a shot, Sparky's happy mood dimmed. He scowled, glancing back at Saphira with betrayal.

"I know, but it's only a little shot!" Saphira coaxed. "Only a little one! And my golu-molu is so brave," she said, speaking to him in her baby voice. Sparky wasn't happy, but he acquiesced, settling down.

Lavinia administered the shot quickly and, while Sparky wasn't the happiest baby dragon about it, he was a long way from how upset he had gotten during his first visit. Saphira, too, was much more confident and secure.

"See? That wasn't so bad!" Saphira said. Sparky gave her what could only be described as a dirty look before bumping his head into her hip. Saphira stumbled. "Hey!"

That seemed to amuse Sparky, and he cheered up. His mood improved further when Lavinia gave them both lollipops: a big one for Sparky, and a small one for Saphira.

"I can chat for a few minutes, then I have to bounce, but tell me! How are things?" Lavinia asked.

"Good!" Saphira replied. "So good!"

"How has it been, officially being moved in with Aiden?" Lavinia asked.

"At first it was a little weird, even though I have obviously been at his place so much, but to properly move?" She sucked on her lollipop. "It's only been two days, but it's been so much fun! It's like having a sleepover with your best friend every day. It's just such a joy—to know that he's always around. And even when he isn't, to know that he'll be coming home to me, or that I'll be coming home to him."

"Aw." How sweet. She loved that. She loved love! Even so, loneliness echoed through her, a dull ache. She yearned for that desperately.

"Sparky loves it, too, of course," Saphira said, petting her dragon's black scales. "He was getting too big for my old apartment, anyway, and now he doesn't have to worry about that."

"Sparky is such a good boy," Lavinia said, petting him. "Aren't you?" He cooed in response, pleased.

"What about you?" Saphira asked. "How's school—and Biter! The picture you sent me yesterday was too cute!"

"She is adorable!" Lavinia replied. "I love having her around. And it's good practical learning for school, as well. You know—I should be getting extra credit!"

After chatting for a few more minutes, Saphira and Sparky left, and Lavinia returned to her work. At the end of the day, when she checked her phone she saw that she had a new message from Calahan.

Excitement fizzed through her. She opened the message.

"What do you call a dog magician?" she read aloud to herself before responding with a few question marks. She watched her phone screen, waiting for a reply until a new message appeared: **a labracadabrador**.

Lavinia laughed out loud, then texted back: **stop that was horrible!**

His response was immediate: **Noooo, i've been working on that all day, please tell me you at least giggled.**

**Only a little,** she messaged back, smiling to herself.

The rest of the week passed with classes and interning and assignments and notes, and she found professor jokes to send Calahan, while he sent her veterinary jokes. She was setting the stage, planting the seeds, etc., though she did detest the mechanics of the modern dating scene.

Then, finally, it was Saturday, the day she would be at the Baby Dragon.

It was time to commence Operation Calahan.

# CHAPTER 9

Lavinia got to the Baby Dragon, wearing the outfit that Theo had disapproved of, the one with the leather skirt. Because she had liked it, she had video-called Genevieve for a second opinion on Sunday night, and Genevieve had loved it, saying she looked like an absolute babe, so Lavinia had gone with it.

She didn't understand why Theo had told her not to wear it.

It was almost as if he was trying to sabotage her chances—but why would he do that? She was being absurd.

She needed to stop being such a hopeless romantic. It was bad for her mental health. She needed to switch gears and be a *realistic* romantic. That would keep her heart protected. Yes, a realistic romantic sounded good. She would trademark that and make it a thing.

When Lavinia entered the cafe on Saturday morning, Calahan was nowhere to be seen; he must have been in the kitchen. She quickly took off her light jacket, setting it down with her purse under the counter, then started taking down the chairs from the tables. She was just finishing up a table when Calahan came out from the kitchen.

A little jitter shot through her. He was wearing a navy blue sweater with beige trousers, and when he saw her, his eyes widened behind his glasses. He stopped in his tracks, jaw slackening.

She gave him a wide smile. "Good morning."

He blinked twice. "Morning," he replied, voice awed.

That put a little pep in her step. She bounced around, taking down the rest of the chairs, and Calahan came over to help her. His gaze kept straying her way, which only made her excitement grow.

Calahan paid attention, and he was caring. The day at the cafe was busy, as usual, but throughout, Calahan kept making excuses to come over and ask if she needed help, or offer to take orders to the tables for her. Then he would chat with her for a bit at the counter.

Butterflies fluttered in her stomach, and she felt like dancing.

She always got like this in the beginning of a crush, when it was all exciting and hopeful. She mapped out the ways it could turn out perfectly. Sunday was Calahan's day off, as well; maybe they could go to the farmers' market together sometime! She could imagine it now, walking hand in hand through the stalls, sipping an autumnal drink and trying out various snacks.

They could go on study dates together at the library ... or, oh, the ceramics store had just started a new date-night pottery class! That would be fun!

This would be the moment Theo would tell her to calm down and not get ahead of herself, but it was just so fun imagining things going well. It was the only thing that kept her going—hope.

Around midday, the rush gave way to a slow period, and

Lavinia yawned, feeling tired. She leaned against the counter, rolling her ankles to stretch them, the chunky platform loafers heavy on her feet. Calahan came out, his shoulder brushing against hers as he came to stand with her against the counter.

"Tired?" he asked. She nodded. "It always hits me around midday, too."

"We need sugar," Lavinia said, turning her gaze to the display case of bakery items they sourced from the Rolling Pin. She grabbed a butter pecan chocolate chip cookie, then split it in half.

Calahan's eyes brightened. "Yes," he said. "One hundred percent yes, but we need to enjoy it properly."

She raised a brow, intrigued. "Meaning?"

"Give me a second," he said, flashing her an easy smile.

He grabbed napkins and disappeared with the cookie halves on each, then came back a little while later, gingerly holding the napkins in his hands. They were warm.

"Ooh, yes," she said, as he handed her one. The heat seeped into her palm, and she inhaled the nutty aroma of brown butter.

"And don't forget the cold milk," Calahan said, opening the fridge and pouring them both small glasses of milk. A bolt of pleasure beat through her. They were so similar!

"You are speaking my language right now," Lavinia said. "I don't trust people who can have warm chocolate and wash it down with water."

"Diabolical," Calahan agreed.

They both bit into their warm cookies, into the crunch of the pecans and soft chocolate chips. At the same time, they took sips of their cold milk, and she hummed, content. After they finished off their cookies and milk, Lavinia crumpled up her napkin, tossing it into the bin.

"That was divine," Lavinia said. Calahan looked like he was about to agree, but then he laughed. She furrowed her brows. "What?"

"One second." He grabbed a fresh napkin and wet it by the sink. She furrowed her brows, confused, but then he got closer. He wiped the napkin on her chin, shaking his head with amusement.

"Chocolate," he said.

"Oops." She giggled, feeling fizzy inside.

Then a customer came up to the counter, and she got busy taking their order, while Calahan disappeared back into the kitchen.

As she made the customer's drink, she couldn't help but feel pleased with herself. Operation Calahan really was a fantastic idea. She had been so silly about Theo; she must have been confused. She had *wanted* romantic love, so she had probably latched onto Theo because he was always there.

There was no time to be confused now. She only had a few months until winter, when she would be the same age her mother was when she met her future husband. Theo wasn't the one written for her—obviously. If he was, he would have kissed her that night. He hadn't—which was a harsh but necessary reminder.

On the other hand, Calahan did seem to like her, and for once, she wanted to be loved and not have to worry about how the guy felt. Love was supposed to be easy, Mama always said.

But it never was. The last two times Lavinia had been in love, it hadn't worked out. Once was in high school, with a lacrosse player who was popular and funny. The second time was in university, with an art major who was insightful and deep. Both times, the boys concerned had liked her a lot while they were dating—she could tell they did! Until they eventually got tired of her and dumped her.

That was a train of thought she could not dwell on for too long or she'd ruin all her makeup with crying.

The workday continued, and a little while before closing, she saw Theo enter through the front doors as she was wiping down a table. He wore a beige utility jacket with black jeans, hair mussed from the wind. She waved, and he waved back, coming over. As he got closer, his gaze swept over her, taking in her outfit.

His eyes widened, his steps faltering. She could feel him staring and her skin flushed with heat. But he was only staring because it was the outfit he had advised her against; there was no other reason he would be looking at her *so* intently.

"Did you get off work early?" she asked, going back behind the counter while he came up to the other side. Just as Theo was about to respond, Calahan popped out to the front. Theo's expression changed, darkening so slightly that Lavinia must have been imagining it.

"Hey," Calahan said to Theo. He didn't wait for a reply before turning to Lavinia: "What are you up to later?"

It was almost time for closing. "Nothing much," she said, heartbeat quickening.

"Do you want to go to the town movie night?" Calahan asked. "Maybe grab dinner after?"

Lavinia resisted the urge to squeal out loud, but she most

definitely squealed inside her head. She pretended to think for a moment, not replying as immediately as she wanted to.

"Sure," she replied, smiling. "Sounds fun."

"Great." He touched her elbow, then disappeared back into the kitchen.

Lavinia turned back to Theo, mouth splitting into a grin. She loved when things went perfectly according to plan. It gave her a huge high. "Ah!"

Theo made no response.

"The stars are aligning!" Lavinia told him. "Operation Calahan is working!"

It was just as she had imagined; maybe she had manifested this. Actually—maybe she and Calahan were meant to be? Everything was working out—and on a quicker timeline than she had originally accounted for! That had to be a sign.

Theo grunted in response, and she furrowed her eyebrows at him. He was so quiet. She wondered if he had had a phone call with his parents. She knew that he had a difficult relationship with them—a horrible one. She didn't hate many people, but she did hate his parents. They always made Theo so sad.

"Hel-*lo*," she said, waving a hand in front of Theo's face. "Earth to Theo."

He blinked. "Hm?"

"No reaction?"

He ran a hand through his wavy locks. "Dinner?" he said, eyebrows furrowed. "Isn't that, like, a lot? So soon?"

Now it was her turn to furrow her eyebrows at him. "No?"

He huffed. If she didn't know any better, she would even say he seemed annoyed. But what did he have to be annoyed about?

"Did we have something planned for tonight that I forgot about?" she asked. He blinked, the irritation washing away from his face.

"No," he replied. He scratched the back of his neck. "I was going to say we could go to the town movie together but . . ." He trailed off.

"Oh." They had been to loads of town movie nights together. "Rain check?" she asked.

"Yeah, fine," he mumbled.

"Oookay."

He was being moody, that was all. She would ask him about it later; at the moment, he didn't seem too keen to discuss anything.

"Anyway. You got off work early?" she asked. He nodded. "Did you want me to make you something?"

He shrugged. "I don't really want anything anymore."

She narrowed her eyes at him. "Let me get you some chai."

Maybe he just needed a little cozy drink to soften his mood. She went to the kitchen and made him a cup, then brought it out in a mug, handing it to him. He sat down at the bar and took a sip. She got busy with other customers while he pensively drank his chai, and when he was about halfway done, the dark cloud over his head seemed to have vanished.

Now, he just looked tired. "Was work okay?" she asked.

"Yeah . . ." He trailed off, rubbing a hand over his face. "I don't know." He sighed.

"You're still feeling like you don't enjoy it anymore?" Lavinia asked. He had mentioned it to her last week, and then again on Sunday during dinner at her place. She could sense that he was still figuring out how he felt, so she didn't want to push or pry, but she did want to be here for him if he wanted to talk to her about it.

"I don't know what's wrong," he replied. "I love baking. I love working for Suki. So why am I not happy?"

Lavinia thought about it. "Maybe you need a change of scenery?" she suggested. That only seemed to stress him out further.

"But I could never leave the Rolling Pin," he said. "Not after Suki took a chance on me. Besides, I wouldn't even know what to do if I did leave the bakery. I just . . ." He broke off, exasperated. Lavinia frowned. She hated seeing him like this.

"Do you want me to cancel with Calahan?" she asked. She would feel bad, but Theo was her priority. "We can do something together."

Theo's face brightened—then immediately darkened. "No, don't," he said, voice quiet. "I-I hope you have fun tonight." He forced a smile.

She beamed. "Thanks."

"Can I get a cookie?" he asked, and she got one out of the display case for him.

His phone was on the counter, so she tapped the screen to check the time. His background was a photo of both of them, and above that, she saw the time. The cafe would close in ten minutes, then Calahan would come to the front to help her with closing up.

Excitement ran through her. She reached under the counter for her purse, opening it to pull out her lipstick and compact mirror. She held both up, reapplying her lipstick.

As she did, she felt Theo's eyes on her, his gaze intense. He had finished his cookie and was sitting completely still, watching her. Her pulse quickened, her hand shaking ever so slightly.

Swallowing, she clicked the cap back onto her lipstick, putting it back in her purse with her handheld mirror. She pressed her lips together, both to smooth the color and out of restlessness. She turned away, unable to bear Theo's eyes on her and the heat that scorched through her as a result.

"Wait a sec," Theo said. She turned back to him.

Her skin prickled with goosebumps as he walked around the bar, walking behind the counter toward her. She was so shocked, she didn't even tell him he technically shouldn't be behind the counter.

He stepped straight in front of her. Nerves spiked through her, both sharp and sweet. She felt her heart pounding loudly in her ears.

"What is it?" she managed to say, voice breathless.

He didn't respond. His eyes were hyper-focused and trained on her lips. Involuntarily, her mouth parted. He brought his hand up to her face, and her throat went dry.

He cupped her face in his hand, and then, ever so gently, ran his thumb across the very edge of her bottom lip. The movement was achingly tender. Sparks shot up her spine.

Her eyelids fluttered. Desire lit through her, and she inched closer, unable to stop herself, drawn toward him like a moth to a flame, not caring if it would be her demise.

Slowly, he pulled his finger away, then held it up for her to see. She saw a streak of crimson color.

"Your lipstick," he said, voice rough. "Fixed it."

His gaze dropped to her mouth, his eyes lidded. Lavinia stared at him, unable to speak. When he brought his eyes back up to meet hers, she saw they were dark, burning. He looked as if he wanted to say something. Lavinia held her breath as he opened his mouth.

But then it was as if he thought better of it.

"See ya," he said, voice strangled.

He abruptly left, leaving her feeling unsteady.

# CHAPTER 10

After work, Lavinia went home to freshen up before the date. The movie wasn't until eight, when it got fully dark in the park, and she had about an hour before then. She realized it might get a bit late for dinner after the movie, so she filled a tote bag with pretzels and candy; she was already getting hungry.

Lavinia also grabbed a blanket for her and Calahan to sit on, then stole one of her mother's expensive shawls to wear because she knew it would get cold.

After she was ready, she texted Genevieve that the outfit had been a success, informing her of the date tonight. While Lavinia was touching up her makeup, her phone rang. She swiped on the video call, setting her phone against the mirror.

"Hiii," Lavinia said, applying a layer of mascara.

"Ooh, are you getting ready?" Genevieve asked, her bare face filling up Lavinia's phone screen. "Let me see." Lavinia walked back, spinning for Ginny. "Love it."

"I'm going to head out soon." Lavinia had to stop applying mascara because she was smiling and her eyelashes would smudge. She glanced down at her phone, where Genevieve looked very pleased.

"Exciting!"

"Is that Lavinia I hear?" Saphira's voice called from behind Genevieve. Genevieve lifted her phone from her position on the couch, which Lavinia recognized as the couch at Saphira and Aiden's place. Saphira came into view, and Lavinia waved.

"Ooh, you look hot," Saphira said, squishing next to Ginny. Now both of their faces filled the screen. "Where are you going?"

"I have a date," Lavinia said, giggling. Saphira gasped, eyes wide.

"A date?! With who?!"

"Calahan!"

Saphira's jaw dropped, voice increasing an octave. "*Calahan* Calahan?"

Lavinia nodded. Saphira blinked, surprised.

"This is great," Genevieve said to Saphira. "I always knew he liked her."

Saphira blinked. "It is," Saphira agreed, then paused. "I had an inkling he might like you too, but I thought you were interested in . . ." She trailed off, shaking her head. "Never mind." She gave Lavinia a bright smile. "I hope you have lots of fun!"

"Me too," Lavinia said, trying not to think about what Saphira was going to say. She chatted for a bit, then blew Genevieve and Saphira a kiss goodbye and headed out.

She drove over to Starshine Public Gardens, where the town movie night would be. It was always set up on an inflatable screen in the field, and everyone either brought camp chairs or sat on the ground. She had been coming with her family ever since she was a kid, and of course, then Theo would join as well. It was a popular spot for families and couples alike; this was not her first time going on a date here.

When she got out of her car with her things, she saw Calahan at the front of the garden's entrance, holding a tote bag and a box. He had thrown on a brown overcoat over his blue sweater and she thought he looked especially handsome; when he saw her, his face lit up. She smiled, walking over, trying not to skip with excitement.

"Hey," she said.

"Hi." He held up the box in his hands. "I brought pizza since I figured it might get too late for dinner."

She appreciated the foresight, and she didn't mind that they weren't going out for dinner; dinner dates could be stressful with how formal they felt.

"Oh, yum!" she said. "I had the same thought and brought snacks!" She held up her own tote bag.

He smiled, dimples showing. "We'll have an entire feast, then."

They walked over together, where there was already a decent crowd set up in the field. Calahan had brought a blanket as well, so they used her blanket to sit on, and he put his blanket over their legs. Which was also good because this leather miniskirt was not made for sitting on the ground and was riding up. The night was a little chilly, cloudy, and windy; she wrapped her mother's shawl loosely around her shoulders.

They chatted for a bit, eating the pizza, which was still warm, then the candy she had brought. Soon thereafter, the movie began, and the crowd quieted, attendees snuggling closer if they wanted to make commentary on the film. The showing was one of those action-fantasy movies—it was the type Theo loved, so Lavinia had seen it already. Lavinia was hardly paying attention to the screen.

She was hyper-alert to every movement she made, not to mention every movement Calahan made. This close, she caught his scent, which she realized was familiar to her after working together for so long at the cafe: he smelled like ink and paper.

As the movie progressed, she slowly inched closer to him, her knee brushing against his under the blanket. Then, finally, he scooted over entirely, until he was right beside her. He put his arm behind her, and she leaned back, against his chest, in a way that felt very natural and normal. The contact warmed through her core.

After the movie finished, they sat for a bit longer, even as people stood up and left. They ate the rest of the pizza, which had long since gone cold, and finished off the candy as well.

"We should probably head out," Lavinia eventually said, when most of the field had cleared and even the inflatable screen had been dismantled. Calahan rose to his feet and offered her his hand with a dimpled smile. She took it.

He packed up their things, throwing the garbage out, and they walked back to the parking lots, where there were only a few cars left, two of which were theirs. He walked her to her car, putting her bag away.

"I had a lot of fun tonight," Calahan said, not quite going just yet. Her heartbeat quickened as she gazed up at him, the shawl dropping from her shoulders. A shiver ran down her spine.

"Me too," she replied, smiling. His gaze went to her mouth,

and he took a step forward. Anticipation fizzed through her body, and she waited, holding her breath until he bridged the space between them completely.

He kissed her, lips soft against hers. Lavinia hummed, relishing the contact she had been craving and had been denied by another. Going on her tiptoes, Lavinia wound her arms around his neck, kissing him back, bringing him in closer. He held her waist, hands steady.

The kiss was sweet. A perfect ending to a perfect first date.

He pulled back, and they both grinned. She unwound her arms and he let go of her waist, reaching for her hand.

"Goodnight," Calahan said, squeezing.

"Goodnight," she replied, squeezing back.

She got into her car, and he waited until she drove away, lifting a hand up to wave. Once she was out of his sight, Lavinia squealed in her car. She put on some upbeat music and sang alone as she drove home.

Everything was happening exactly like she wanted it to! There was nothing to worry about at all! She was on track to find love, and before her deadline, too.

When she got home, she went up to her room and got ready for bed, busy with washing off her makeup and changing. After all that was done, she returned to her bedroom, finally catching a moment of quiet for the first time that day.

And in that silence, a little spike of anxiety pricked her. She rubbed her chest, frowning.

Things had gone perfectly, as well as she could have imagined. Calahan was sweet and fun.

Why did she feel so . . . she didn't even know what she felt. But it was making her stomach hurt.

She took the things out of her purse, putting them on top of her vanity. Taking the lipsticks, she put them away in her drawer, and as she did, she saw Theo's cologne.

Her hand itched. She was tempted to spray it—but no, she shouldn't.

Lavinia shut the drawer, but her hand lingered on the handle. Biting her lower lip, she pulled it open, taking out the cologne and spraying it in the air. Theo's scent immediately comforted her, calming her nerves.

She grabbed her phone, calling Theo. She wanted to discuss the date with him, the way she did everything. The phone rang and she waited. Her gaze strayed to the clock, but it wasn't so late that he would be asleep already.

Finally, he picked up.

"Hey," he said, clearing his throat. He sounded a bit off, but she heard sheets rustling and figured he was probably in bed, about to sleep.

"Hi! I just got back from my date! It went so well!!"

"Oh. That's good. I'm glad." He cleared his throat. "Was it cold?"

"A little, but Calahan brought a blanket, so we shared that. He also brought pizza so we didn't end up going for dinner, but it was really fun at the movie! After the movie, we sat and talked a bit, and mostly everyone had gone by then. When we went back to the parking lot, he walked me to my car, and then he kissed me and—"

"I'm tired," Theo said abruptly, cutting her off. "Can we talk later?" His voice sounded pained.

"Oh. Yeah. Are you . . . Are you okay?" she asked, concerned.

He was quiet. Then, finally, he said, "Mhm."

He hung up before she could ask or say anything else. Lavinia's heart pounded, unease spreading through her. She felt strange, as if she had upset him—but what about her having a successful date could be upsetting to her best friend?

It had to be something else. She'd ask him about it later.

Sometimes he needed time alone to collect himself; she knew when not to push. When they were kids and he was overstimulated or needed a break, he would pace around her backyard or sit under the apple tree, watching the branches rustling.

At first, Lavinia would follow him out there, but then he'd get irritable, and she'd stomp back inside, annoyed. Until finally Beena explained to her that he probably just needed to recharge, and she should let him.

"But why?" Lavinia would ask, pouting. Beena would hold her face in her hands, brushing back her hair.

"Patience, gudiya, patience," her mother would respond. "Sometimes people get overwhelmed."

The next time it happened, Lavinia let Theo be. She stayed inside, coloring at the kitchen table, and a half an hour later, Theo came back inside, right as rain.

Lavinia was sure that this now was one of those moments; he just needed to recharge.

Even as she told herself that, she felt unsettled. If she was Theo, this would be a moment she'd start pacing, like he did whenever he felt restless, but instead she turned off the lights and went to bed, curling into a ball. She grabbed a throw pillow and hugged it to her chest, trying to go to sleep.

A little while later, she still felt strange. With a groan, she grabbed her phone and texted Genevieve that the date was a success.

Genevieve replied almost immediately with an abundance of exclamation points: **Tell me EVERYTHING!**

Lavinia smiled, giving Genevieve the entire debrief and rundown, replaying every moment. As she did, she grew happy and excited all over again, giggling to herself.

**I love all of this**, Genevieve texted back. **This is FANTASTIC!**

Yes, this *was* fantastic, Lavinia told herself.

She ignored the little voice in her head telling her something was wrong.

# CHAPTER 11

A few days later, Theo was at the Rolling Pin, aggressively kneading cookie dough. His thoughts returned to the memory of fixing Lavinia's lipstick, how heat had swept over him at the contact of her skin against his.

He'd had to leave immediately before he did something stupid, but that didn't stop him from pressing the lipstick stain on his finger against his mouth, as if he could transfer the feel of her lips to his own. Desire beat through him at the thought, as it had every time he had recollected the moment over the past few days.

He had no business thinking these things. Not when Lavinia had had such a successful date with Calahan. He'd felt nauseous hearing her talk about it, which meant he truly was an awful friend. He should have been happy for her, overjoyed at how jubilant she sounded. Instead, he'd had to hang up, unable to bear it.

Since then, he had changed the topic every time Lavinia had brought Calahan up, and she seemed to get the sense he didn't want to talk about Calahan because she stopped bringing him up.

Not that it changed anything. Not that it helped. Theo kept imagining the two of them together, the romantic scene of them sharing a blanket. Him, kissing her—

"Theo." He felt a hand on his arm, and he jolted. He turned to peer into Suki's concerned dark eyes. "Let's not overwork the batter," she said, looking at the mess he'd made of the cookie dough.

He winced. "Sorry." Embarrassment flushed through him. He felt like a student getting a low score on an exam in his favorite class.

Instead of being disappointed, Suki only looked concerned. "It's okay. Why don't you take a coffee break?" she suggested.

He nodded, throat thick. Sometimes people's kindness made him want to cry. Suki gave him a smile, and he took off his apron, going to wash his hands. When he was done, he headed out, going in the direction of the Baby Dragon.

Wind cut through the air, and he rolled down the sleeves of his flannel shirt, his hands shaking. Leaves skittered across the ground, crunching beneath his boots as he made his way over to the cafe.

He entered, immediately inhaling the scent of coffee. A pang beat through him; Lavinia always smelled like coffee. He shook his head, walking to the counter, and his mood brightened when he saw who was there.

"Theo, hi!" Saphira said, giving him a big smile. She was at the counter, and when he came over, she went on her tiptoes and leaned across to kiss his cheek. Her presence dulled some of the ache in his chest.

"Hey, Saph," he said. "I'm happy to see you."

"I'm happy to see you, too!" she replied, then she pouted. "It's been too long."

"I know."

"I miss the good old days," she said. Now that he had been promoted, he didn't do deliveries anymore. Even his fusion recipes were sent with the other deliveries.

"How were the seviyan cream puffs?" he asked. He had tested out the recipe, then perfected it before making them as part of this week's order for the Baby Dragon Bakery, as Beena liked to call it. He did only one fusion recipe each week—sometimes new, sometimes tried and true.

"Super yummy!" Saphira replied, dark eyes warm. "I had to sneak some away just for myself before they finished." He smiled. "You're so creative with these recipes," she continued, voice amazed. "I would have never thought of that!"

Hearing her say that almost made him feel proud of himself. Almost.

"Anyway. What can I get you?" Saphira asked. "Are you on a coffee break or did you only work half the day today?"

"Coffee break," he replied with a sigh. "Can I get a butter pecan latte, please?"

"Of course!" After he paid, she set about making that. He sat on one of the barstools, waiting.

"How have you been doing?" he asked, while she pulled the espresso shot.

"Good! Busy. I'm usually not even here, but I missed working the counter, so I popped in today. Otherwise, I mostly do managerial stuff now, and it's a lot. The business is doing really well, which is wonderful, but it feels like there are always a million little things that could be optimized or done better. It's busier than ever, so there's more to think about."

"It's great the cafe's doing so well," Theo said. "But, yes, managing a business can't be easy." He knew how complicated it could be from the classes he took for his undergraduate degree.

"Aiden helps out a lot with the math, since you know I'm hopeless at that stuff," she said, pouring steamed milk into his to-go cup. She finished the latte off, powdering cinnamon over a heart stencil, then handed it to him. "But he has his own business to run!" Aiden had a gardening company called The Bloomsmiths. "So I don't want to put more work on his plate. He says he doesn't mind, but still. He suggested that I could hire a business managerial assistant to help out, but there's no one I trust, and no one has been here since the beginning, except for Lavinia, but you know how busy she is with school, obviously."

Theo listened, making a thoughtful sound. "I could help out, if you wanted?" he said, taking a sip of his latte. The words were out before he had a chance to second-guess them, and he realized the prospect of assisting the management of the cafe interested him. "I do have a business degree," he continued. "My knowledge might be a bit rusty, but if you wanted . . ."

"Aw, that's so sweet! Thank you." She squeezed his forearm. "But I know you're really busy, too, with the Rolling Pin, and I don't want Suki to think I'm exhausting her best baker."

Saphira's words made him immediately sober. *Suki.* How could he have forgotten? Guilt pricked at him.

"Yeah. Right." He cleared his throat. "Speaking of, I should head back," he said, standing with his drink. She slid him a lid, and he stuck it on. "Thanks for the latte."

"One more thing before you go!" Saphira said. "I need help. I've been trying to come up with a puppuccino equivalent for the baby dragons, but they don't really like whipped cream or sweet milk like that. Any suggestions?"

"Um," Theo tried to think, but he could hardly come up with any coherent thoughts. He had been scatterbrained since Saturday—that moment with Lavinia, then the news about her date.

He must have looked as lost as he felt because a moment later, Saphira waved a hand, her massive engagement ring sparkling in the light. "Never mind." She looked at him closely, voice turning gentle. "Are you okay?"

*Was* he okay? Not really. He wanted to be supportive, to be a good friend to Lavinia and help her in her love life because that was what she always did for him, but he was unhappy with the entire situation.

He was begrudgingly grappling with the fact that perhaps the reason he was in a bad mood every time Calahan was mentioned was because he was jealous. And if he was grappling with that fact, he had to additionally grapple with the fact that he was jealous because he wanted Lavinia to feel that way about him.

Because *he* felt that way about *her*.

Theo was realizing that he'd had feelings for Lavinia all along, that moment at the engagement party had just brought it to the surface. And now it was too late because she was finding happiness with someone else, and all he wanted, truly, was for her to be happy, even if it wasn't with him.

That didn't stop it from hurting.

Why, oh *why*, hadn't he realized sooner? How could he have missed something so obvious? He wished he was more confident, but he wasn't like Lavinia. He wasn't raised in a loving household among people who always encouraged him.

He knew if he fell, there would be no one there to catch him, so he was always twice as careful. What if—in being so careful—he had missed his chance?

Another voice flickered to life, reminding him that he probably had never had a chance to begin with. Compared to Calahan, Theo was hardly a contender. Lavinia deserved a swoon-worthy romance, and Calahan was perfect.

"Theo?" Saphira asked again, brown eyes worried.

"Sorry," he said, shaking his head. He sighed, unsure about how to talk about what he was feeling. It felt wrong to discuss anything with anybody when he hadn't discussed that thing with Lavinia. "I'm just tired, I think."

"Sit for a second," Saphira said. "Suki won't kill you if your coffee break lasts a little longer."

Theo was too tired to protest. He sat down, releasing a long breath. "I don't really feel much like going back, to be honest," Theo said, taking a sip of his latte.

"What do you mean?"

"It used to be exciting, working there, but now, there's no spark." He rubbed a hand over his face. He didn't really know why he was working there anymore.

"Maybe you're just in a funk," Saphira said. "You love baking, and you're so good at it!"

"Maybe. Besides, if I'm not baking, I don't know what else I would do. I don't know who I am if I'm not baking." He fiddled with the lid on his to-go mug.

"It doesn't have to be your entire identity," Saphira told him. "You can explore other things."

But that would feel too much like failure. He wasn't allowed to fail. He wasn't allowed to make mistakes.

Saphira thought for a moment, then asked, "Have you decided what you're going to bake next for the cafe?"

"I'm thinking of trying something new," he replied, because this was something he'd planned out. He didn't want to disappoint Saphira. "I was thinking of gulab jamun cheesecake cups."

Her face lit up. "Ooh! What would that be like?"

"A classical cheesecake with gulab jamun inside, but about the size of muffins, so they're easily sold individually. I love cold gulab jamun, and I think with the cold cheesecake it would pair really well. The textures, too: the silky cheesecake with the moist and melt-in-your-mouth gulab jamun."

Saphira smiled. "You sounded excited just then," she told him. "You lit up!"

"That was different," he replied. "I love experimenting and sourcing stuff for your cafe." He smiled a little. "You know Lavinia's mom, Beena? She calls the desserts I make for the cafe the Baby Dragon Bakery."

"Aw, I love that!" Saphira said, holding a hand to her heart. "I should make a little sign over the display cases that says, 'The Baby Dragon Bakery,' that would be adorable!" She pulled out her phone. "I'm making a note to myself right now." She paused, looking up at him. "As long as you don't mind me stealing the idea?"

"No, not at all," Theo said. "I would be proud."

"You should be! You're incredible. I love the stuff you make for us here."

He smiled, touched by her words. He stood up again, gaze straying to the clock. "I should really get back now."

"See you soon?" Saphira asked. Nodding, he went on his

way. Outside, cold wind blew against him, but the sun was warm, and he felt a little better, having talked with Saphira.

Until he felt his phone buzz. He pulled it out; his mother, Amaya, was calling. He had never called her back the other night. He should pick up now and get it over with. He watched his phone ring, bracing himself. Finally, he picked up.

"Hey, Mom," he said.

"Theo, hello," Amaya said. "You never called me back."

"Sorry, been really busy," he said. He got to the Rolling Pin but walked straight past it; he would talk to his mother for a few minutes while pacing up and down Main Street, then head back in.

"What are you busy with?" Amaya asked, sounding confused.

"Just work," he replied.

"And how is work?"

"Fine."

"You're still at the bakery?" she asked.

"Yup."

She made a thoughtful noise. He bristled, his pace quickening.

"Your father says hello," she said.

"Tell him I said hi back," Theo replied.

"Come visit soon," Amaya asked. "Surely work at a bakery can't be so busy that you can't even visit your family."

He wondered if she said that out of formality or if his parents really wanted to see him. He always hoped for the latter, but realistically, it was probably the former.

"Sure. I'll try and visit this weekend."

"Good."

"I have to get back to work now, Mom," he said.

"Okay. Goodbye."

He hung up, then did another lap around Main Street, just to calm his nerves a little. He was always so full of energy, and as a kid, it made him hyperactive. His parents were calm, and that was what they had wanted from their only child, as well, but he couldn't be still or quiet. All those years had dulled some of his radiance, to be sure, but it was never enough.

He rubbed a hand over his face, then went back into the Rolling Pin, getting back to work. It was a good thing he had football with the guys later that evening. The sport helped a bit with his restless energy.

Unfortunately, no matter what he did, he couldn't clear his head entirely. He kept thinking of Lavinia, her going out with Calahan. He couldn't get the image of Lavinia and Calahan kissing out of his head.

Even though it was driving him crazy to think about it, his thoughts returned again and again to the two of them together. It was like picking at a scab, and he couldn't stop, no matter how much it hurt.

# CHAPTER 12

Lavinia was at the Animal Hospital, preparing for an appointment. It had been a hectic week between work and school and spending time with Calahan, and she felt like there weren't enough hours in the day for everything.

She followed Dr. Quan to the patient's room. She would be seeing Luke Hayward, who was here with a chimera. She hadn't seen many baby chimeras in her time interning here, so she was excited to see this one today.

Lavinia recognized Luke's name and vaguely knew of him because he was on Genevieve's cousin Emmeline's hit list for trying to poach Saphira's business from her. Luke owned a coffee-roasting company called Tempest, which rivaled Emmeline's own coffee-roasting company, Inferno.

While Emmeline's company had dragon-roasted coffee, Luke's had chimera-roasted coffee. A chimera had the body of a lion with the head of a goat and the tail of a snake; they had wings and breathed fire, just like dragons, though they weren't as coveted as dragons. Dragons were rarer, a status symbol of power and privilege, but Lavinia liked all animals equally.

Luke was in today with a year-old chimera, who must have been the baby of one of his fully grown chimeras that roasted Tempest's coffee. When she entered the patient room behind Dr. Quan, he gave them both a charming smile, and she felt a little weak in the knees, if she was going to be honest.

Luke Hayward was supermodel gorgeous, clothed all in black. He had deep, rich brown skin and a clean-shaven face that showed off his sharp jawline and high cheekbones. The top buttons of his shirt were undone to reveal glittering chains against his chest.

"Good afternoon," Dr. Quan said. "This is my intern, Lavinia. She'll be conducting your visit today."

"It's a pleasure to meet you," Luke said, standing with the baby chimera in his arms.

"Who is this little angel?" Lavinia asked, as Luke set the baby down onto the patient bed. The chimera bleated.

"This is Barnabus," Luke replied, scratching behind the chimera's ears, beneath Barnabus's little horn stubs.

Lavinia smiled, inspecting Barnabus. She checked on the baby chimera's vitals, and almost immediately, she deduced what the problem was.

"I believe Barnabus has selenium deficiency," Lavinia said. "It can cause weak rear legs and also keep the baby from swallowing properly."

She turned back to confirm with Dr. Quan, and he nodded, gesturing for her to continue. "See how he's holding his legs; that's the telltale sign." She pointed for Luke to see. He nodded, understanding.

"We'll give him an injection now, and then you can bring him back in a week from now for another checkup and possible further injections," Lavinia told Luke. She turned back to Dr. Quan. "Anything to add?"

"Nope, that's perfect," he replied, giving her a proud smile. "I think you've got it from here." Dr. Quan took his leave, and Lavinia left to retrieve the injections.

Satisfaction coursed through her. She loved her work, applying the things she had learned in school. It made her feel accomplished and competent that Dr. Quan trusted her to run appointments alone. Even though school was difficult and trying, she did love learning.

That was something she and Calahan shared, she reminded herself. They were definitely fated to be together.

Lavinia returned to the patient room and administered the shots, while Luke held the baby chimera in his arms. The baby made a bleat of displeasure, and Luke stroked his little goat-head with his ringed fingers, soothing.

"All done," Lavinia said. She petted the baby chimera's furry head, then brought him a bunch of thin crunchy carrots, which he happily ate. "You can make the follow-up appointment in the front."

"Perfect." Luke stood, giving her that winning smile again as he held onto the baby chimera with one muscled arm. He made as if to leave, then paused by the door, turning around. "You work at the Baby Dragon Cafe, don't you?" Luke asked, cocking his head. "I think I've seen you there before."

"Yes, I do," Lavinia replied. His lips spread into a smile, eyes glittering with mischief.

"Tell Emmeline I said hi." He looked pleased with himself.

"Sure," Lavinia replied, and then he was off.

There was no way Lavinia would be telling Emmeline

that, or Emmeline's blood pressure would shoot through the roof. Lavinia didn't see Emmeline Sterling often, but she knew enough that Emmy was triggered every single time she heard Luke's name. Saphira had mentioned once that the two went to university together and there was some history between them, but Lavinia didn't know the whole backstory.

After Luke left, Lavinia went back to Dr. Quan's office, sitting down at her desk. She typed up her notes and filled out paperwork. There were no more appointments for that day, so she did the work at a leisurely pace, preparing for tomorrow's appointments.

When her phone lit up, she turned her attention to see a text from Calahan. She opened the notification, which was simply a photo. A smile spread across her face.

It was a photo from last night, of her sleeping on her books. They had gone to the Tales & Tails Bookshop off Main Street on Elderberry Lane for a study date; the bookstore was a bit rundown, but quiet and devoid of distractions.

It was a lovely place, and the study date had also been lovely, until they'd gotten to the actual "studying" part. Then, Lavinia had in fact fallen asleep on top of her books while she listened to a playlist titled "you're daydreaming while you're lost in the palace gardens." In the picture, Calahan had taken her glasses off and set them aside, tucking her hair behind her ear, but she still looked ridiculous, mouth open, a dribble of drool spilling out.

**So rude, delete that!!** she texted him.
**No thanks, you look too cute,** he replied.

She giggled to herself. It had been ten days since their first date. She and Calahan had gone out two more times since then, once to the farmers' market, and once to study. It was just as she had planned, just as she had imagined, sweet and easy. So easy! Mama always said love was easy.

She was moving on from Theo, no, really, she was. Calahan was so clever and mature. Being with him felt very grown-up. Like the right decision.

The *wrong* decision would be to pine over someone who wasn't interested in her and jeopardize the most important relationship in her life in the process.

For a moment, Lavinia worried she was simply using Calahan to get over Theo, but no, that wasn't true. She knew with absolute certainty it would not happen with her and Theo, and she really did like Calahan. Maybe this was what was always meant to be.

Besides, she didn't have any time to waste, not with the winter just a few months away. She had wasted enough time already!

Beena and Lavinia both had birthdays in May, so it was easy to imagine the ghost of her mother's past as Lavinia's companion. She had met Garrett on a cold December day, and they had started dating immediately after, everything happening so seamlessly.

Lavinia wasn't sure yet if she would want to spend forever with Calahan, but she still had some time to figure that out. Until December, at least.

Calahan was wonderful. He really liked Lavinia, and she knew they should be content, but she just felt . . . She didn't know what she felt, what was making her hesitate.

Nothing was perfect, not even her feelings for Theo, if she was being fair, which she was really trying to be. There were too many fireworks, which could be beautiful, yes, but they could also blow up in her face. She didn't ever want to imagine her life without him.

With Theo, there was too much risk—too much to lose.

With a sigh, she went home, where homework was waiting for her. Graduate school was an endless cycle, and she hardly felt like she had a moment to breathe. After saying hello to her family and giving Biter a quick kiss and cuddle, she went to her room and did her assignments while listening to a playlist called "writing poems to your forbidden lover at three a.m." which was surely what she would have preferred to be doing instead of categorizing different infectious diseases.

Luckily, she lived at home, so in the evening she came downstairs to a prepared dinner and the company of her family members, as well as the adorable Biter, who was practicing flying on the carpet with Alfie.

"Come on, Biter, come on!" Alfie coaxed, rattling a toy. Biter's red eyes widened. She took unsteady steps toward Alfie, her tiny wings flapping. She made it a few steps before falling forward onto her face.

She hissed, and Lavinia scooped her up into her arms. "Aw, Alfie is making you do so much work, isn't he?" Lavinia asked, scratching Biter's scales. Biter hummed, wagging her tail. Even though Lavinia had spent all day with various baby animals, then even more hours reading about animals, she still loved this time with the baby dragon.

"I'm making her practice!" Alfie protested, coming over. "Mama said I can't bribe her with candy, so I used the chew toy."

"She's a baby, Alf," Lavinia said. "She can't eat solids yet, let alone candy!"

"Oh." Alfie looked sheepish, and Lavinia laughed, mussing his hair.

"Dinner!" Beena called.

Lavinia set Biter down in her bassinet with a few toys, then went to the table with Alfie, which Garrett had already set. Beena brought over a dish of lentils and a dish of boiled rice. The yellow daal was topped with a butter, brown onion, and coriander tarka; it was the perfect fortifying food.

After dinner, she helped clean up, then went back to study for a bit, until Beena called her downstairs.

As Lavinia made her way to the kitchen, she inhaled the warm scent of cinnamon and sugar. Her mother had baked pumpkin snickerdoodles, which were so yummy and cozy with a cold glass of milk.

She handed some to Alfie, who was sitting at the kitchen table doing his homework, then joined her mother in the living room with a second plate, having had enough of studying for the day.

They got cozy on the couch, and while Beena switched on the television, Lavinia spread a throw blanket over their legs. It was mid-October now and properly chilly, true autumn in full swing. She loved it.

Her mother put on the next episode of the show they were watching together, a period drama with an actress her mother loved. Once or twice a week, Lavinia sat and watched television with her mother; it was a nice way to spend time together, especially as a weekly ritual in the midst of her hectic school/work schedule.

Lavinia wasn't big on period dramas, but she enjoyed watching them with her mother and was fully invested in the storylines. There was something so swoon-worthy and grand imbued in these stories, something so romantic. Sighing, she watched as the hero wrote his heroine a beautifully worded love letter.

After the episode was done, Lavinia brought over a bowl of warm oil. It was a mixture of coconut oil, almond oil, and castor oil. She handed it to Beena, then sat down on the floor, by her mother's feet.

"Tch, your hair is getting so thin," Beena tsked, running her hands through Lavinia's hair. "You're taking too much stress from all your studying. And what have I told you about tying such a tight ponytail?"

"I know, I know," Lavinia said, head rattling as her mother massaged oil into her scalp.

"We'll have to do this twice a week now," Beena said. Lavinia ordinarily got oil put in her hair once a week. "Then you'll notice a difference."

"Mmm."

Beena continued to oil Lavinia's hair, and Lavinia closed her eyes, enjoying it, though her mother could be a tad aggressive at moments. While it was heavenly to get her head massaged, she also loved sitting at her mother's feet, feeling close to her.

When Beena finished, she brushed Lavinia's hair, then pulled it back into a loose braid, so it wouldn't move at night when she slept. Lavinia would wash it out the next morning.

"All done," Beena said, smoothing a hand over Lavinia's oiled braid.

"Thank you, Mama," Lavinia replied. Even though she was done, she did not get up right away. She leaned against her mother's knees, thinking.

Theo's behavior had been different lately. Every time she tried to bring up Calahan, Theo seemed unhappy. It looked as though Theo didn't like the fact that she was going out with Calahan, but there was no reason for him to be upset by that. Calahan was great, and Theo had always liked him.

A hesitant little voice rose in her mind: *what if he's jealous?* Was she reaching? Or was that a possibility?

"What's up, gudiya?" Beena asked. Lavinia shook her head, clearing her thoughts.

"What do you mean?" Lavinia asked, twisting to look back at her mother.

"You've been sighing all day," Beena replied. Lavinia felt her face fall. She couldn't hide anything from her mother, and she couldn't talk about this with anyone, so maybe Beena was the right person to talk to.

"I thought I had feelings for Theo," she said. Saying the words out loud made her feel humiliated by his rejection all over again. She swallowed hard. "But he wasn't interested in me—at least, that's what I thought. Now? I don't know." She threw her hands up. "I just don't know. What to do, or what's right, or what will happen." If she knew how things would play out—how the story would end—she could act accordingly.

Beena was quiet, and Lavinia could feel her mother thinking. She got up off the floor and joined Beena on the couch, sitting with her legs up so she could face her. Beena played with the end of her braid, a pensive expression on her face.

"What you and Theo have is extraordinary," Beena finally said. "It's special and rare—you should protect that as much as you can." She paused. "It seems like you're a bit confused, and it's best not to do anything you're not certain about."

"Right," Lavinia said, disappointment spreading through her. "No, of course. Yes."

She swallowed, and Beena released a long breath. "Aren't you seeing someone right now? That boy from the cafe? Calahan, right? I thought that was going well."

"No, it is." She ignored the pit in her stomach. "It absolutely is." She forced a smile, shaking her head. "I don't know what I was thinking."

And she didn't, truly. She wanted things to work out with Calahan—she needed them to, or there would be no hope at all—and for that to happen, she needed to stop being delusional and selfish, wanting things that couldn't be.

She needed to be responsible.

# CHAPTER 13

Lavinia was keeping her chin up. It was full steam ahead on Operation Calahan, and she was positive everything would continue to work out, so long as she did not sabotage herself.

They had a pottery date tonight but, before that, she was meeting Theo for coffee at the cafe after they both got off work. She felt as if she hadn't seen him much lately and had texted him to meet her, which he had immediately agreed to. He seemed so busy recently, and whenever he was free, she was busy, and vice versa.

She missed him the way she would miss her morning coffee.

When she finished up at the Animal Hospital, she said goodbye to Dr. Quan. Theo was already waiting for her outside. His brown hair was messy from the wind, and he was wearing a forest green shirt-jacket.

"We match!" Lavinia said, pointing to the forest green overalls she was wearing over a long-sleeve ribbed crop top. She fell into line with him and they started walking.

"Copycat," he said. She bumped his hip with hers, and he stumbled. She giggled, and they continued walking.

She loved living in a walkable small town with such a great Main Street, filled with places like the live theater, the stationery store, the pizza parlor, the florist, and more. Theo was a foot taller than her, but he knew to take shorter strides when they walked together, so she didn't have to run to keep up. They walked at a leisurely pace, enjoying the crisp autumn air, the warm sun, and the sharp breeze.

She had gotten used to his height now, but at first, it was jarring. They used to be the same height, until the summer they were sixteen. Then, every day it seemed like he was growing taller and taller. He didn't believe her when she told him that; he felt the same as always. She started measuring him every time she saw him, using marks on the back of her bedroom door to keep track, and those had proved her point.

Things changed even when you didn't notice.

They walked over to the Baby Dragon, which smelled like coffee, heavenly. She caught the waft of warm brown sugar and cinnamon, autumnal scents. The cafe was mostly full, and baby dragons ate little snacks from their position on the floor by their owners' feet, or they slept up on bed nooks. A few were even in their owners' laps. She thought of Biter, missing the little draggo.

The cafe used to be a bit more chaotic during the early days, but now things were more harmonious as the patrons and their dragons adjusted to the cafe's space and knew how to behave. Lavinia loved coming here, again and again.

They went to the front to order, and Lavinia spotted a new detail above the display shelves. She grabbed Theo's arm. "Look!"

There was a new sign in the same font as the cafe's logo,

except it said *The Baby Dragon Bakery* and had an illustration of a cupcake with wings. "Wait, I need a picture of you with this." She grabbed his shoulders and, despite Theo's protests, made him stand next to the sign and display cases. Lavinia pulled out her phone.

Theo gave her a toothy grin and two thumbs-up, and she snapped the picture. "Perfect." She immediately sent it to her mom, who replied back with about fifty heart eyes. Lavinia snorted, showing Theo, and he smiled, pleased.

They both ordered karak chai, as well as the new fusion recipe that Theo had made. It was ras malai tiramisu, and there were only a few orders left. Lavinia was interested to try it out, so she ordered that, while Theo got a maple spiced butter cookie.

Having picked up their orders, they sat down on a table by the exposed stone wall, a candle flickering between them beside a vase of yellow sunflowers.

Lavinia took a pensive sip of her chai, then inspected her dessert. "You know, this really feels like a stretch to me," Lavinia said. "Ras malai tiramisu?"

"I think it came out good, but I'm interested to see what you think," Theo said, taking a bite out of his cookie. Crumbs fell onto his jacket, and he brushed them away.

"I'm sure I'll love it, I love everything you make," she said. "I'm very easy to please like that."

"Still," he replied, waiting anxiously. "Your opinion matters to me."

"So if I said it was awful, you would throw it out and never make it again?" she joked.

"Yes," he replied, completely serious.

"What? Why!" She shook her head. "You're so silly! I don't even know what I'm saying half the time. My opinion doesn't matter that much."

He looked at her like she was being absurd. "Your opinion is the only thing that matters."

A current ran through her spine at the intensity with which he said those words, how earnest his brown eyes were.

She was touched. She reached across the table and squeezed his hand. It was warm from holding his mug of chai, and he held onto her fingers. She felt all gooey inside.

Then, she broke the moment by kicking him under the table.

"Well, if you told me I sucked at my job, I certainly wouldn't quit."

The tension broke as he laughed. "Come on, try it already."

She did, knowing that it would be delicious. She planned to act as if it was terrible, just to annoy him, but once she took a bite, she couldn't.

"Oh my god," she said, mouth full. "I'm in love."

Ras malai was made of disks of chenna, which was a type of cheese like cottage cheese, then soaked in sweet milk flavored with cardamom, but in this version, the disks of chenna replaced the lady fingers of the traditional tiramisu in the middle layer, and the cardamom sweet milk was mixed with the coffee soak for the lady fingers. The combination was divine.

She was thoroughly impressed. "How do you even come up with stuff like this?" she asked, awed. She took another bite. He was pleased and sat back in his seat, relaxed. After having another bite, she passed the ras malai tiramisu his way, while he slid her half of the cookie.

He ate a spoonful of the tiramisu. "It really is good," he said. They shared both desserts until they finished, then drank their chai, talking and people-watching, pointing out all the cute baby dragons. Then, Lavinia told him stories about Biter, and Theo told her the latest gossip between his coworkers at the Rolling Pin.

After some time had passed, Lavinia checked her phone to make sure she wasn't running late for her pottery date. That was when she noticed she had a text from Calahan, from about an hour ago.

"Oh," she said out loud, disappointed after reading his message.

Theo straightened. "What is it?"

"Calahan got roped into some last-minute tutoring session, so he can't come tonight," Lavinia said, frowning. "He's really sorry."

"Oh," Theo said, though he didn't look particularly crushed from the news. "Maybe you can go another time?" he said. His tone was bright. He was trying to be positive, which she appreciated.

"I might go anyway," Lavinia said, nibbling on her lower lip. "He booked it in advance, so it's already paid for, and I've wanted to go for so long. My parents went last month and loved it. They made the cutest little bowl!"

"I could go with you," Theo said, and was she imagining it, or was there eagerness in his voice?

"Oh." She hadn't been expecting that. Nerves ran through her, though she didn't know why. He was her best friend; they had done loads of activities together over the years. This would be no different.

She shouldn't overthink it. "Okay, great!" She smiled.

Theo stood. "Shall we?" He offered her his arm, and she hooked her elbow with his. They left the Baby Dragon and walked over to the ceramics store, which was on Main Street and a short walk away. As they entered the store, Lavinia became excited all over again.

The front of the store had various clay products to purchase, such as dinnerware or vases and the like, and they went to the back, where a studio was set up for pottery classes. There were six stations, and most of them were already filled. There was one free in the middle, and Theo and Lavinia made their way over to the empty station.

All the attendees were couples: one old couple, two her parents' age, and the rest in their twenties and thirties. While it was a class for couples, Lavinia was sure it wouldn't be anything too intimate. Theo didn't seem bothered, so there was no reason for her to get weird.

Lavinia and Theo sat down on the little stools. "Move your legs," Lavinia said, bumping his knees with hers. His legs were so long, and he was practically smushed against her on their tiny seats.

"Move yours," he replied, knocking his knees back. She laughed. There wasn't much room for anyone to go.

The instructor was a white-bearded older man with a kind face, wearing a smock covered with dried clay streaks. He waited for the last couple to arrive, and for everyone to put on their smocks and settle down, then he stood at the front and the room quieted.

"Good evening, everyone, my name is Gabriel, and I'll be leading the workshop," he said, smiling. He continued to tell them a bit about himself and his history with clay making, and then they got started.

"First, we will throw the clay onto the wheel," Gabriel said. "You want it to be as close to the center as possible and firmly set."

Gabriel had already cut blocks of clay and set them on each workstation, and Lavinia grabbed one. She threw it onto the wheel—and totally missed.

Theo snorted. "Nice one."

"Shut up," she replied, though she was biting back a laugh, too. The clay was only about six inches off. She pried it off the wheel, handing it to Theo. "How about you try?"

"You know what, I will." He threw the clay, and it landed pretty perfectly in the center.

Her mouth fell open in shock. "No fair!"

"Once you've got your clay thrown, you want to center it," Gabriel instructed. He explained how to dip their hands in water and spin the wheel, moving the clay until it was perfectly centered.

Theo went first, dipping his hands into the bucket of water, gently pressing on the pedal to get the wheel going. It spun, and he moved the clay until it was mostly centered. She narrowed her eyes at him.

"Why are you so good at this?"

He gave her a smile. "I'm good with my hands."

Heat flushed through her. She forced herself to get her mind out of the gutter.

"Here, you try," Theo said, stopping the wheel and removing his hands, which were covered in gray slip. Lavinia rolled her shoulders, taking a deep breath. Theo bit back a laugh.

She dipped her hands in the water, then slowly pressed on the pedal. The wheel began spinning, and she brought her hands to the clay, trying to move it, which was much more difficult than expected.

"Why is this so hard?" she asked, muscles straining. She really had to push, and it was so slippery!

Theo laughed, and she looked over her shoulder to glare at him. "Don't laugh!" she scolded. "You're going to mess me up!"

She shouldn't have taken her focus off the clay; it moved off center and slip splashed over her, splattering onto her face. Theo was further amused. She swiped her clay-covered finger over his cheek.

"Let me try again," Theo said, elbowing her arms off the clay. She let him, but this time he got cocky and applied too much pressure. The entire clay block flew off the wheel. Lavinia bit back a squeal while Theo narrowly caught the clay. They both turned to each other, eyes wide.

At the same time, they burst into laughter.

"Oops," Theo said, holding the mangled mess in his hands. Gabriel's back was turned as he tended to another couple, so he didn't see, and Lavinia gestured for Theo to put the clay back on the wheel.

"Quickly!" she said. It would be embarrassing for Gabriel to see the mess they'd made when everyone else's was perfect. With haste, Theo threw and centered the clay again, fixing it just before Gabriel made his way over to check in on them.

Gabriel gave them an approving smile, then moved on, and Lavinia let out a breath.

"Phew." Theo exhaled. They both giggled like kids who had

just narrowly missed getting into trouble—something they did in fact spend a lot of time doing as children.

Gabriel explained the next step, which was to make a hole in the center with their thumbs, then mold the clay into either a mug or a bowl. For this part, they would work together.

"You want to make sure you have a good bit of water on your hands. Keep the wheel nice and slow, until you get into a steady rhythm together," Gabriel explained.

Theo and Lavinia began, her left arm over his right, their hands interlinked.

"You must work in harmony," Gabriel continued. "Apply pressure together."

They sat closer, their thighs pressed together. The room quieted as everyone focused, and Lavinia felt his breath light on her neck, the warmth of his body behind hers. She inhaled the scent of sugar and dough from him. As they applied pressure, she could feel the muscles in his arms moving.

Slowly, they worked the clay, their hands covered with slip as they moved together. The clay formed into a cup, smooth against her palms. They molded it, their hands covered in slip, until she could no longer see where their hands were separated from the clay, or where they were separated from each other.

When they finished, they slowed the wheel until it stopped entirely. Their hands drew closer together on the cup, moving up until they released it, but they did not let go of each other's hands. The slip was wet and soft, and a small smile spread across her face as they played with each other's fingers.

Then, he entwined their hands. Theo blew air on their joined hands, and the clay dried a little. If they didn't move, it wouldn't crack. They had become a work of art themselves.

Tenderness spread through her, and she looked up to find him looking at her.

Their eyes met, and the moment seemed to extend out until it felt as if there was no one else in the room but them. A quiet intimacy hushed over them as they gazed into each other's eyes. Lavinia felt each beat of her heart.

"Once you're finished, you can cut your creation from the wheel," Gabriel instructed, and his voice brought her back to the studio, the moment between her and Theo breaking. She pulled her hand away from his, the dried clay on their skin cracking.

Her heart ached, bringing her back to reality. Tears sprung in her eyes, and she blinked them away, admonishing herself. She needed to stop this. She was supposed to be here with Calahan, the guy she was seeing. She needed to stop this ridiculousness about Theo.

After the pottery class, they cleaned up and headed out. The sun had set. The evening was brisk, but the sky was clear.

"Do you want to grab a bite to eat?" Theo asked before Lavinia could even think of leaving. "Should we get tacos?"

"Ooh, yes! I haven't had one in forever!"

They walked to the taco place, which was on Elderberry Lane off Main Street. Inside, they sat down at one of the empty tables, which was painted in many different colors. The restaurant was lit with fluorescent green and red lights, casting a glow over their faces and those of the other patrons there.

Theo and Lavinia used to come here loads when they were teenagers, and again during their university years whenever Theo would come to visit, but they hadn't been here in a while.

They ordered food, replaying the events of the pottery class, even though they had literally just come from there, but she loved to recollect moments with him, see how they could become funnier and brighter. They were killing themselves laughing and—not for the first time—Lavinia said, "We need to start a podcast, we're so funny."

Theo laughed, and before he could agree, she added, "Except there are already too many men on podcasts. So it'll mostly be focused on me."

He laughed harder, and she laughed, too. It was so much fun—it was always fun with Theo. Lavinia had forgotten just how spicy the salsa was, and when she took a bite of her taco, her eyes sprang with tears.

"Oh my god." She fanned herself, and Theo snickered, so she snuck some of the salsa onto his food as well, and then he was dying too, both of them with tears in their eyes, cackling. Theo drank a big gulp of lemonade, then choked, some of it spluttering out of his mouth. Lavinia laughed harder.

"What is wrong with you?" she asked, taking a sip, but then she realized why he had choked because she choked as well. "Why is it so sour?"

Her vision was blurry with tears. She could hear Theo wheezing.

"I'm in so much pain," Theo gasped.

"Me too," she cried. She pressed her hands against her ribs, which hurt from laughing, but she couldn't stop.

Eventually, feeling returned to their tongues, and they calmed down enough to order dessert. The plate of freshly fried churros rolled in cinnamon sugar arrived soon thereafter, and the scent alone made Lavinia salivate. The sweet churros were perfect, one of her favorite things ever, and she couldn't believe how long it had been since she'd last had them.

"I would kill someone for these churros," Lavinia said, reaching for a second. "Like, commit actual murder."

"And I would one hundred percent support you in that," Theo replied, dipping his churro in chocolate. They toasted each other with their churros, continuing to talk and joke around. She hadn't laughed this much in a long time, and she felt buoyant.

Afterwards, they walked around Main Street, which was quiet and dark, most of the places closed for the night. There were only a few people around under the clear night sky. They walked over to the white gazebo in the center of the square, where there was some reprieve from the evening wind. She leaned against the railing, looking out at the stars.

A few times, both of them attempted to leave, but each time, they kept getting distracted with talking. Even when they left the gazebo to walk back to their cars, they ended up sitting on the slanted ground in front of the gazebo, the grass crunchy and cold.

Theo talked to her about work, how it was all so uninteresting to him now, and she listened as he explained how it wasn't the way it used to be. There wasn't much she could say, but she just listened, and he had a lot to say, as if he, too, was waiting to just talk to her.

"Saphira mentioned how she could use a business assistant, and I thought . . ." He broke off, shaking his head. "But how could I ever leave Suki? After she took a chance on me? I mean, I didn't go to culinary school, I had practically no experience, but she still saw something in me. She nurtured that. Would it be ungrateful to even consider leaving the Rolling Pin?" He sighed, falling back onto the grass. She leaned back on her arm, thinking.

"I wouldn't say it's ungrateful of you," Lavinia finally said. "Plus, Suki adores you—I'm sure she just wants you to be happy, wherever you are."

He blew out his cheeks, looking up at the stars. She lay down next to him, nestling close and leaning her cheek against his shoulder. They watched the stars in silence, huddled together to keep warm.

"We should probably go," she suggested at some point.

"Yeah," he agreed, though neither of them moved.

She turned her face up to look at him rather than at the stars, and he turned toward her, too, until they were both looking at each other. Half of his face was awash with starlight, the other half in shadow.

He was so beautiful. The thought was unbidden and made her pulse race. Tension hummed through her. She forced her heart to calm, blurting, "Do you think everything is okay with me and Calahan?"

Theo sighed, turning his face.

Insecurity pricked her, and she sat up. "What if he stood me up today because he didn't want to come, and the tutoring thing was a made-up excuse?"

"Why would he do that?" Theo asked.

"What if he's getting tired of me?" she asked, nibbling on her lower lip. "This always happens; boys always get tired of me. I'm easy to like, but hard to commit to."

He dragged himself up into a sitting position. "Okay, let's take a deep breath." He inhaled, gesturing for her to mimic him, and she did, though that hardly helped. "I don't think any of what you just said is true."

"But what if it is?"

"Well, it's not." He rubbed a hand over his face. "When was the last time you guys hung out? Walk me through it."

She told him about their study date at the bookshop a few nights ago, how everything had seemed fine. "Then, at the end, we kissed, and he said goodbye," Lavinia finished. As she spoke those last words, Theo made a face, frowning, and something struck her.

"Oh my god. Do you think that's it?" she asked. Theo furrowed his brows. "Do you think that he thinks that I'm a bad kisser?"

She had never had any complaints before, but it had been some time, so maybe she was rusty. They hadn't made out that much, and maybe this was why!

"No, definitely not," Theo replied, sensing she was spiraling.

"How would you know?" she asked.

"Well, we can test it, if you're so worried," he said.

Lavinia froze.

# CHAPTER 14

The words were out before Theo even realized. Lavinia's eyes widened.

"It doesn't have to mean anything," he quickly added, absolutely lying, but he didn't want to back down now—not when the possibility of kissing her was in front of him. A desperate thrill shot through him like a lightning bolt, burning and bright.

"Okay," she said, tone cavalier. She didn't look at him, but he couldn't tear his gaze away from her. She fiddled with her fingers, then took a deep breath. "But only because I need a second opinion."

Theo's heart pounded. "Okay."

Finally, she looked at him. The breath lodged in his throat. Sitting in the grass, her face wasn't so far away, and her features were awash with starlight. His chest tightened painfully. She moved closer, until she was right in front of him, close enough to touch.

She smelled like coffee and caramel, sweet and strong. He wanted to take a bite out of her, and any thought that this was a bad idea went out of his head because, having her so close, he wondered how could this be anything but the very best idea?

He brought a hand up and brushed her hair back, fingers grazing her neck. She stared at him with big, open eyes, waiting. Suddenly, he felt nervous—something he hadn't felt in a long time. He'd had casual hookups here and there, and he'd always been confident in himself—but now? With Lavinia? His stomach was in knots.

"Is this okay?" he whispered, touching her face with his hand. She nodded slowly, eyelids fluttering. He stroked her cheekbone with the curve of his thumb, his pulse quickening. This might be his only chance to kiss her; he wanted it to be good.

So as much as he wanted to kiss her right then, he waited, moving his hand down from her cheek to run his thumb across her bottom lip, feeling the softness of it against the pad of his finger. He heard the sharp intake of her breath, and desire swept over him.

"Close your eyes," he whispered, voice rough.

She did, and he took the moment to appreciate her face without her watching, to take in every detail. The fan of her dark eyelashes, the slope of her nose, her full cheeks. He cupped her face with both hands and brought her closer, then brushed his lips against her forehead.

She released a shuddering breath, her hands going to his waist. He kissed her left cheek, then her right, and her grip on him tightened. Heat scorched through him, white-hot. He could feel her pulse racing in her throat. It was agonizing being this close to her.

Finally, he brought his lips close to hers, though not quite kissing her yet. As torturous as it was to hold himself back, he was savoring this, unsure when he would get the chance again.

When he could bear it no longer, he kissed her. It was a soft brush of his lips against hers, slow and sweet, but then she made a little whimper, fingers digging into his waist, and his restraint snapped.

He kissed her properly, his blood roaring. His entire body lit aflame. A moment in and he was already desperate for her, to explore every inch, to touch her everywhere.

Surely he had enough experience now to let her know she wasn't a bad kisser. Surely he should stop. The decent thing to do would be to stop.

But then she grabbed hold of his shirt and pulled him closer, and he couldn't help it, he went with her, chasing her mouth with his. Then they were horizontal, his hands over her shoulders on the grass as he kissed her and kissed her, his every movement frantic and hungry.

His heart pounded fiercely as he slipped his tongue into her mouth, and she made a low sound in the back of her throat. He wanted to find out everything she liked, and only do that for the rest of his life. He could picture it so clearly, doing this again and again. Doing everything with her.

He needed to stop. Right now, or he never would.

Theo pulled away, his breathing ragged. He sat down, catching his breath, trying to remember his own name. He had no idea of anything, let alone what they had been talking about before this, until slowly, it came back to him.

She had been worried she was a bad kisser. This had only been an experiment.

Theo cleared his throat, trying to find his voice. "So. I don't think your kissing is a problem," he managed to say.

Lavinia didn't respond. For once, she was quiet.

Theo had half a mind to say she needed practice just so she would practice with him, but then he glanced at her, the swollen pink of her lips, and he couldn't pull off such a deceit. He couldn't bear it if she thought she was a bad kisser, because she wasn't, she really, really wasn't.

And he was falling in love with her.

Fear beat through him at the realization.

Without another word, he bolted.

# CHAPTER 15

Lavinia could not believe she and Theo had kissed. She and Theo!

She was in her car, driving, and still thinking about it two days later. Every time she did, her entire body hummed with desire, a tingle going down her spine. She pressed her fingers to her lips, recalling the feel of his mouth on hers, and the memory made her pulse quicken.

The way he had kissed her. She had dreamt about it the last two nights, but in her dreams, they hadn't stopped there. At the thought of her salacious dreams, she opened the window, getting some cold air in and trying to catch her breath.

Lavinia had hardly remembered her own name after, let alone what had even transpired to bring about such a situation.

"He only kissed you to make you feel better," Lavinia reminded herself. To assuage her qualms, to reassure her that she was in fact a good kisser, and that that wasn't the issue with Calahan.

"He's your best friend!" Lavinia scolded herself. "Why else would he volunteer to kiss you?"

Even so, she couldn't shake the feeling that there was something between them, something undeniable and fierce. She had felt it, deep in her bones. She thought he might have felt it, too, with the desperate way he had pressed her body into the grass with his.

Until he had pulled away first.

He had bolted. He had run as if he couldn't get away fast enough.

He hadn't even said goodbye! Or walked her to her car! This was the first time she could recall in their entire seventeen-year friendship that he hadn't said bye to her.

He had texted her the next morning to apologize for that, but he hadn't given any explanation. She had just thumbs-up reacted to the message because she didn't know what to say either.

Ugh! It was all so confusing!

There was no time to dwell on it any longer; Lavinia had arrived at her destination. She was at Aiden's cottage, where Saphira had invited Lavinia over for Friday-night dinner along with Genevieve, Emmeline, and Theo.

Aiden's cottage—now his and Saphira's—was a cute little place not too far away from Main Street. It was nestled in the hills, and the houses in this area were spread apart and private. As Lavinia stepped out of her car, it was nice and secluded; she listened to the crickets chirping, the leaves rustling.

She knocked on the door, and it opened to reveal Aiden and Saphira, his hand on her waist. Saphira was wearing a pleated brown skirt with a pink sweater on top, while Aiden wore dark brown trousers and a beige top, his outfit complementing hers. They looked gorgeous together, picture-perfect.

"Welcome to our home," Aiden said, giving her a warm smile.

Saphira hugged Lavinia, holding on tight. "I'm so happy to see you!"

"Thanks for inviting me!" Lavinia handed Saphira the small bag she was carrying, which Saphira peeked into to see a spiced pumpkin candle.

"I was going to bring flowers but figured that would be redundant," she said. Aiden smiled sheepishly, moving aside to let her enter their home. When she did, she knew her previous statement was right. Almost every surface was already covered with vases of beautiful bouquets of flowers, each one carefully crafted; she could easily see Aiden's hand. The perks of being engaged to a gardener!

"A candle is perfect," Saphira said, going to grab a lighter. "I'm going to light this right now."

"Come sit," Aiden said, and she looked around. She had been here before, but not since Saphira fully moved in, and it was funny to see how his cottage had changed with Saphira's touch.

Before, it was simple and tidy, but now it was full of life. The one story had a spacious living room and kitchen, as well as two bedrooms, and it seemed as if every inch was full of artwork, potted green plants, colorful throw pillows, and trinkets.

Lavinia turned into the living room, where two guests were already present. Genevieve and her cousin, Emmeline, stood up to greet her. Lavinia hugged Genevieve first, who was wearing a variation of her usual outfit, fuss-free but expensive black trousers and a simple top, this time a light sweater with the sleeves rolled up.

Then she hugged Emmeline, going on her tiptoes, for Emmeline was the fanciest in sharp heels, even though she was already pretty tall. She wore a lace dress with dramatic sleeves. While Genevieve was bare-faced, as usual, Emmeline's makeup was stunning, smoked-out kajal eyes and blood-red lipstick. She had an elaborate gold nose-piercing as well, adding to the striking look.

"How on earth do you ride in those outfits?" Lavinia asked, awed.

Emmeline laughed. "I don't—I change when I arrive."

"I respect the commitment to serving looks."

"Lavinia! Look at who Emmy brought with her!" Saphira said, setting down the candle and joining them in the living room. She was practically giddy. Lavinia watched as Emmeline brought over a wicker basket full of blankets. It wasn't until Emmeline brought the basket closer that Lavinia spotted a black-scaled baby dragon, sleeping soundly.

Lavinia gasped. "Oh my god! Who is this?"

"My brother's new baby dragon, Motu," Emmeline replied. "He just hatched a month ago, and I'm babysitting." Lavinia had never seen such a young basalta dragon. Even at this age, he was bigger than other baby dragon breeds.

"Isn't he the *cutest*?" Saphira asked. She crowded around the basket with Lavinia.

"Adorable," Lavinia agreed before looking up at Emmeline. "I didn't know you had siblings."

Aiden snorted, entering the living room. "Being an older sister is Emmy's full-time job," he said, coming over to stand with Saphira. "The coffee-roasting business is her side gig."

Emmeline laughed, though she looked a little irritated. "Yes, I have a little sister, then two younger brothers, all in their twenties. My sister got married and moved away, and neither one of my brothers drinks coffee, so you've never met them at the cafe."

Emmeline set the basket and sleeping baby down on the side, then sat down with Saphira and Aiden. Lavinia sat with Genevieve on the other couch, and they chatted while Emmeline and Saphira had a conversation of their own.

"Oh my god, I forgot to tell you," Lavinia said, grabbing Genevieve's hand. She looked over to make sure Emmeline wasn't listening, then lowered her voice. "I saw Luke Hayward at the Animal Hospital. He said to say hi to Emmy."

Somehow, Emmeline heard, and she was immediately triggered. "Lavinia!" she cried. "What am I hearing!"

"Um, you shouldn't be hearing anything because I was whispering," Lavinia replied, laughing.

Emmeline glowered. "That *heathen* dared to tell you to say hi to *me*."

Saphira tried not to laugh. "What heathen?" Aiden asked, looking confused.

"The owner of Tempest," Emmeline replied. She couldn't even bear to say his name.

"Oh, Luke?" Aiden said.

Emmeline made a disgusted face.

"I totally feel like they've hooked up or something," Genevieve whispered to Lavinia. Again, Emmeline heard. She made a cry of absolute offense, face red.

"Ginny, he is literally evil," Emmeline said, though she didn't deny the theory. "Evil!"

"What does that have to do with anything?" Ginny replied. "He's super hot. He's old, otherwise I'd totally go for it."

Aiden's expression turned pained. "Please stop," Aiden said, uncomfortable with the topic of conversation.

"Now I can't even appreciate a gorgeous man without you being a big baby about it?" Ginny asked.

"No," Aiden replied flatly.

Genevieve ignored him; she and Emmeline loved bothering him, which was amusing to watch. "Ginny, *no*," Emmeline said, voice hard. "He broke Millie's heart, and Millie cried for a week." To Lavinia, Saphira added as an aside, "Millie is her sister."

"Yeah, but Millie cries over anything," Ginny said. Emmeline scowled, and Lavinia sensed she was very protective of her younger siblings.

"*Anyway*," Saphira said, changing the topic of conversation to something else. Lavinia listened as the others carried on talking, but her focus was frayed.

Her gaze kept straying to the door, waiting for Theo to arrive. She hadn't seen his car out front, but he would probably be arriving any moment, and she braced herself.

Until Saphira said, "Pity Theo couldn't join."

"Hm?" Lavinia blinked, and Saphira looked confused.

"Theo," she said. "He told me he couldn't come. I thought you would know."

"Oh! Um, we haven't talked today," Lavinia said. "He probably texted me, but I haven't checked my phone." She played it off, but Saphira gave her a strange look, brown eyes concerned.

Lavinia gave her a bright smile. "I'm going to grab some water."

She went to the kitchen and ran the tap, waiting for it to

get cold. She listened to the water rushing, trying to stay calm. She knew for a fact Theo had no plans today. She was his main friend, so who else would he be hanging out with? And he didn't have football, either, because Saphira had asked before setting the date.

Which meant he didn't come on purpose because he was avoiding Lavinia. Her eye twitched.

She mentally scolded herself; she shouldn't have even been thinking about Theo, anyway. He was not part of her plans or her operations. She should have been thinking about Calahan, about her deadline.

She drank the glass of water, then joined the others, who were heading for the back door.

"We can all say hello to Sparky, or he'll be upset," Saphira said, and they followed her out to the yard, which was beautiful and spacious.

The yard was big, with lots of room to play for the dragons. There was also a vegetable garden and flower bushes, and strings of fairy lights that crisscrossed over the patio. Sparky was flying overhead with Torch, Emmeline's dragon. When he spotted them, he headed down, landing in front of them with flapping wings to receive pets and kisses from everyone. Emmeline held the basket with Motu, and Sparky came over to lick the baby.

"Sparky, no," Emmeline chided, laughing. Sparky's tongue was the size of the baby. Still, Sparky watched the baby with big eyes, bouncing on his feet with excitement.

"He's still a baby, but he thinks Motu is so cute," Saphira said, smiling fondly. Then, Sparky came over to Saphira, nudging her shoulder with his head. He looked at her with big purple eyes, and Saphira laughed, seeming to understand whatever it was he was communicating.

"Alright, alright," she said, then turned back to them. "He wants me to saddle up and show you our progress." She looked at Lavinia. "As long as it's alright with the good doctor?"

Lavinia laughed. "The good doctor thinks it's completely fine."

Aiden grabbed the saddle, strapping it onto Sparky with an apprehensive look on his face. Once the saddle was set, Aiden checked all the buckles again, then a third time, just for good measure.

"Aiden," Saphira said, gently pushing her fiancé to the side. "It's fine!"

He furrowed his brows as Saphira approached Sparky, then put his hands on her waist, hoisting her up, though surely Saphira could have done it on her own. Once Saphira was safely atop Sparky, Aiden's hands lingered, until Saphira nudged him away with her foot.

Purple eyes bright, Sparky lifted his chin, trotting proudly. "He's just getting used to my weight right now," Saphira explained. "We haven't started flying yet—the most he does is jump."

Hearing the word jump, Sparky jumped up. Aiden let out a loud gasp, reaching out with both hands, but Saphira only threw her head back, giggling. She was giddy as she petted Sparky's black scales.

"Aiden! Stop stressing out," Genevieve said, hitting his arm.

"Honestly," Emmeline said, voice disapproving. "You're acting like you've never been around a dragon before!"

"Dragging the good Sterling name through the mud," Genevieve added, shaking her head.

Aiden frowned, crossing his arms over his chest. "Excuse me for caring about the love of my life's safety," he said.

"Aiden, it's okay," Saphira said, voice coaxing as she and Sparky trotted over to him. Sparky licked Aiden's cheek, and Aiden scrunched his face, though his lips did twitch with affection.

Sparky did another lap, bouncing around, and Saphira held on tight to the pommel. The girls cheered, and Sparky began showing off, flapping his wings this way and that like a prize dragon.

"I think that's enough for today," Aiden said, waving his hand. "Sparky, come on."

"You are such an old man," Genevieve said. "You do realize you're practically at death's doorstep now that you're turning thirty in a few months, don't you?"

Aiden rolled his eyes. "This from the girl still in her cradle. How do you even know how to talk? Shh. Babies don't talk so much."

"Excuse me! I'm turning twenty-one in a few months, and then I'll have a baby dragon of my own," she replied, a dangerous glint in her eyes.

Genevieve turning twenty-one suddenly made Lavinia feel *ancient*. Aiden was turning thirty, so twenty-four was young in comparison, but Aiden was already happily settled with the love of his life.

The winter was fast approaching. She needed this to work with Calahan, or she would miss her chance at true love and everlasting happiness. The morning after that calamity of a kiss with Theo, Calahan had called Lavinia. He had been apologetic for missing the pottery class and had immediately scheduled another date.

Which meant that he *did*, in fact, like her. He hadn't stood her up; he wasn't trying to get rid of her, and she *certainly* wasn't a bad kisser. These were all good things, and yet, they did not feel like it.

Saphira dismounted from Sparky and skipped over to kiss Aiden's cheek. He pulled her into him, hugging her close. "Don't worry," she said, looking up at Aiden. "I already know thirty is going to be incredibly sexy on you."

Finally, Aiden smiled. Sparky skipped over, wrapping them both in his wings. Aiden and Saphira laughed, falling into Sparky.

"Barf," Genevieve said, going inside, but Lavinia thought it was sweet. They were their own little family. She wanted a love like that—one that was strong enough to take root and grow.

Her thoughts strayed to her parents, and then, inexplicably to Theo. Her heart ached, and she shoved the thought of him aside with vehemence, going inside with Emmeline. Aiden took Sparky's saddle off and put it away, while Sparky flew up in the sky, free.

Inside, Saphira set the food on the table until Aiden came inside and took over, and then they all went to the table, looking at the delicious spread: a hearty chicken pot pie; an autumn salad with sweet potatoes, apples, and a maple vinaigrette, and a loaf of bread with clove butter.

The table was decorated with burgundy candles and a vase of sunflowers, as well as bud vases with marigolds and daisies. The table-scape was completed with little assortments of pinecones and pomegranate seeds. Even their place settings were autumnally themed, the porcelain plates rimmed with a gold and cornucopia design along the border.

"Everything looks amazing," Lavinia said, taking her seat. "I need to take a picture for my mom." Lavinia pulled out her phone; Beena would love this.

"Send it to Theo, too!" Saphira said, sitting on Aiden's right. "Tell him we miss him."

Lavinia's stomach flipped. She forced a smile. Truthfully, she didn't just want to send him a picture, she wanted to video-call Theo, but after their kiss, she didn't know how to proceed.

And as the dinner party continued, everyone eating the delicious food and chatting, Lavinia couldn't help but look over to the empty seat beside her, where Theo was supposed to be. Everything felt unbalanced without him here. She bit her bottom lip hard, trying not to focus on his absence, but it was impossible not to.

Lavinia turned her attention to Aiden and Saphira, to them in their home. The love between them filled this entire house and made it radiate warmth. Lavinia knew she wasn't stupid to believe in love, in *true* love—not when the evidence was right in front of her.

"So Lavinia, how's school going?" Emmeline asked, taking a sip of her blackberry mint cocktail. She was seated on Aiden's left; Genevieve was beside her and across from Lavinia.

Lavinia laughed. "It's good! I mean it's been really busy and a lot of work, but still, it's okay," Lavinia said, tearing off a piece of her bread. "Grad school is no joke."

"*I*, for one, can't wait to be done with school," Genevieve said, stabbing a piece of sweet potato. "It's so tedious."

"Barely a semester and a half left now, Ginny," Saphira said with a smile. "Now, use those brains to think of a dragon puppuccino equivalent for the cafe. And that's an order for all of you!"

"Hmm," Lavinia considered it, but nothing was coming to her at the moment. No one else had any suggestions, either, and Saphira let out a breath.

"I should have been able to come up with something by now, but I've just been so busy with managing everything!" Saphira played with the end of her wavy hair.

"I'm telling you, darling, you need to hire a managerial assistant," Aiden said. "Someone to help with the business side of things." Theo had mentioned this.

"But I don't trust anyone!" Saphira pouted. "The cafe is my baby."

Lavinia wanted to suggest Theo for the job, but she didn't want to speak for him, especially not when he wasn't sure himself. Instead, she said, "In another life, I would love to be your business-partner-in-crime, but unfortunately, in this life, I love being a vet (in training) too much."

"Ugh, in another life, that *would* have been so fun," Saphira said. "But don't worry, I know, and I love you being a vet, anyway. Don't forget about my private island."

Lavinia smiled. Being around her friends did help her feel better but, at the same time, it also underscored just how much she was missing Theo.

She had no choice but to grapple with that fact when she got home at the end of the night.

In her bedroom, Lavinia met her gaze in the mirror above her vanity, and she saw just how sad her eyes were, though she had no reason to be sad.

What was wrong with her? She never could stop thinking

about him, and after that kiss it was just a hundred times worse. Tasting him had unlocked all this desire from deep inside of her, the intensity of which astounded her.

Kissing him had been better than she could have ever imagined or dreamed of, and now she wanted more. She was desperate for it, and just the thought sent the blood racing in her veins. Her entire body ached.

Lavinia's phone lit up on top of her vanity, and her stomach flipped. She snatched her phone, looking at the notification—but it wasn't Theo. The energy that had shot through her dissipated.

It was Calahan, texting to confirm that they were still good for their date tomorrow. She was a tornado of mixed emotions. While kissing Theo wasn't cheating on Calahan because she and Calahan were not boyfriend/girlfriend or exclusive or anything that serious, she still felt . . . guilty. And she felt even more guilty by how much Calahan cared for her, even though that shouldn't have made her guilty, but happy!

The part of her that was mature and logical had been upset when she thought Calahan was growing tired of her, but the delusional and silly part of her that still liked Theo was relieved when she had thought it wasn't working out with Calahan.

She needed the different parts of her to start aligning real quick, because while they didn't, she was getting a headache!

The lines were blurring between all her shifting emotions and feelings: burning desire from their kiss and her subsequent outright lewd dreams; the feelings for him from her crush that she perhaps never moved on from entirely; and the fact that he was her best friend, so of course she missed him and wanted to see him all the time.

What she knew for certain was that she needed *something* to work. She needed her happily ever after. Especially with the way time was moving—winter was creeping closer, and she needed to find her person by then, the same way her mother had. If she didn't find her person by then, she never would, and she would just be alone for the rest of her life.

Lavinia released a groan, throwing open her vanity drawer. She needed to get her hair out of her face, and she gathered it up into a ponytail, reaching into the drawer with her free hand for a scrunchie.

As she did, she saw a little bottle in the corner. Hidden, but not hidden enough.

Theo's cologne. Lavinia dropped her hair, letting the strands fall forward. She reached for the bottle, her fingers touching the cool glass. She was tempted to spray it, to inhale the smell of him.

"*No,*" she scolded herself.

She shoved the drawer shut with a resounding snap.

# CHAPTER 16

The next day, Lavinia went on her date with Calahan. It went well, and at the end they kissed, and it was lovely, really, it was—but she couldn't help making comparisons. Kissing Theo had made her feel like she was a tree being struck by lightning, lit aflame for a long while afterward, while kissing Calahan was as sweet and comforting as eating a slice of warm pie.

She couldn't decide which was better, but maybe love wasn't supposed to feel like a calamity. Even so, as she got ready for bed that night, she found there had been nothing memorable about the day's events. Surely that wasn't a good thing?

Or was she overthinking it? Besides, this wasn't exactly the time to be so picky. If she couldn't make things work with Calahan—who was basically perfect—she wouldn't be able to make them work with anyone.

Confusing feelings aside, Lavinia missed Theo. Before going to sleep, she sent him a text: **Come over tomorrow for a fall day.**

She waited to see if his response would come immediately, the way it usually did. It wasn't even that late; she knew he wouldn't be asleep. But no matter how intently she stared at her screen, his reply did not come.

Yet, somehow, she knew he would show up tomorrow, and so she put her phone to the side and got into bed, going to sleep. The next morning when she woke up, she had a text from him, a few hours after she had fallen asleep: **Okay, i'll come by around 1.**

She was twitching, but she was sure everything would be fine.

A fall day was something they did every autumn without fail. They went out to the farms, which were especially festive this time of year. Weekends there were always packed in the months of September through November. As such, they always got stuck in standstill traffic on the one-lane road, but it was always worth it.

The farms had apple picking and tractor rides for kids and a corn maze—they used to do all of that as kids with her parents, and then again when Alfie was a kid, but ever since Lavinia started university, she and Theo went just for the food: roasted corn bathed in sweet butter and doused with sharp salt; perfectly baked potatoes topped with butter and Cajun seasoning; and fresh apple-cider donuts, pillowy on the inside and crisp on the outside, covered in a pound of cinnamon and sugar. There were also farm stands that Theo loved to buy fresh produce from, especially apples and butternut squash and figs; things he could use for baking.

After eating brunch with her family, Lavinia got ready. She was so comfortable around Theo that she never put extra effort into her appearance when it was the two of them, and the same was true today, despite all that had transpired between them.

She was glad for that, at least. She would hate to feel hyper-aware of her appearance in front of him.

She dressed in chocolate brown corduroy pants with a cream-colored blouse that had embroidered flowers on the collar and little gold buttons down the front. She tucked her hair behind her ears and put on some makeup, then grabbed her purse before heading downstairs, where she grabbed a light jacket and her new heeled booties.

It was nearly one, and a few minutes before, she had received a text from Theo. He was here. He was always on time. She replied that she was coming out, putting on her shoes. They clicked on the tiled floor as she went to the front door.

"I'm going!" she called back to the house. "Bye!"

"Make sure you're back by five!" Beena called back from the living room. Lavinia was watching Biter in the evening while her parents took Alfie to a football match. "Have fun!"

As Lavinia stepped out of her front door, she felt a jitter run through her spine that had little to do with the brisk autumn weather and more to do with nerves when she spotted him in his car. Taking a deep breath of crisp air, Lavinia walked over, getting in.

"Hi," she said, sitting down and looking at her best friend. Theo was wearing a soft flannel shirt that was navy blue and beige, the sleeves of which were rolled up, displaying the muscle of his forearm as he gripped the wheel with one hand.

"Hey," he said, looking over. He gave her a smile, which was perfectly normal. This would be fine!

Lavinia smiled back, and his gaze flicked down to her mouth, snagging there. She bit her bottom lip, nervous, and his eyes jumped away. His grip on the wheel tightened. Heat swept through her, and she busied herself with putting her seatbelt on, feeling only slightly nauseous.

Memories of their kiss resurfaced in her mind: the feel of his mouth against hers, the taste of his tongue.

"Ready?" he asked, voice rough.

"Mhm!" she all but squeaked.

Theo put the gear shift to drive and they headed away from her neighborhood. Lavinia grabbed his phone, which was connected to the car, and hit play on his music. She scrolled through his playlists, putting songs up on queue; after a few songs, they both relaxed.

They drove out to the farms. Most of the trees had changed from green now, and the multicolored landscape was breathtaking as they drove. Some of the roads were covered with yellow leaves that looked like shavings of sunlight. As a breeze lifted the air, leaves twirled and fluttered as they fell, shimmering.

Lavinia started singing along to the music, and Theo looked over at her, a smile twitching his lips. Then she put on songs they used to listen to in high school, laughing as Theo groaned.

"Why are we listening to this?" he asked, wrinkling his nose. "This is painful. I can feel all the teenage angst seeping back into my pores."

Lavinia only turned up the volume, belting out the words, and eventually Theo joined in. She cackled and they sang together, the way they used to on the drive home from school when they were seniors and Theo would drive her home everyday. A wave of nostalgia hit her at the memories. That was so long ago now, yet, in the car with him at this moment, she felt like no time had passed at all.

They made it to the farms, and even though the traffic had

been rough, she had hardly noticed. Theo parked, and they got out of the car. The sun was shining now, so she left her jacket in his car, tilting her face up to the sun's heat, relishing the feeling.

When she turned back to Theo, she saw he had been watching her, a fond expression on his face. His gaze was warm, and she felt shy all of a sudden.

Lavinia looked around at the masses of cars in the parking lots, the tons of people walking around. "There's so many here," she said, and he came around the car to walk with her.

Most of the rush was for the farm activities, not the food, but still. Theo smiled, throwing an arm over her shoulder as they walked towards the barn, where the food was sold from a window-counter. They approached the food line, where there were at least a dozen people in front of them: parents with young children and old couples and groups of friends.

"The donuts'd better not be finished," she said, peering at the line.

"Don't worry," he said. "If they are, I'll steal some from the first person we see."

She looked up at him, arching a brow. "Even if it's a kid?"

He nodded. "Even if it's a kid."

"You're awful," she said, laughing.

"Just for you," he winked.

They continued chatting until they made it to the front of the line, where they ordered baked potatoes and roasted corn. Luckily, the apple-cider donuts were still in stock. "Thank god," Theo said, paying. "I really didn't want to make any kids cry today."

"As opposed to every other day? When you are okay with making kids cry?"

Theo laughed, bumping her shoulder with his, and they walked over to the benches with their food, sitting down with their feast. There was a band playing live country music in the background and kids running around with baskets of apples.

They ate, people-watching. When they were finished and about a pound heavier for it, Theo did his shopping at the farm stands and Lavinia bought an armful of pumpkins to decorate her front door. Theo ran the groceries back to his car so they wouldn't have to carry them around and, when he returned, they walked over to the area where games were set up, playing a round of cornhole, which Lavinia was abysmal at.

It was a fun day, but by the time they were walking back to his car around four in the evening, her feet were aching. The heeled booties were new, and she had not broken them in yet, and as such, she was losing feeling in her toes.

Lavinia winced, walking gingerly, and Theo's gaze went to her shoes.

"Who said to wear heeled boots, huh?" he asked.

She pouted. "But they're *soooo* cute." She took another step, limping, and Theo stopped in his tracks.

"Come on." He turned around and crouched down. She laughed when she saw what he intended.

"A piggyback ride?" she asked. Since he was a foot taller than her, he used to give her piggyback rides all the time. "You haven't given me one in forever; not for years probably."

"Don't worry," he said. "I won't drop you. You're bite-sized."

"So not eating those vegetables when I was a kid *did* pay off!" She climbed onto his back, putting her arms around his neck, and his hands came up under her legs, lifting them around his waist. A jolt ran through her body.

He straightened, and she wrapped her arms around his collar, chest flush against his back. She inhaled the scent of his shampoo, the ends of his hair tickling her cheek as she leaned her chin on his shoulder. He was so warm.

His hands on her thighs were strong, his grip steady. He was holding her up so easily.

"You're huffing and puffing a lot less than you used to," Lavinia noted. He used to be so scrawny, but that was evidently not the case anymore.

"I've been training," he said. "This is my Olympics."

"Really?" She moved her hand down to his arm as a joke, but wow, his bicep really was solid. Again, she thought of their kiss, the feel of his body pressing hers against the grass.

Probably not the best thing to think about as she was latched onto his back with his hands under her legs. Desire lit through her as quickly as a match catching flame. Her mouth went dry. She focused her attention up to the sky, trying to think of chaste things.

They made it back to the car, and he let her down. Luckily, by then, she'd calmed down a bit, so she could look him in the eyes without combusting. She hopped off his back, and he turned to give her a mock bow. "My lady."

She did a mock-curtsy in response. "Why thank you, noble steed."

He drove them home, but the fall day was not done, and she didn't need to invite him in for him to know. He parked and then followed her inside, just as her parents were by the door with Alfie.

"Perfect timing," Garrett said, lifting Alfie's football bag onto his shoulder. "We're heading out for Alfie's match—

Biter is your responsibility until we're home." Lavinia nodded, kicking off her shoes, then Garrett turned back to the house. "Alfie, Beena—come on!"

Beena appeared, already prepared in her coat and shoes, carrying a thermos of chai. Alfie was beside her, Biter in his arms. The baby dragon was asleep, her red scales matching his red uniform.

"Mama, take a picture of me and Biter," Alfie said, whining in a way that informed Lavinia he must have made this request three times already. "We match!"

"Okay, okay, one second," Beena said, rummaging around her purse with her free hand.

"I got it," Lavinia said, taking her phone out. Alfie's face brightened, and he grinned, holding Biter up. Lavinia snapped the picture.

"Give Biter to your sister," Garrett said. "We've got to get a move on—we need to pick up Logan, too." One of Alfie's teammates.

"Oh yeah." Alfie approached Lavinia, and she took the sleeping dragon from his arms. Beena put Alfie's jacket on his shoulders, and he slipped it on. After quick kisses, Garrett, Beena, and Alfie headed out, leaving Theo, Lavinia, and Biter.

"I'm going to put her in the bassinet," Lavinia said.

"I'll grab your pumpkins," Theo told her.

"Thanks, pumpkin," she said. Theo snorted. Lavinia carefully placed Biter back into her bassinet, but the moment she did, Biter's tiny face scrunched. She opened one ruby eye, then the other. "Uh oh."

Biter growled, angry to be awake. She scratched at her face with her tiny paws, hissing.

"Okay, okay," Lavinia coaxed, picking her up again. Biter snuggled into Lavinia's arms, immediately latching her mouth onto one of the gold buttons of her blouse. "Uff, Biter, no!"

Lavinia grabbed one of the baby dragon's chew toys, easing it into Biter's mouth. She walked Biter over to the front door, where Theo was putting down her pumpkins. She had gotten two large, three medium, and seven small ones.

"Here," Lavinia said, handing Biter over to Theo. Biter cried out in protest, until Theo cooed at her.

"Hi, angel," Theo said, voice sweet. Lavinia's heart melted, and his tone seemed to have the same effect on Biter. The baby dragon perked up.

Lavinia couldn't help but watch as Theo took Biter onto one forearm, then moved his arm up and down like he was doing workout curls. Biter held onto his forearm, tail wagging as she made a sound of glee. When Theo stopped the movement, Biter climbed higher and bit his bicep, and honestly, Lavinia couldn't even blame her.

Shaking her head, Lavinia focused on the pumpkins, arranging them on either side of the door and down the two steps with the pots of radiant red and yellow mums. Theo sat down on the step while she finished up, letting Biter down.

Biter quickly crawled over to the biggest pumpkin, which was double her size. She tried climbing up, but slipped down the round side. Biter hissed, trying again. She slid down once more, and Biter snarled, scratching at the pumpkin with her tiny claws, irritated.

"Alright, darling, let's try this one," Theo said, scooping her up with one hand and positioning her closer to a medium-sized pumpkin. Biter attempted climbing up, and she made it to the top. She bounced by the pumpkin's stem, holding onto it with her paws, wings flapping.

Too cute! Lavinia held a hand to her heart. She looked up at Theo, who was watching and smiling as well, face fond. Then Biter began chewing the stem, aggressively gnawing at it.

"I think she might be hungry now," Lavinia said with a laugh. She scooped Biter up and they headed inside, where Lavinia fed her with a bottle. Soon thereafter, Biter fell asleep, and Lavinia laid her down in the bassinet.

"Now I'm hungry, too," Lavinia said, heading for the kitchen. She pulled her hair up into a ponytail and pulled out a bag from the freezer. "Gnocchi?"

Theo nodded in agreement. "I'll make dessert."

While Lavinia threw together a brown butter sage gnocchi (one of the few things she knew how to make because it was so simple), Theo made apple crisp with apples from the farm.

They ate dinner, then had the apple crisp, which was gooey with a crumbly crust and perfect topped with salted caramel ice-cream. The sun set over the backyard, turning all the clouds pink and gold, and then it was nightfall. The temperature dropped, bringing a chill into the house, and they moved to the living room, huddling together on the couch, sharing a blanket.

They made popcorn and put on a movie, and as they watched, she looked over at him, thinking of all the times they had done this, year after year. So much had changed except for this—never this.

Lavinia couldn't let anything jeopardize her and Theo's friendship.

It was better if she forgot about their kiss entirely.

# CHAPTER 17

Theo and Lavinia had become friends in the fall the year they were seven years old, and Lavinia thought back to that time now.

They were in the same class that year, just as they had been the year before. While they were friends, Lavinia had other friends as well, and so Theo wasn't her very best friend just yet.

Until they were eleven and, one day, she was hanging out at his place. His parents weren't home because they had to go somewhere, but she hardly ever saw his parents, anyway, no matter how often she and Theo hung out. They did not stick around the few times she came round to his place, unlike Beena, who was constantly watching the kids, making them snacks every little while, ensuring that Theo had eaten and was comfortable.

It used to annoy Lavinia how Beena wouldn't leave them alone, so she didn't mind when they hung out at Theo's and his parents weren't there. Lavinia's parents could be too nosy sometimes, and she thought it was pretty cool that Theo's parents trusted him on his own—she and he could be little grown-ups.

That day, it was October, and they were playing outside after having eaten a casserole his mom had left for them. Lavinia had a sweet tooth, and wanted something for dessert, and an idea popped into her mind when her gaze fell upon the apple tree in Theo's backyard.

"Theo, get some apples," she'd said, tugging on his sleeve. "We can have caramel apples!"

Back then, they were the same height, but he was half her size because he was so thin and wiry. He had a lot of hair, as if his parents had forgotten to take him to get a haircut, and his eyes were huge on his gaunt face. He looked a little lopsided, like a character from a cartoon, but in a good way, like he was her sidekick, and they were important enough to have a show about themselves.

At Lavinia's words, a worried expression came over Theo's face, even though she hadn't asked anything too demanding. All she wanted were some apples!

"Come on!" she urged. He looked as if he was going to say something in response, but she pouted.

"I haven't done it before," he said, bouncing his leg.

"Don't worry!" she reassured him. "I have an apple tree in my backyard, too, and I climb it all the time, you know I do! I can pick them, just come with me."

"No!" he said in a panic. "No—I'll do it."

She shrugged. "Okay. I'll dip them in the caramel, then."

He looked scared but nodded. Taking a deep breath, he walked over to the apple tree, and she skipped behind him, excited. "They're going to be so yummy!"

Theo stood at the bottom of the tree. He tipped his head back, looking up, his throat moving as he swallowed.

"You can do it," Lavinia said, giving him a little push forward. She didn't get what he was so scared of. He took a deep breath, then started to climb. "Woo! Go Theo!"

She cheered him on until he got to the branch with ripe red apples hanging. "See! That wasn't so hard!"

Theo's eyes were wide as he looked around, as if he couldn't quite believe where he was. She thought for a moment he'd be upset she had made him go up there, but then he smiled. He closed his eyes, tilting his face to a patch of sunlight between the branches, and his brown skin glowed. He looked so happy that she smiled, feeling happy, too.

He opened his eyes, then reached for an apple. He picked one and threw it down. She lifted the end of her dress and caught the apple; it bounced on the fabric, and she laughed. He smiled, grabbing another apple, and the both of them made a little game out of it—they could make a game out of anything.

He kept throwing and she kept catching. Lavinia's dress was getting stretched out, apples falling; they had more than enough, but they kept going, laughing, giddy. He climbed onto a higher branch, reaching, and it all happened so fast—

The branch snapped, and he fell. She heard his high-pitched scream, and then saw his crumpled body. There was so much blood.

"Theo!" she shrieked, running to his side. She saw that he had split his knee open against a sharp rock. There was a flash of white amongst the red, which must have been his bone. He was crying, and she started crying, too.

They were both sobbing: him in pain, and her because she

was scared. She had never seen so much blood before and she worried that he was dying or something; she didn't know! She took off her cardigan and tried to wrap it around his leg, ruining her favorite sweater in the process.

Theo continued to cry, his face wet with tears and sweat, and her cardigan changed from a soft pink to a bloody, bloody red. Lavinia searched Theo's pockets for his phone, her hands shaking. He had gotten a cell phone early—which she had been jealous of—because his parents often left him home alone.

Lavinia swiped open his phone, saying, "Don't worry, I'll call your parents."

"No!" he cried out. His expression was panicked, and he grabbed her hand, squeezing it so tight it hurt. "No, you can't tell them, Lavinia, you can't." And he started crying harder, which only made her chest hurt.

"I won't," she said. "Theo, I won't."

She squeezed his hand back, then called her parents. Her father's number was the only one she had memorized; he had made her memorize it in case of emergencies.

Garrett picked up after the first ring. "Hello?"

Hearing her father's voice made her start crying all over again.

"Daddy," she sobbed.

"Pumpkin!" he said, his voice frightened. "What is it? What happened?"

"It's Theo," she said, hardly able to get the words out. "He fell."

"Hey, don't worry, okay?" He was trying to sound calm, but she could feel that he was freaked out. She heard a commotion in the background, as if he was running. "I'm coming. I'm coming right now."

"Okay." She sniffled, unable to say anything else, and hung up. She turned to Theo. "My daddy is coming, okay? Don't worry."

That seemed to calm Theo down a little, and he nodded. Lavinia bit her bottom lip, unsure what to do. She pressed on the wound with her sweater, since that was what her mom always did when she got a cut, she would press down—but this wasn't doing much, her sweater was already wet and it made a squishing sound when she pushed on it, which made her feel sick.

Luckily, her parents arrived shortly thereafter, and she didn't have to think about anything. Garrett gathered Lavinia into his arms, inspecting her to make sure she wasn't hurt while Beena went to Theo.

"He fell," Lavinia said, holding onto her dad. Now that her parents were here, she knew everything would be okay, and she stopped crying. "Theo, don't worry, okay? They're going to take care of you. My mom's a nurse, remember?"

Theo nodded, but his eyes were wet with tears. Beena turned back to Garrett, and Lavinia didn't hear them say anything, but they seemed to understand each other perfectly. Her parents always did that, talked without really saying anything.

Garrett left Lavinia's side and, in the same moment, Beena came next to her, the two switching. Garrett scooped Theo up, and he shrieked with pain as they moved him.

"Mama!" Lavinia cried, admonishing.

"It's okay," Beena said. "We're going to take him to the hospital, okay?"

Lavinia nodded, and Beena went to hold Theo's leg, keeping it wrapped in Lavinia's sweater. Lavinia ran to her father's other side, reaching for Theo's hand. He held onto her hand as they made it to the car, and she held on the whole car ride to the hospital.

She felt so horrible—it was all her fault. She had told him to get the apples!

When they arrived at the emergency room, everything was so busy, people running around, the white lights of the hospital blinding.

"I'll take him in," Beena said, after Garrett had deposited Theo onto a hospital bed. "Stay with Lavinia."

"No!" Lavinia shouted. "I'm coming, too." She didn't let go of Theo's hand and gave her parents her absolute scariest face, so they wouldn't dream of refusing her.

"Okay, gudiya, okay," Beena said. "We'll all go together. Okay?"

Lavinia's face softened. "Okay." Her voice was small.

They all went, but Lavinia wasn't focusing much on what the grown-ups were saying or what was going on. She was holding Theo's hand with both of hers. Soon, a doctor came in to stitch his wound, and she saw how scared Theo was.

He moved his face all the way to the side so he wouldn't see, and she put a hand over his eyes just for good measure, then squeezed her own eyes shut.

Her parents were there, holding on, too, but Lavinia hardly noticed, until Beena said, "It's done. You can open your eyes."

She released a sigh, opening her eyes, but she didn't move her hand from Theo's just yet. She looked at his leg, which was covered with a massive bandage, no longer gruesome. Then, she moved her hand from Theo's face. His hair was matted down with sweat.

"You're almost there, sweetie," Beena said, brushing Theo's hair aside. "They just need to put a cast on, and then they'll be done."

Theo nodded, barely moving his head. Lavinia had never been more unhappy in her entire life.

Eventually, another doctor came and put on the cast, and Lavinia tried to think of games to distract Theo while the doctor did so.

"What number am I thinking of?" she asked. He didn't respond, and she said, "Come on, guess."

"Sixteen," he replied in a whisper.

She gasped dramatically. Her mouth fell open in amazement. "How did you know that?"

Finally, a very small and very tired smile appeared on his lips. "I can read your mind."

The truth was, she had been thinking of the number three, but she wanted him to smile, so she had pretended. Finally, the doctors finished, and Theo was looped up on pain medications by then, so he had a dazed look on his face.

Until his parents came in. When they entered the room, they saw Theo, and Lavinia heard her parents telling his what happened, since Lavinia had told them everything, and she'd never forget—Theo's parents sighed.

"Come on, pumpkin, let's let Theo rest," Garrett said, prying Lavinia away from Theo's side, even though she didn't want to go, and Theo didn't want her to, either. He tightened his grip on her hand, but her fingers slipped through his.

"Come on, gudiya. His mom and dad are here, right?" Beena rubbed Lavinia's shoulders. "They'll take care of him."

But Lavinia wasn't so sure. She didn't think anyone could take care of him, no one except for her. Theo was quiet, his eyes downcast. He didn't outright ask her to stay, so she went.

The next day, she went to visit him at his house, running straight upstairs to his room once his mom let her in. When she entered his room, he was asleep, and he looked terrible.

"Theo," she whispered, not sure if she should be waking him. He roused, and his eyes were so *sad*.

She thought he was mad at her for a second, since she was the one who said to get the apples. "Do you want me to go?" she asked, voice breaking.

He shook his head. "Please don't." So she stayed, crawling onto his bed. She had brought cards and she dealt them out. They played, and she stayed the whole day, but he was still so down. And she saw that his parents weren't doing much to make him happy.

Whenever Lavinia was sick, she got the most special princess treatment ever: Beena made her favorite foods, and Garrett would bring her a stuffed animal or new toy, and she was allowed twice as many sweets. Her parents even let her sleep in their bed with them! Which she wasn't allowed to do since she was bigger now, but when she was sick, they did anything to make her feel better.

Theo's parents were not doing that. When Lavinia went home after visiting him for the second day, she begged her parents to have him stay at her place.

Beena and Garrett shared a long look before Garrett sighed.

"Pumpkin, he has to be at his own home," he said. "With his parents."

"They won't like it if he stays with us," Beena added. Lavinia couldn't believe her parents were saying no.

"They don't care about him!" Lavinia yelled. "You don't care either." She started crying, and Beena hugged her close.

"Of course, we care, gudiya," Beena said, stroking her hair. Lavinia felt awful, and yelling at her parents only made her feel worse. "He has to be in his own home, but you can visit again tomorrow. Visit as much as you'd like. I'll bake cookies and you can bring them for him, how does that sound?"

Lavinia sniffled, acquiescing.

The next day, she visited Theo, bringing her best stuffed animals and her favorite blanket and a variety of books and the cookies that her mother had made. She stayed with him all day, setting up camp in his room, crawling into bed with him. His parents had set up a television in his room, and they played video games and cards and read books.

She tried her best to distract him and make sure he was comfortable, and she did the same thing every day for the next few weeks. She went straight to his house after school, bringing him the classwork he missed, and she stayed until dinner, sometimes even after, the both of them falling asleep together until her parents came to pick her up, waking her.

Funnily enough, even though she practically lived at his house, she hardly saw his parents, and even then, she could see how quiet his house was. She understood a little about why he could get quiet sometimes, too.

She felt a fierce protectiveness of him then, and they became inseparable, and remained that way, even after he got better.

He still had a scar on his knee, and every time she saw it, she was reminded of that time, how much blood there had been. Of course now, looking back, she knew such an injury wouldn't have killed him, but at the time, being eleven years old, she had truly thought she might lose him.

She and Theo had never fought, so that was the closest she'd ever been to losing him.

Just the thought sent a shiver down her back, and Lavinia turned to look at him beside her, no longer eleven years old but twenty-four. She moved closer, leaning on his shoulder. He slid down on the sofa so she would be more comfortable, tapping his head against hers.

He put a handful of popcorn in his mouth, then offered her the bowl, his gaze still on the movie. His face was lit up with light from the television, a small smile on his face.

"I love this scene," he said.

"Me too," she whispered, but she wasn't looking at the screen—she was looking at him.

# CHAPTER 18

After the movie finished, Theo offered to clean up in the kitchen, since he knew Lavinia had studying to do.

"You're the best," Lavinia said, giving him a quick hug. She checked on Biter, who was still asleep in her bassinet, before heading upstairs, leaving him alone.

He didn't mind; her house was home to him, so being alone here didn't bother him. He shut the television off and folded the blanket, setting the pillows back into their proper positions on the sofa before switching off the lights in the living room. He went to the kitchen, picking up their plates and glasses from dinner, taking them to the sink.

He washed the dishes, looking out to the backyard from the window above the sink. It was a full moon, and the milky moonlight shone over the trees, making the branches silver. The tree that stuck out to him the most was the apple tree, the fruit ripe and round, while some of the apples had already fallen to the ground.

It made him think of the apple tree in his own backyard—to that day over a decade ago when he'd split open his knee at eleven years old.

Theo wasn't allowed to climb the apple tree; his parents were very strict about that. They were very strict about a lot of things. There was to be no fooling around or playing inside of the house. Outside, he was only to kick the ball around if he did not hit anything but the net. There would be no climbing of fences or trees, no getting dirty, and no making any noise that would be disruptive.

Overall, he was not to fuss. He was to be on his best behavior, all the time.

He tried so hard to be good, to be still and quiet, but he just couldn't. He was hyperactive, something he knew was a bad thing in his parents' eyes, so he thought it was bad, too—until he met Lavinia, who was so much worse than him.

And Theo loved her energy, how she was always bouncing and skipping and twirling and talking, always talking. She was so *loud*. And he thought maybe all the energy he had wasn't so bad, after all. They became friends, and he was even worse with Lavinia, the both of them hyper and obnoxious.

With her, he was no longer the quiet, well-behaved child he was with his parents; he was carefree and *fun*, and he liked that version of himself best, the version he could be with Lavinia.

Which was why he had climbed the apple tree, even though he knew he wasn't allowed. And he'd paid for it dearly. His parents made sure of that.

After the hospital, Rishi and Amaya were quiet the entire car ride home. They helped him to his room. After he was settled, his parents stood by the door, both of them frowning.

"This is what happens when you don't listen," Rishi said. Amaya was silent.

Their disappointment was worse than if they had hit him. The moment they left, he began crying, his entire body shaking until finally he fell asleep.

He went to a dark place—until Lavinia was there right after school, a shooting star landing in his room. A few days later, she brought an arsenal of things so he wouldn't be sad, and she took care of him.

After the injury, they spent so much time together that it cemented them as best friends, and even though he'd had other friends at school or at football, it was then that he realized he didn't need any of them—he only needed her.

It was why, secretly, he hadn't even been sorry he'd split his knee open. It had made them best friends, and since then she had been the best thing in his life, without a doubt.

In school, they always liked asking hypothetical questions like, "If there was a fire what would you take?" or, "Name one thing you can't live without" or, "If you were stranded on an island, who would you want to be stuck with?"

The answer was always the same: *Lavinia*. She was always the first thought that popped into his mind. If he had her, he didn't need anything else.

It had always been platonic between them, but now, after that kiss, it felt like much, much more, in a way that utterly devastated him. He was miserable with the way things were between them, and it hurt just like it had that day he split his knee open. At least then, he'd had Lavinia. Now, it felt like he was utterly alone in what he felt.

But . . . what if he wasn't alone? A little voice dared to hope, and he clung to it, fanning the flames.

Lavinia was much too good for him, but she *had* kissed him back. She had pulled him closer—he hadn't imagined that, had he?

What if she also felt for him even a fraction of what he felt for her?

"She's seeing someone," Theo reminded himself. He aggressively scrubbed at a dish.

But what if she didn't like Calahan that much? She hadn't brought him up at all this evening.

She didn't have to fall in love with Theo yet—but *could* she? Did he dare to hope?

She deserved a prince from a fairy tale, or a knight in shining armor, or one of those fancy titled lords from the period dramas her mom liked watching, and he was just a guy, but maybe, for her, he could be something more.

As Theo finished cleaning up, the front door opened, and in came Alfie, along with his parents behind him. Alfie bounced into the kitchen, still in his football uniform, the red jersey and shorts dirty with streaks of grass.

"Oh, Theo! Leave it!" Beena fussed, setting down her purse on the counter. Garrett took her coat, disappearing to hang it. "I want to say that I can't believe Lavinia made you clean up all on your own, but I really *can* believe it."

"No, it's alright," Theo replied, setting down the last dish. "I don't mind. It helps clear my head." He turned to Alfie, drying his hands with a towel. "How was the game?"

"Amazing!" Alfie exclaimed. "I scored!" Garrett returned in time to hear that and raised a brow. Alfie looked at his dad, then back at Theo. "Well, I passed it to the guy who scored, but that's basically the same thing!"

"That's great!" Theo held up a hand and Alfie shot over to give him a high-five, cheering for himself.

"And we got pizza after! And ice-cream!" Alfie bounced.

"In case you couldn't tell we had sugar," Garrett added, lips twitching.

"We saved you some apple crisp, too," Theo said. Alfie gasped, running to the fridge.

"Excuse me!" Beena said, giving Alfie a warning glance. He froze with one hand on the fridge door. "You've had enough sweets, thank you."

"You're going to rot all your teeth out," Garrett added. "Then how will you eat anything?"

"We'll have to feed you banana mush and milk like when you were a baby!" Beena added.

Alfie looked harassed. "Please!" he begged. "I don't even need all my teeth! Please, please, please!"

"You definitely need all your teeth, kid." Theo snorted. He and Garrett exchanged an amused glance at Alfie's theatrics.

"Why don't you have a shower and get your things ready for school? And we'll let you have a little bit."

"Yesssss." Alfie pumped his fists in the air, then shot out of the kitchen. Theo heard his feet running up the stairs, and Garrett followed after him, kissing Beena's cheek as he exited. Beena remained in the kitchen, coming over to the sink to pour herself a glass of water.

"So what do you need to clear your head about?" she asked, taking a long sip.

"Hm?"

"Earlier," she said, tucking a loose strand of hair behind her ear. "You said cleaning helps clear your head, but what's going on in that head of yours?" She set the glass down, touching his cheek, and even though her fingers were cold, he still felt their warmth. "Is everything okay?"

Beena looked at him with such motherly fondness and concern that Theo felt tears prick his eyes. He could lie to his own mother, but he couldn't lie to her.

He gave her a sad smile, swallowing the lump in his throat. "You know, I can't remember the last time my own mother asked me that," he said. "If she ever did, really."

Beena frowned. "Your parents are blind. Is that what's bothering you?"

Theo shook his head, shrugging. "It's fine." What was really bothering him was this whole thing with Lavinia, not his parents, anyway.

"It's not fine," Beena replied, brows furrowed. "No one is allowed to make you upset."

She pinched his cheek, the way she used to when he was a kid, and that got a smile out of him, which made her expression brighten as well.

He had always been able to talk about things with Beena: if he should try out for the school's football team or not; what colleges he should apply to; if he should take culinary courses in addition to his business degree.

Maybe he could discuss his feelings for Lavinia with her, too? She had never steered him wrong before.

"So, what did you guys get up to yesterday?" Theo asked, leaning against the counter. He figured he would ease into it.

"Oh, nothing much," Beena replied, taking a sip of her

water. "Lavinia was out with Calahan, and Alfie had plans with his friends, so Garrett and I stayed in reading together."

Theo's stomach twisted. "Oh." Lavinia hadn't mentioned she'd had a date yesterday. "Calahan—have you met him?"

Beena nodded. "We've met him at the cafe, and he seems like a wonderful boy! He has a good head on his shoulders, and I think he's great for Lavinia." She smiled, and it was clear just how happy she was.

His heart catapulted and crashed.

Beena was right; Calahan *was* wonderful. And in comparison, Theo was . . . not. Of course Beena wanted her daughter to go out with an accomplished adult. Of course she was pleased.

Just like Theo should have been, just like he *should* be. Instead of being selfish, hoping that things weren't working out between Lavinia and Calahan so that Theo could have a chance.

"Yeah . . . Yes, he's great," Theo agreed, swallowing the lump in his throat.

Theo needed to give up now, before he went too far. He knew that was the wise thing to do, the *right* thing to do, and yet . . . it still made him sick. He wanted her, and he didn't know how to stop wanting her.

He didn't think he could.

# CHAPTER 19

Lavinia remembered when she was a kid, maybe about six or seven. She was meant to be asleep, but she'd heard her parents laughing downstairs. So she had tiptoed down, following the noise.

She had hid behind the wall, and peered around the corner at her parents in the kitchen, where Beena had been washing the dishes and Garrett was drying them. Beena had laughed at something Garrett had said, and he'd taken her soapy hand, twirling her around, and then they were dancing, both humming along to the same tune.

Lavinia had stood and watched, smiling to herself at how happy they were. She'd giggled, then clapped a hand over her mouth, since she was supposed to be sleeping, but Beena had heard. Rather than scolding Lavinia, her parents had both held out a hand for her, and she'd bounced over to join them, the three of them dancing together.

Garrett had lifted her up onto the kitchen table, and her parents had danced around her, singing together while Lavinia twirled on the tabletop in her pajamas and bare feet.

That moment had felt like it was made of gold, even as she'd lived it, and now the memory was shiny and radiant every time she returned to it.

Even then, she knew what her parents had was rare and precious. Since then, she'd dreamed of finding a love like that for herself, a love that turned the mundane into magic.

Now she was with Calahan, and she was so sure he was everything a good partner should be: kind, caring, attentive. Not to mention handsome and a good kisser, too.

But she wasn't sure if what they had could be called true love.

Maybe she was thinking too much—which she decidedly shouldn't have been doing because it was only making her doubt, and there was no time for doubts. If she couldn't make things work with Perfect Calahan, she was resigned to being alone for the rest of her life.

She knew that not everybody found romance in their life, and that to live without romantic love was not the worst thing in the world, but the prospect frightened her as it seemed to presage the worst kind of future: the idea of a very long life without any of the companionship that she had grown up witnessing in her parents.

Lavinia groaned, focusing her attention on what was in front of her. She was in the library at university, her laptop and textbook spread in front of her, and she was supposed to be studying. She pushed her glasses back on her nose.

"Focus," she muttered to herself, but her gaze strayed to the windows lining the walls.

It was drizzling outside, the atmosphere misted and foggy. Gray clouds marbled the sky, adding a dull cast to the school grounds. The wind rustled the branches of the trees, some of which had already lost all their leaves. Autumn was passing quickly, bringing winter closer and closer.

She was listening to a playlist titled "you're writing love letters in an ancient library during autumn" and she wished that was what she was doing here, instead of studying the particulars of administering anesthesia to griffins.

Lavinia loved what she did—she loved learning and studying and working hard—but sometimes, she was just so tired. She sighed, leaning on her arms, the sleeves of her light sweater soft against her cheek.

She wanted to be done already, to have reached the end, but she knew also that to reach the end without any of the hard work required wouldn't be as satisfying. So she continued studying until it was time to head home.

She walked across campus. While it was evening by then, the university was bustling. She passed ivy-covered buildings as students and faculty members walked along the pathways, big bags on their shoulders and hot to-go cups in their hands. There were students sitting on benches reading books or eating snacks or just catching a break.

When she entered her home, it was warm, and she heard sizzling coming from the kitchen as dinner was being cooked. The familiar scent helped ease some of her fatigue; what a joy it was to have a comfortable home to return to.

"Pumpkin, is that you?" Garrett called from the kitchen. Lavinia closed the door, kicking off her shoes.

"It's me!" Lavinia called back. She walked into the house, where Beena stood at the stove in the kitchen, stirring a pot. Garrett was at the counter beside her, chopping up cauliflower.

She went over and kissed her parents hello, then went across to the living room, where Alfie was lying down on the carpet with Biter on top of him. He giggled as the little red draggo walked across his stomach, tickling him with her tiny paws.

"Give her to me," Lavinia said, scooping Biter up off him. She cuddled with Biter, who was getting a little bigger now, pressing her cheek against the baby dragon's. "I need this."

Alfie sat up, watching her.

"Being a grown-up is very difficult," she told her little brother. "I wouldn't recommend it."

He gave her a confused look. "You're a grown-up?"

Honestly, a valid question. "Technically?" she replied. "I am twenty-four."

Alfie's eyes widened. "Wow, you *are* old."

"Thanks." Then she lay down on the rug, putting Biter onto her stomach, squealing as Biter's paws moved.

Alfie lay down six inches away from her. "Biter, jump!" he said, pointing to his stomach. Biter cocked her head. "Come on, jump!" Biter prepared, then hopped across, wings flapping as she landed on Alfie. Lavinia smiled.

It wasn't all so bad.

After dinner, she had Beena put oil in her hair before going up to her room to study for her anatomy class. It was her hardest class—and the one she was currently doing the worst in. While she ordinarily got As, she was barely making a B in this class at the moment, and most of her final grade hinged upon the massive midterm she had coming up in two weeks.

Taking a deep breath, Lavinia put on a playlist titled "watching the stars on a quiet night" before opening up her notes. After she had done an hour of uninterrupted studying,

Lavinia took a break. She rolled off her bed, landing on her feet, then went to her vanity to get her phone.

She realized she should probably call Calahan, since they hadn't talked today. Embarrassment flushed through her at the fact that she hadn't thought of him sooner.

When Lavinia picked up her phone, she saw that she had missed a video call from Theo from half an hour ago. She called him back, and he immediately picked up. His face filled the screen and she smiled.

"Hey!" she said, but the word came out funny and she realized she had already put her retainer in for the night. "One sec, let me take this out."

She put the phone down and dashed to the bathroom, pulling her retainer out and sticking it in her retainer case. Then, she glanced in the mirror. She was wearing a stretched-out T-shirt from middle school and had her oiled hair back in a braid that made her look like a seventeenth-century lord.

She didn't mind that Theo was seeing her like this; she just thought it was funny. She could be any version of herself with him; she never had to be self-conscious about herself.

"I'm back," she said, picking up her phone again. She'd been right, Theo was totally unfazed by her appearance. "How was your day?"

"Busy," he replied. "We got a last-minute order, so I had to stay after to help. Just got back and showered, then I called you."

His hair was still a little wet, the brown of his locks darker. He was wearing a black hoodie, and he looked tired, but his eyes were bright as he talked with her.

"Ooh, sounds like a lot," she said, going back to her bed.

She kicked her books to the side and got comfortable. "What was this big last-minute order about?"

Theo told her about it, explaining in detail how hectic things were all day, and how each of his coworkers was behaving and reacting. She knew each of them by name—she'd heard Theo talk about them so often—just like Theo knew all her professors by name, and even the names of some of her classmates, particularly the ones who annoyed her or who helped her out.

As Theo gave her the play-by-play, Lavinia listened. Video-calling like this reminded her of when they were undergrads. He had gone to university a few hours away to get away from home, and they would talk on the phone almost every day, giving each other a recap like this. She remembered talking to him while walking between classes, or on her way to grab lunch, or during a coffee break.

"Anyway," Theo finished. "We figured it out and everything got done, but now my arms are like jelly, we did so much."

He sighed, looking exhausted, the way he had every time he talked about work lately. Before, he would be tired after a long day, but he would be satisfied and accomplished, too, proud of the work he'd done. Now, he was just tired, and she didn't think it was just a funk he was in.

He was unhappy, and she knew how difficult it was for him to take big steps. Maybe he needed a little push.

"If you're still feeling bleugh about the Rolling Pin, maybe it's time to do something," she suggested. "Saphira mentioned needing a business assistant the other day at dinner—have you thought about that further as a possibility?"

He rubbed a hand over his face. "November and December

are our busiest months after the summer season," he said. "I couldn't leave."

Though he sounded like he really wanted to.

"Do you want to?" she asked.

Slowly, he nodded. "Honestly? Yeah." He groaned, falling silent, but she could almost hear the thoughts whirring around his head.

"Tell me what you're thinking," she said. She was always interested in every single one of his thoughts.

"Would I even be good as a business assistant?" he asked, nibbling on his lower lip.

"I'm sure you would be," she replied without hesitation. "You're smart and hard-working; I think you'd succeed at anything you set your mind to."

He looked at her like she was being idealistic. "Come on."

"I mean it!" she protested. She really did.

He made a thoughtful sound, and she could tell that he didn't really believe what she was saying. He never believed her when she told him how wonderful he was. Sometimes, like now, it seemed like he *wanted* to believe her—but he just couldn't.

His parents had really messed him up. She couldn't imagine what it was like for him to grow up in that environment. She saw it firsthand when he split his knee open when they were kids, and she thought maybe his parents would ease up as Theo got older, but they never did.

Even now, they were just as harsh and disappointed.

The thought devastated Lavinia. She wished there was some way to shield him from all that hurt. She wanted him to be happy.

She and her family had always done all they could to make him feel loved, but of course, they could only do so much. There were limitations—even now.

She couldn't love him fully, the way she wanted to, wholeheartedly, and being unable to do that hurt, too.

"You do have a degree," she reminded him.

He looked like he wanted to argue but then conceded the point. "What am I going to do? Make a career change at this age?"

"This age?" she repeated, gobsmacked. "As if we're fifty! Please. Anyway, you can make a career change whenever you want if you're not happy with what you're doing. There's nothing wrong with focusing on different things in different phases of your life."

He blew out his cheeks. "I'm not happy," he admitted. "I keep trying to convince myself that I am, that this feeling will go away, but it won't."

He furrowed his brows, his expression growing dark. For some reason, she had a sense that she didn't fully understand the meaning of what he was saying.

"Maybe you can talk to Saphira," Lavinia suggested. "I think you'd be perfect for what she's looking for."

Theo looked unsure. "But she's our friend," he said. "If I ask, she'd feel bad saying no to me, and then she would be stuck."

Lavinia genuinely did not think Saphira would say no; actually, she thought Saphira would jump at the opportunity. It would solve both of their problems! But she knew Theo; he couldn't see the value in himself, so he thought that merit didn't exist.

Resolve bounded through her. Lavinia would talk to Saphira tomorrow herself.

Theo needed a little boost of confidence.

The next day, around midday, Lavinia was in the office at the Animal Hospital. Dr. Quan was out with a patient, and Lavinia was meant to be writing up the notes from her last patient's visit, but instead, she pulled out her phone, dialing Saphira.

"Lavinia, hey," Saphira said, picking up. "What's up? Aren't you at your internship?"

"Hi! Yes, but shh, don't tell," Lavinia said, keeping her voice lower than usual. "I had an idea, and I wanted to discuss it with you."

"Please do!" Saphira said. "I love your ideas."

"Okay, so, you know how you want to hire a managerial assistant to help with the cafe?" Lavinia asked, tapping her nails on her desk.

"Mhm."

"And we both agreed that I couldn't do it . . . But, I've been thinking—what about Theo for the role?" she said. "He's a bit unhappy at the Rolling Pin and looking for something new, and he's been around since the cafe opened, just like me!"

"Oh my god, really? I didn't think of Theo because I knew he was busy with the Rolling Pin, but if he's looking for something new, that would be perfect!" Saphira exclaimed, as excited by the idea as Lavinia was, just like Lavinia knew she would be. See, she *was* always right! "He has been around as long as you, and I completely trust him."

"Exactly!"

"You know, last year, he did offer to help out with managing when I was struggling with getting things situated so I could pay off the last of the mortgage on the place. I didn't have any funds to hire him for a proper job at the time but *now*, if I run the numbers—by which of course I mean if *Aiden* runs the numbers—I'm sure I could afford to hire him!"

"Yes!" Lavinia said, sitting up. "I think that could work. You should talk to him about it and see what he says. He won't bring it up himself because he doesn't want to put you in an awkward position, but I knew that you'd think it was a good idea, which is why I'm meddling a little."

Saphira laughed. "Don't worry, I appreciate the meddling. And he actually did mention it to me before when I brought it up with him, but I didn't think about it too seriously because I didn't realize he actually wanted to leave the Rolling Pin. But now—this could be perfect! You really do have the best ideas!"

"Yay!" Lavinia loved when things worked out the way she wanted them to. "Okay, now I have to get back to work before Dr. Quan comes back in here and finds me yapping. Talk soon!"

"Okay, byeeee."

They hung up, and Lavinia got back to work, thankfully before Dr. Quan returned to the office.

When she was done with her internship about two hours later, she went to her car and called Theo while she drove to campus for class. He picked up after two rings, then said, "Wait, one sec."

She heard a little muffled noise, then heard his voice again. "Hey, sorry, was just putting my headphones in. Am currently kneading cookie dough."

"Ooh, yum," Lavinia said. "I could go for some cookies right now."

"When are you not in the mood for cookies?" he asked, laughing.

"Fair point. *Anyway*. I called because I was just casually talking to Saphira, and she said she had something she wanted to talk to you about—so did she?" Lavinia asked.

"Casually, huh?" Theo laughed. "Yes, I did talk to her. I was going to call you when you were done with class in the evening. Are you driving over to school now?"

"Yup," she said. "So . . . what did she say?"

Theo snorted. "As if you don't know," he said, though he didn't seem upset. On the contrary, his tone was fond. "I can recognize a Lavinia Williams Plan from a mile away."

"Maybe I know a little bit," she admitted, giggling. "So what do you think? Isn't it a great idea?"

"It is!" He paused. "But what if it doesn't work out? What if I'm not good at it?"

"You will be good at it!" she said. "You're good at everything." She paused. "Well, except for bowling. You're pretty bad at that."

"Hey! You know I had a hand-cramp that day!" he objected. "But seriously . . . I've never worked a business type of job, you know?" He released a breath. "And what about Suki? Plus, what if I miss the Rolling Pin when I leave? Things are comfortable as they are. What if I ruin a good thing and regret it?"

"It's a big step!" she said, understanding his qualms. "You obviously don't have to decide this second. Change is scary, and even if things are *comfortable* right now, you said you weren't *happy*, so maybe a change is necessary."

He groaned. "Ugh, I know you're right. Thanks for the push—I'll definitely think about it."

"Good! I just want you to be happy, you know that, right?"

"I know." His voice went soft. "Thank you, Lavinia." He paused, and she heard him swallow. "I don't know what I'd do without you."

This was usually the moment she would tease, saying something like, "You'd be lost without me!" or "Of course you don't!" but there was something in his voice.

Something she didn't understand.

## CHAPTER 20

For the next week, Lavinia devoted her time to studying for her anatomy midterm. It was going to be her hardest exam, and she was genuinely worried she wouldn't pass.

She and Calahan met at the university library for studying dates, and at the end of the night, they'd walk back to their cars together. He'd carry her bag, and she'd feel giddy.

Tonight was the same. They packed up their things and, before she could take her bag, he picked it up.

"Ready?" he asked. She nodded, and they walked away from the lamplit wood tables, passed the shelves of books, and went out into the main entryway.

"I feel bad," she said, as they headed toward the door. "I'm carrying nothing and you're carrying both of our bags."

He wrinkled his nose at her. "It's nothing," he said, laughing.

"Really?" she asked. "Because my shoulder is always *killing* me at the end of the night."

He was carrying her bag easily, though, holding the tote straps in his left hand while his leather messenger bag hung down his right shoulder.

"So I take my offer back—you can definitely hold onto that," she said. He smiled.

They walked out into the cold evening, heading in the direction of the parking lot. It was late, and most of the campus was empty and quiet. Moonlight shone over the darkened buildings, casting the stone walls in white light.

They had taken a break for dinner earlier in the evening, before doing more work, and now, when she got home, there would be nothing to do but sleep. She couldn't wait to collapse into her bed.

A breeze lifted the air, and a chill ran down her spine. She shivered.

"You didn't bring a jacket?" he asked, looking over at her. The rain the last few days had made the temperature drop further, and the warmer autumn days had given way to chillier ones.

"Um, no," she said. "But it was so nice during the day!"

"Because the sun was out." Calahan stopped walking.

"What are you doing?" she asked, facing him. She watched as he set down both their bags. He took off his coat. "Oh, you don't have to!" she assured him.

He came over and draped his coat over her shoulders; it was still warm. "I insist," he said. She was hit with a wave of fondness for him.

"Thank you," she replied, putting her arms into the armholes of his coat, a tweed blazer. It smelled like a museum, lovely and old. "Do I look like a professor?" she asked, putting a hand on her hip to strike a pose. "I mean a tweed blazer—it's so classic!"

He smiled. "It's cute on you."

"It was pretty cute on you, too," she said. "Maybe it's just the blazer."

"Nah, I don't think so." He came closer, and she bit back a smile, excitement sparking because she knew what was about to happen next. Calahan drew closer, hand on her waist as he pulled her in for a kiss.

He kissed her slow and sweet, and a soft feeling spread through her. This was what it was supposed to feel like, easy and calm.

Not intense. Lavinia was already an intense person, and maybe it was good to be with someone who made her a quieter and calmer one. She didn't need to be so loud and obnoxious all the time, the way she was at home, and with Theo, or with Saphira.

She could be demure and mature. Maybe that was what an adult relationship was supposed to be like.

She tried not to think about it too much as she kissed him back. He pulled back, then kissed her cheek, wrapping her into a hug. Being enveloped in his arms was cozy, like being in a warm bath.

Someone walked past, giving them a look. "Oops," she said, giggling. "We are in fact in the middle of the walkway."

"Don't worry," Calahan said, looking over her shoulder at the retreating figure. "That was one of my students." He picked up their bags, and they began walking again. "He's probably just pissed because he failed the quiz I gave this week."

Lavinia laughed. They continued talking until they reached her car, at which point she took her bag back. "Thank you, again," she said, handing him back his coat.

"Of course." He reached out and took her hand, and she squeezed. "Do you want to meet again tomorrow after class?" Calahan was working on his thesis, so he spent most of his time at the library doing work.

"Sure," she said with a smile.

"It's a date."

He kissed her goodnight, then was on his way, and she got into her car. Sitting down, she started the engine, and as the car warmed up, she pressed the cold fingers of her left hand against the vent while her right hand pulled out her phone from her bag. She touched the screen and it lit up, and she scrolled through her notifications.

Disappointment echoed through her. There was no reply from Theo. She had messaged him earlier today when she was going to the library to ask if he wanted to join her and Calahan, but he hadn't replied, which meant no, obviously, but he could have just said that.

She had tried inviting him to join her and Calahan since she didn't have too much free time with exams coming up, and this way, she could see both of them, but he either responded too late or made some excuse.

This was the third time in the last week, and she was starting to think it was on purpose, which was not good. If Calahan was going to be her person, the way she wanted him to be, Theo needed to be better friends with him!

As she drove home, she wondered what Theo's problem was. He was being so moody, almost as if he was avoiding Calahan on purpose. Every time she even mentioned Calahan, he got this weird expression on his face, like he was pissed off and trying not to be and failing.

Ordinarily, he was never this weird with the guys she dated—he was usually so supportive! Something had changed, and she couldn't pin down what, no matter how hard she thought about it.

A part of her did consider that maybe, just maybe, it was the kiss they had shared—but that was probably just her being delusional, and she didn't need to entertain those thoughts because it only hurt.

Instead, she tried to think back to other instances he had behaved like this. Being friends for most of their lives meant she could usually track his behavioral changes based on their history. She knew him.

"What is going on?" she asked herself.

And then she remembered. This one time, in high school when they were seniors, he was really busy with the school's football team, and she was really busy with the debate team. To make matters worse, they only had one class together, so they hardly ever saw each other.

She did, however, have almost every class with another girl—Ayushi—and they were on the debate team together as well. Lavinia and Ayushi became close, spending a lot of time together, and she recalled that Theo had acted strangely towards Lavinia for a few weeks.

He never wanted to hang out with her when she was with Ayushi, and when Lavinia finally asked him why he was being so weird, he admitted that he was scared she was replacing him.

She had laughed, thinking he was joking at first, but then she realized he was deadly serious, his face pinched with an expression of pain. "Theo, of course not!" she had told him, genuinely baffled he could think such a thing. "I could never replace you—I wouldn't be able to."

It took some time for Theo to truly believe her—but what if he was having a similar thought now? That she was replacing him with Calahan? She had been busy this past week, and it was easy to see Calahan since he was already on campus and they could meet up to do work together.

But of course Calahan couldn't replace what Theo was for her—no one could! And no one ever would. Theo was her brightest star, her constant.

Plans needed to be made.

The next day, on Wednesday, when she was supposed to be paying attention in her Principles of Surgery class, she opened the messages app on her laptop to send a text to Theo: **Earth to Theoooo where are youuuu.**

His reply came a minute later: **Hiya, sorry, been busy.**

She rolled her eyes to herself, but decided not to be petty and say something sarcastic in response. Instead, she wrote, **What are you doing later today?**

He replied that he had a football match, and another message came immediately after: **Do you want to come?**

Lavinia smiled, no longer annoyed with him. **Yes!** she replied, **Send me the time and place xx**

He sent a smiley face back, and Lavinia opened up her to-do list, rearranging her tasks so she'd be free in the evening for Theo's game.

"Oh shit," she muttered to herself, remembering she was meant to be meeting Calahan at the library for a study date after class. Lavinia bounced her leg. She *really* should have been paying attention in class, since she had a midterm coming up for this subject as well, but now she needed to text Calahan.

**I can't meet at the library tonight, sorry! I forgot Theo**

invited me to one of his football matches, and I already told him I'd go.

This was technically not true, but it would look bad if she canceled on Calahan after the fact. Lavinia shifted her focus back to her professor, quickly jotting notes down from the PowerPoint before the slide changed.

After Principles of Surgery, she had her anatomy class, and Lavinia turned all her attention to the reproductive practices of dragons, turning her phone to silent so she wouldn't be tempted to check her messages during her hardest class. As such, she didn't see Calahan's response until she was leaving class, heading in the direction of the parking lot. He hadn't texted anything; she had a missed call.

Lavinia called him back, walking. "Hey!" she said. "Sorry again to cancel, but I'm sure you'll have a much more productive evening without me distracting you, anyway."

Calahan laughed. "That's probably true, but I was thinking—mind if I tag along?" he asked. "I could use a break from thesis work, anyway, and maybe we can grab dinner after?"

"Oh!" A variety of emotions clashed through Lavinia. She was pleased at the effort Calahan made; he really was swoon-worthy. Then there was guilt: she should have suggested that! And then there was something else, a little voice that told her that maybe this was a bad idea.

*But why would it be a bad idea?*

"Yes, definitely!" she found herself saying, because it had already been too long of a pause. "I don't think the game will be super long, anyway."

"Great, send me the address," he replied. "I'll meet you in the parking lot there and we can walk in together."

"Perfect!" she squeaked. Lavinia hung up, then sent him the location, a strange feeling spreading through her like a chill. But maybe that was just the weather, reminding her how close winter was.

These plans with Calahan were good. The more time they spent together, the better. While she still wasn't sure yet that he was The One, she was determined to make things work with him. Besides, it wasn't like she had other options.

Lavinia rolled her shoulders, making it to her car. She sat down, closing the door against the cool autumnal air. The weird feeling remained, even as she drove over to the field.

She *was* happy with Calahan, and she knew that as long as they were together, she would be happy.

But was she the happiest she could be? She didn't know what to do. She wanted to see the map of her entire life and make the right choice. Being unable to was debilitating.

Shouldn't it have been easy?

The thing was, it *would* be easy, if it was up to her. She didn't allow herself to think it, but deep down, in the shadows of her thoughts, tucked into the darkest corner of her heart, she knew she would choose Theo. She wouldn't hesitate, and there would be nothing to second-guess.

But would he choose her? She already knew the answer.

So then why . . . *why* would she jeopardize things with Calahan? Ruin something good for someone who didn't even want her!

Tears pricked her eyes, and she squeezed them shut. She rubbed her temples, releasing a long breath. It was almost the end of October. She'd had all this time, all these years, to find her person—if she wasn't settled by the winter, she never would be.

Calahan liked her, and he didn't seem to be getting tired of her. He seemed—dared she say it—committed. It had almost been a month since they had started seeing each other, which wasn't long, but his affections only seemed to be growing, not lessening.

And she wanted to be loved. She wanted to be loved so badly. Didn't people always say it was better to be loved? She couldn't remember who exactly these *people* were, or where she had heard that, but she was sure it was a thing.

*Stop thinking so much*, she mentally scolded herself. She was getting exhausted at herself and all these emotions.

Things would work out, and she would get used to it. These doubts would go away, and she would be settled.

Lavinia arrived at the location of the match, then waited in the parking lot for Calahan. She could see the guys out on the field, warming up, and about fifteen minutes later, Calahan's car parked beside hers.

He got out of his car, then walked around to the passenger seat, which was next to the driver's seat of Lavinia's car. She stepped out, and he smiled at her. "Hey," he said, kissing her cheek. "Brought you something."

He opened the door to the passenger seat and pulled out two coffees, as well as a bakery box, the goods all decorated with the Baby Dragon Cafe logo, a coffee cup with wings. The other side of the bakery box was decorated with the words *The Baby Dragon Bakery* and a cupcake with wings, which was adorable.

"Ooh, yum," she said, as he handed her a drink. She took a sip; it was a latte, one she hadn't had before. "What is this?" she asked, trying to figure out the taste.

"S'mores latte," he replied, shutting the door of his car. "It's a chocolate mocha topped with roasted marshmallows and crushed graham crackers."

"Oh! You know, usually I'm a mocha hater, but this is pretty good," she said. They began walking over to the field.

"Why are you a mocha hater?" he asked, holding the bakery box with one hand and his drink with the other. "I thought you loved coffee."

"No I do, but mochas just taste like chocolate milk to me," she said. He laughed, and they made it to the field, where there were a few other friends and partners of the players on the sidelines, watching. The viewers were sitting on blankets on the grass or on folding outdoor chairs.

"So," Calahan asked, turning to the field. "This is a league or something?"

"Yes," Lavinia said, taking a sip of her mocha. "All these guys get together to make a team and practice and then meet up with other guys who have also gotten together to make a team and practice. Just for fun."

"Who's the ref?" Calahan asked. There was in fact a man in a referee outfit with a whistle hanging around his neck.

"I think they all pay for someone to come," Lavinia said.

"Very official," Calahan said, taking a sip of his coffee.

"Oh, very," she agreed. Calahan met her gaze, and she laughed. This was obviously not the World Cup; it was just for fun. But Theo took it very seriously, and she knew that he loved whenever she came to watch him play.

Lavinia drew her attention away from Calahan to look for Theo, who was warming up with the other players on his team.

They were all wearing black T-shirts and shorts, while the other team was wearing gray T-shirts and shorts.

She gave Theo a big smile and waved. His face lit up and he jogged toward her, smiling—until his gaze shifted to Calahan beside her. His brow knitted together, something dark coming over his expression.

Theo slowed his pace, walking over. "Hey," he said, the word flat.

"Hiya!" she replied, going over to hug him with her coffee-free hand. He hugged her back with one light hand, his shoulders stiff. "Who are these guys?" Lavinia asked. "Have you played them before? Give me the rundown."

Theo usually explained the other teams and their stats to her: which players were good, which were bad, how many games they had won, how many they had lost. Today, however, he was quieter than usual.

"They're not bad," Theo said. He looked over his shoulder. "I should probably get back."

Her heart sank. "Oh. Okay." She took a breath, forcing a smile. "Have fun!"

"Good luck," Calahan added, and Theo jogged back onto the field.

Once the football match began, Lavinia's attention was focused on the field. Calahan tried to chat with her, but she didn't really respond; she was so invested in the match.

She loved watching Theo play. It was one of the few times he was wholly stress-free, similar to how he got when he was baking. He simply enjoyed himself without worrying or thinking too much.

Though something was off. Usually, Theo was pretty good

at the sport, but today, he was all over the place. As the game continued, Lavinia wondered if he was off his game because Calahan was here.

Maybe it had been a bad idea to invite him.

A little while later, Lavinia finished her mocha, and she walked over to the garbage can to throw out the to-go cup. As she was walking back, she saw Theo had the ball on the field, and he was running.

She cheered. "Go Theo!"

He weaved between players, growing closer to where she was standing by the opposite team's net, and Lavinia's heart rate picked up with excitement as she watched him play. She whistled with her fingers, hooting as he got closer and closer.

He took the shot—and scored!

"YES!" she screamed, jumping up and down. "WOO!"

For the first time since the game began, Theo smiled. He ran straight to her, and before she knew it, he had scooped her into his arms, hugging her.

"Ew, stop," she shrieked, "you're so sweaty!"

He hugged her tighter, his sticky skin pressing against hers as he picked her up off the ground. He spun her around, and she screamed, laughing. Theo whooped.

"Okay, okay, get back to your match," she said, hitting his shoulders. He set her down and ran back to the field, looking over his shoulder to flash a crooked grin her way. She felt like she was floating, and she skipped back over to Calahan.

"He scored!" Lavinia said, smiling wide. Calahan furrowed his brows ever so slightly.

"I saw," Calahan said. He looked a bit surprised by how

she'd reacted, and she calmed down a little bit, realizing how obnoxious that had probably been.

Calahan hadn't seen her so hyper, especially since most of their dates took place at the university library. It was true that she could be loud with Saphira at the cafe, but that had been back when Calahan didn't know her that well, and then Lavinia had started working less at the cafe anyway, and so had Saph.

Lavinia felt a little self-conscious, then, and she fussed with her hair, letting it fall out from behind her ears to cover her warmed cheeks.

They continued to watch the game, and a little while later, Theo scored again.

He immediately looked over to see her reaction, but this time, Lavinia didn't jump up and down or yell. She just clapped, smiling widely at him.

Theo frowned, and she knew he had noticed her toned-down reaction. She willed him not to say anything about it. She couldn't be that obnoxious with everyone, anyway.

Theo's gaze shifted from Lavinia to Calahan. His expression darkened, and she felt her stomach twist.

She looked over at Calahan, who was noticing the look on Theo's face. Then, it was Calahan's turn to frown.

Anxiety spiked through Lavinia. She felt stuck in between them.

Maybe it was good that the three of them hadn't hung out together.

Now she just needed to get through this match in one piece.

# CHAPTER 21

It was towards the end of the game now, and Lavinia had sat down on the grass with Calahan, both of them huddled together as the sun set over the field, bringing a chill into the evening. They hadn't opened the Baby Dragon Bakery box Calahan had brought, and finally Lavinia reached for it.

"What did you bring?" she asked, opening the box to reveal two cupcakes with swirls of frosting on top. They smelled divine. She pulled a cupcake out of the box; it was dark orange and spongy.

"I was told they are pumpkin spice vanilla chai latte cupcakes," Calahan replied, really working to remember that whole name. She snorted.

"Why is that so hyper-specific?" she asked, pulling the wrapper off the cupcake.

"I have no idea," Calahan replied. "But it sounded like something you'd like."

"And you're absolutely right, I love all of those things." He bumped her shoulder with his. She took a bite, not caring about the frosting getting on her face. It was sweet and perfectly spiced, all the flavors mixing together effortlessly. "Ohmygod, soooo good."

Calahan laughed. "I can tell," he said, reaching over to swipe her nose. He held up a finger, where there was a huge dollop of frosting.

"Oops." She reached forward to lick the frosting off, and he pulled his hand back. "Hey!" she cried, grabbing his wrist. "That's my frosting!" Calahan laughed, letting her lick the frosting off his finger. "Mmm," she said, as the sweet buttercream melted on her tongue.

"Insatiable," Calahan said, shaking his head fondly. She laughed, letting go of his wrist.

She turned back to the field, still laughing—until she saw Theo. He had stopped in his tracks in the middle of the field and was watching her and Calahan.

The smile vanished from her lips at the expression on his face. Time seemed to slow around them, until all she heard was the loud roar of her blood rushing in her ears.

Then, Theo got rammed into.

Lavinia gasped, watching as he went flying into another player. Three bodies collided, crashing to the ground in a tangled heap. The referee sounded the whistle.

Lavinia shot to her feet. "Theo!"

She dropped her cupcake, running to the field. All three guys were groaning as they rose to their feet, and Lavinia reached between them for Theo.

He was in the worst shape, his face covered with blood that seemed to be coming from his nose and lip. He stood up, swearing profusely to himself.

"Oh my god, Theo," she said, going to his side. Another guy

in a black jersey jogged over—Lavinia recognized him. He was the team captain.

"Do you still want to play?" the captain asked Theo.

Theo shook his head, and the captain nodded, jogging off. Theo limped off the field, Lavinia walking with him, but he didn't look at her. Once Theo was off the field, the referee sounded the whistle again, and the teams resumed their match.

When Lavinia returned to the sidelines with Theo, Calahan stood.

"Shit," Calahan said, holding out a napkin for the blood. Theo didn't take it, not looking at Calahan.

Lavinia turned to Calahan. "I'm going to take Theo home," she said. Calahan paused, as if he wanted to say something, and she remembered too late that they were supposed to get dinner after the match.

Calahan swallowed. "Alright," he said. He reached over and kissed her cheek. "See you later."

Calahan left, but she hardly spared him a glance as she turned back to Theo. "Where's your bag?" she asked. He was standing very still, but his hands were shaking, and there was a stormy expression on his bloodied face. "Theo," she said. He wasn't looking at her, nor did he meet her gaze.

"Forget it," he said, voice low. "I'm fine."

He stalked away from her, and hurt slashed through her chest. Why was he being so cold? She watched as he went over to where his bag was with the rest of the other players' things, then she chased after him.

"I said I'm fine," Theo said, glancing over his shoulder but not quite looking at her.

"Theo, stop," she said, pissed off. Her body was buzzing

with restless energy. She was worried and didn't have time for him to be fussy.

Finally, he looked at her. Something in his expression broke. She softened her voice. "Come on, I'll drive you home."

She was concerned—not because he was injured, because it didn't look terrible enough that he needed to see a doctor, but because he was so quiet. He looked wounded in a way that wasn't just physical.

The only time she had ever seen him get hurt and not crack any jokes was that first time, when he'd fallen from the apple tree in his backyard.

"Okay?" she asked. He nodded, then followed her to the parking lot, walking a few steps behind her. They got to her car, and he threw his bag in the back. As she got into the driver's seat, he collapsed into the passenger seat with a sigh.

She started the car, pulling out of the parking lot.

"You didn't have to leave your date," he said, grumbling. "You don't have to do all this."

"Stop talking," she snapped. "I mean it."

She looked over to glare at him, and he sank into his seat, crossing his arms over his chest.

"Everything hurts, and now on top of that, you're being mean to me." He pouted.

"I'm not being mean to you, I'm just telling you to shut up," she told him, driving toward his place. "Let me take care of you."

He went quiet. He turned away from her, looking out the window, but before he did, she caught the way his eyes shone. She glanced over at him again and saw his throat moving.

Something terrible was happening, and she couldn't understand what. Fear clawed through her.

When they got to his apartment, she parked in his spot. They got out of the car, and she walked over to his side, taking his arm and putting it around her shoulder. They walked into his apartment building, taking the elevator up to his floor.

They made it to his place, stopping in front of the door, and he groaned. "My key," he said. "It's in my bag."

Which they had left in the car.

"It's okay," she said, rummaging around her purse. She found the spare key she always kept with her and let them into his apartment.

Inside, she switched on the lights, helping him over to the couch. He sank in, resting his head back against the pillows and closing his eyes. She brought him painkillers and water, which he took.

"Your face," she said. His nose had stopped bleeding, but there was dried blood all over the lower half of his face, and his shirt was in no better condition, the black fabric darker.

With a groan, he stood and pulled his shirt off.

Lavinia paused, pulse quickening. Of course, she had seen him shirtless hundreds of times before, but now the sight made her entire body tense. She had felt the muscles of his chest through his flannel when they had kissed. Her mouth went dry at the memory, her hands twitching.

He walked past her and went to the bathroom. She heard water running, but he must have only splashed water on his face because when he came back and fell onto the couch again, his face was only marginally cleaner.

"You look like shit," she said.

He gave her a thumbs-up. "Feel like it, too," he replied, not opening his eyes.

She shook her head, then went to his kitchen, grabbing a bowl of warm water and some paper towels. She came back and sat on the coffee table in front of him, putting the bowl beside her leg. She dipped the paper towel in, wringing it before lifting it toward his face.

"Let me," she said.

He opened his eyes, gaze shifting to her hand. He paused, throat moving as he swallowed. He nodded slightly, closing his eyes again. She reached over, but he was all the way back on the couch, and she couldn't reach from here. She stood, drawing closer, and she felt heat emanating off his body.

Lavinia's blood pounded as she leaned toward him, resting her left hand on his shoulder. His skin was hot, searing into her palm. Her hand looked so small along the curve of his shoulder, her thumb pressed against the hollow of his throat. She wanted to trail a finger down the slope of his long throat, to trail it lower, over his chest, lower to—

Lavinia shook her head. She swore internally, forcing herself to focus. Carefully, she wiped at the blood on his face. She cleaned his face up slowly, getting a new paper towel when the previous one turned red. The apartment was quiet, save for the sound of his ragged breathing—or was that hers? She couldn't tell.

They had known each other for most of their lives, and she thought she knew everything there was to know about him, all his behavioral patterns and thoughts and feelings, how he would act and react—but this was uncharted territory.

That scared her, but it thrilled her, too, in a deranged way; the way lightning might be exhilarating, despite all the ways it could devastate.

After dipping a new paper towel into the water, she dabbed at the cut on his lip.

He hissed, grabbing her wrist. Her stomach flipped, heat burning through her body. He opened his eyes, and she saw that his pupils were blown wide, his eyes completely dark.

From this close, she could see herself reflected in the dark pools of his eyes. Her chest ached. His thumb pressed hard into the pulse of her wrist, eliciting a delicious sort of pain, and she dropped the paper towel, gasping.

The sound was loud in his quiet apartment, and at the noise, his gaze flicked down to her open mouth, making desire hum through her. He brought his eyes back up to meet hers, their gazes locking.

They were both wholly unmoving, staring at each other. His hand was still gripping her wrist, her hand hovering just above his lips. If she curled her fingers, they would be in his mouth.

But then he let go, and her hand dropped. She moved back.

"Thank you," he said, voice rough.

"Of course," she squeaked. Her face was burning from both desire and shame, and she turned, not wanting him to see either.

She grabbed the dirty paper towels and bowl of water, going to the kitchen. Running her hands under cold water, she washed them, thankful for the sound of the running tap as she tried to catch her breath.

After a few moments, she turned the tap off and went to the fridge. When she opened the doors, cold air kissed her cheeks, helping her cool off. She looked around for something to eat, then spotted a familiar box. Pulling it out, she opened the container to find matar chawal, a brothy rice dish with peas.

"Did my mother make this?" Lavinia asked, turning around. Theo got up from the couch and came over. He sat down on the stool in front of the counter on the perimeter of the kitchen, across from where she was at the fridge.

"She dropped it off a few days ago," Theo said. His face was mostly cleaned up now, which made it easier to look at him without it hurting so much.

Despite the charged moment between them, Lavinia forced herself to act normal. "I was *wondering* where those leftovers went!" Lavinia shook her head. A corner of Theo's mouth tilted into a smile. "I'll warm this up."

She made them both plates for dinner, pairing the rice with keema, the minced meat dish also from Beena. She warmed up their plates in the microwave, then sat down on the stool beside him at the counter. They ate in silence, though neither of them really ended up eating much, Theo even less than her.

"I'm going to my room," he said, getting up.

"Okay," she said. "I'll make you haldi doodh."

He nodded, not saying anything as he walked to his room, disappearing inside. Lavinia released a long breath, then went to the kitchen, warming up milk with turmeric. She didn't really think it did anything, but Beena always made Lavinia drink haldi doodh when she was sick. It was kind of gross, but the warm milk was always comforting, and Lavinia snuck some honey in, too.

After the milk was ready, she brought it over to Theo's room in a mug. He was already in bed, lying down in the middle, staring up at the ceiling.

She set the mug on his side table, looking at him. He looked so . . . *sad*.

"What's wrong?" she asked, heart aching. She hated to see him in pain.

He didn't speak, as if he couldn't. She drew closer and saw that his eyes were wet.

Finally, he whispered, "It hurts, Lav." His chin trembled, and she wanted to cry.

Lavinia sat down on the edge of his bed. "Hey," she said, squeezing his arm. "It's going to be okay. Promise."

He closed his eyes as if she didn't understand. And maybe she didn't. She surely felt lost in a labyrinth of complex emotions, both his and hers. But she did mean what she said. Things would be okay. They had to be.

"Try and get some sleep," she said. She hated the sight of the cut on his lips, the tense furrow between his brows.

She brushed his wavy hair to the side, her hand lingering on his face. Her fingers twitched; she wanted to touch the soft pad of his lips.

Lavinia pulled back her hand as if scalded. She abruptly stood, heart hammering.

She turned to leave, but just when she did, he reached out and grabbed her hand. His finger curled around her wrist. She turned around, pulse racing.

"Can you stay?" he asked, eyes half-lidded as he looked at her. His voice was miserable. "Please."

Lavinia was frozen in place. It was agonizing to be here with him like this, but she couldn't say no to him.

"Okay," she said, voice quiet. "Just for a little while."

She lay down next to him, and he turned onto his side so they were facing each other.

At the same time, they reached for one another, pulling into a hug. For the first time all night, Theo finally seemed to relax, releasing a long exhale.

He still wasn't wearing a shirt, and her hands slid up on his bare back as his arms wound around her neck, one of his hands sliding into her hair. He rested his chin atop her head, holding her against his chest.

It was painfully intimate, the feel of his skin against hers. Every part of her ached for more. Her cheek was against the bare skin of his chest, right above his heart, and she felt his heartbeat.

She wanted to be closer to him, for them to fuse into one. She shifted toward him, heat pooling low in her belly as she felt the hard contours of his body.

An electric current shot through her, making her dizzy. This was dangerous. Everything within her felt unstable.

She pulled back, moving her hands from his shoulders down to his waist, trying to extricate herself from him, despite how much her body protested. She moved back until they were no longer touching and she could look up to see his face.

He opened his eyes, looking at her, his hand moving onto the curve of her neck. His gaze shifted down to her mouth, his lips parting.

"Lavinia," he whispered.

The way he said her name was new, unlike anything she'd heard before, from him, or anyone else. It was almost like an oath or a prayer—something haunted or holy.

Her eyelids fluttered as a shiver ran down her spine, and she involuntarily arched toward him.

"Lavinia," he whispered again, his voice lower, deeper, the

sound barely there, but she heard it as he drew closer. His breath was warm against her open mouth.

Then, his lips brushed against hers as if by accident—but she wished it wasn't an accident, and it was too much.

It was all too much. She pulled back.

"I have to go," she said, voice breaking.

# CHAPTER 22

When Theo's alarm sounded at six in the morning, he felt horrible. There was nothing he could do to convince himself to get out of bed. Instead, he called in sick, and promptly went back to sleep.

His phone rang a few hours later, but he didn't pick up, too tired to do anything. He eventually got up around noon, grabbing his phone. As he scrolled through his notifications, he saw it was Lavinia who had called a few hours earlier.

"Hello?" he said, voice groggy.

"Theo, hi! Did you just wake up?" she asked. His chest hurt and, horribly, tears filled his eyes at the sound of her voice, making his vision blur. "You took a day off? It's good you did; you should rest. I called a few hours ago to check in, but you were sleeping, I guess. Anyway. How are you? I was thinking of popping by after my internship and before class. I can pick up food if you want! What do you feel like having?"

He wiped his eyes, focusing his gaze on the ceiling. "I'm not up for company," he managed to say. "Just going to sleep."

"Oh." Her voice dimmed. "Okay. Well, I have to study,

anyway," she said, trying to sound unbothered, but he could tell that she was hurt. "I have a big midterm coming up in a few days that I'm probably going to fail."

Theo loved listening to Lavinia chatter on, and today was no different, except today, he was in agony. He couldn't find his voice to respond. Lavinia grew quiet on the line.

"Right." She paused. "Rest up," she said. "I'll talk to you later."

"Okay," he said, voice a whisper. "Bye."

She hung up, and guilt needled through him. He rubbed a hand over his face, then got out of bed, going to the bathroom to freshen up. When he glanced in the mirror, he saw that he didn't look too bad. There was just a cut on his lower lip, which was a little swollen, and some bruises here and there.

He felt much, much worse than he looked, but he knew it wasn't from the collision during his match, but everything that had come after. It was why Theo hadn't encouraged Lavinia to come over; he was scared of what he would do or say when he saw her again.

Last night was still fresh in his mind, how he had let himself get carried away by his desire for her. Even as the moment unfurled, he knew he shouldn't have asked her to stay, but it was impossible to suppress his want for her, impossible not to ask.

Having her in his arms was better than any medicine, any balm. The memory sent a shot of heat through his body, and he got into the shower, turning it straight to cold.

After he'd showered, he got dressed in a sweatshirt and sweatpants, going out to find something to eat. He saw their plates from last night, and it reminded him of Lavinia all over again. A futile fight—everything reminded him of her.

He picked up the plates to wash them, and as the water ran, he thought of how she had taken care of him last night. It made him want to cry.

"God," he muttered to himself, blinking fast.

She always took care of him—she was so *good*. So kind and perfect, it astounded him sometimes how she could be real. He was unbelievably lucky to exist in the same world at the same time as her, and luckier still to be in her life—and to be her best friend on top of that! It felt like winning the lottery.

It didn't matter that he had gotten the short end of the stick with his parents because he had her. She was his brightest star, the guidepost from which everything else took direction. If he lived a hundred lives, he'd find her in every one; the way sailors unerringly found the North Star in the night sky no matter the century.

Holding her in his bed last night had driven him crazy. He had leaned in closer and closer, until it would seem like an accident when their lips brushed. He hated himself for taking liberties when she was with someone else, but he couldn't hate himself entirely, either, because he was selfish.

It wasn't an accident: he had wanted to kiss her; he just didn't know how to steal one. During the match, he had seen her with Calahan, the two of them laughing, and the sight had knifed through him, more excruciating than getting rammed into by a guy at full speed on the field.

He wanted her badly, and he couldn't have her.

What was he supposed to do with himself? With all this desire? With all this love he had for her?

He was utterly losing his mind. Theo finished up with the

dishes and threw some sourdough in the toaster, hoping the carbs slathered in butter would rectify his foul mood. The mug of strong chai he made to accompany the late breakfast did help a little.

He went over to his couch, sitting down with his chai, staring out the window. He lasted about thirty seconds before his thoughts wound back to Lavinia, and he outwardly groaned, throwing his head back to stare at the ceiling.

After she had left last night, he couldn't sleep for a long, long time, his blood pounding through his body with unspent desire. He couldn't think of anything else but her, and when he finally slept, it was her he dreamed of. Now that he was awake, it was still her he thought of.

He stared at the ceiling, hardly functioning. He was restless, agitated, and miserable, and he knew he had been strange on the phone with Lavinia. Surely she had noticed, but he didn't know how to stop.

She knew him too well—and yet she couldn't recognize this major thing, how he had fallen irreparably and irrevocably in love with her.

He wondered how it was that she didn't see such a glaringly obvious truth when she otherwise saw him so well, but perhaps she did see it, and she acted as if she didn't.

It didn't matter, either way. The result was the same. She was with someone else—something he had to remind himself about fifty times a day.

He didn't understand what he was supposed to do with himself now that he was in love with her. He suspected that he had been in love with her for some time, he had just never allowed himself to acknowledge the fact. But now that he had, he couldn't think of anything else. He was in love with her! He wanted to shout it from the rooftops.

Theo got off the couch, heading for the kitchen. He pulled out his notebook from the drawer, paging through the notes he'd written down for new recipes he wanted to try. He settled on one, rolling back the sleeves of his sweatshirt.

He was testing out fried kulfi falooda. He'd gotten the basic recipe for kulfi from Beena a long time ago, but this would be a remix of the classic. Kulfi was made of milk, sugar, and condensed milk, and it was a bit denser and fudgier than ice-cream.

Theo grabbed the base ingredients, throwing them together in his blender, along with a bit of cardamom, saffron, and kewra water for taste. At the end, he threw in a half-piece of toast as well, which was a trick Beena had told him about to keep the kulfi smooth and not icy.

Once it was ready, he poured the mixture into little paper cups, using them as molds. He put the tray of cups into the back of his freezer; he would check on them every hour or so, mixing with a spoon to push the thicker cream back to the bottom so the kulfi wouldn't be unbalanced.

As he worked, Theo felt a little bit better. He released a long breath, going to the next portion of the recipe. This part, he hadn't done before. He was going to fry the kulfi to be served the way fried ice-cream was.

He made a wet batter of milk and eggs with a dash of vanilla essence, then a dry batter of breadcrumbs and coconut flakes. When the kulfi was frozen enough, he sliced them into thick disks, dipping them in the wet batter, then the dry.

While that set in the freezer, he took tukmaria—sweet basil

seeds—and added water so they would swell and double in size over the next hour or two. Once that was done, he boiled the vermicelli and took out the rose syrup, which he already had.

It ended up being a lot of components, but he didn't mind it. Baking helped him relax, and this was definitely helping. He jotted down notes as he worked, sketching little pictures beside his notes to help him remember the recipe.

The whole process ended up taking most of the day, since there was a lot of waiting required with the kulfi; it probably would have been better to let the kulfi freeze overnight, then fry it in the morning, adding on the tukmaria, falooda, and rose syrup, but he had nothing else to do.

After he'd eaten an early dinner, he finally fried the kulfi in extra-hot oil, leaving them in for only about twenty seconds until they were perfectly golden and crispy. He topped the fried kulfi with the tukmaria, vermicelli, and rose syrup, then scooped up a bite.

It was delicious. Satisfaction coursed through him, the first positive emotion he'd felt all day.

He did love baking; that wasn't the issue. Perhaps hobbies were meant to stay hobbies, and not careers. There was no pressure when he was just doing it for fun, for the joy of it. At the Rolling Pin, everything had to be perfect and precise, which was stressful.

Theo sighed, picking up his bowl of fried kulfi falooda. He went to the couch, sitting down, thinking again about his career and what he should do. The future was so scary; he couldn't believe *he* was the one responsible for making this key decision.

He had spoken to Saphira about a week ago about helping manage the cafe, and now he thought that maybe it was time to make up his mind once and for all. He had gotten his business degree because his parents had wanted him to, but he hadn't hated it. It was easy, and he was good at it, and he was sure he would love working with Saphira at the Baby Dragon. He could keep up with his fusion desserts for the Baby Dragon Bakery, as well, which would keep him inspired.

But what about Suki? While he had originally hesitated about talking with Saphira because he was afraid she wouldn't want him for the role, now he hesitated because he worried how Suki would react to the idea. Would she feel betrayed? Abandoned?

Consternation spiked through him, and he set down his bowl of dessert. He stood, pacing around his apartment.

He knew he needed to speak with her, but he didn't know how to start that conversation, which was why he hadn't done anything yet, despite wanting to quit. He was always so bad at this sort of stuff. He hated to hurt anyone.

"You're okay," he told himself, but the word didn't do much to reassure him. He continued to pace, until sweat broke out on his neck. He squeezed his eyes shut.

*You're okay*, a voice told him in his mind, and this time, it wasn't his own, but Lavinia's. Theo released a breath, slowing his steps. *You're okay*. He heard her voice again, and it calmed him.

Theo rubbed his temples, trying not to think about Lavinia, which was virtually impossible, but he needed to get his shit together.

He needed a plan. He spent the rest of the evening

considering how to broach the subject of quitting with Suki. He could ease her into the idea, gauging her reaction to the prospect of him leaving the Rolling Pin.

If she seemed amenable to the idea, he could slowly bring up that he was considering quitting and see what her opinion would be, and if she seemed agreeable to that, too, he could let her know that he wanted to leave. And if she reacted badly to the idea, he would just drop it.

Yes, that could work.

The next morning, when he arrived at work, all his plans fell away when Suki called him into her office. Heart beating fast, he followed her out of the kitchen toward the little office she kept for herself.

"Close the door behind you," Suki said, taking off her sage-green apron and hanging it up. She sat down at the desk, which was neat with a computer and papers. Once the door was closed, the small space was incredibly quiet.

"Sit down," Suki said, gesturing to the chair across from her at the desk. Anxiety pricked him, and he swallowed the lump in his throat, doing as she said. He didn't know why he was so afraid; Suki's eyes were warm as she regarded him, her expression one of tender concern.

"I wanted to see how you were doing," she said, leaning forward on her desk. Her gaze went to the cut on his lip, and she frowned. "Are you feeling better?"

"Ye-Yes," he stuttered. He tried to give her a smile. "Just a football scrape-up, nothing terrible."

Suki still looked concerned. "You haven't taken a sick day since you've worked for me," she said. "Surely, you've had worse scrape-ups and still come in, so I just... well, I wanted to know if things are okay with you?" She looked at him closely. "I've been noticing for some time that you seem... unhappy. Is there something I should know about, or is there anything that I can do to help?"

This was the perfect opportunity, and before he could second-guess it, he blurted: "Would you hate me if I said I wanted to quit?"

Suki's eyes widened, and he froze, regret instantly washing over him. He felt awful.

"Theo, of course I wouldn't hate you," she said, genuinely confused. "Why would you think that?"

"You took a chance on me and mentored me, and now it's the busy season, and I'm thinking of leaving you hanging," he said, voice miserable. "I don't want you to think I'm ungrateful or horrible, but you're right, I haven't been happy here lately and, no matter what I do, I can't make myself be. I'm sorry."

"Theo, take a breath," Suki said.

He inhaled deeply, and she waited for him to exhale before continuing. Her face was kind.

"You aren't being ungrateful or horrible!" she told him. "And, yes, it would be a bit of a pinch with the busy season, but we'd survive. If you want to quit, you should quit! I don't want anyone at my bakery who feels forced to be here—that doesn't foster the best environment nor, in my opinion, the best baking."

"Oh." He hadn't expected Suki to react so well, but he realized now that he hadn't given her enough credit.

Suki smiled. "Have you been worried about bringing this up to me?"

"A little," he admitted sheepishly.

"Well, you have absolutely nothing to be concerned about," she said. "You should only stay at the bakery if that is what you want. Is it?"

"No," he replied.

"Okay." She nodded. "So should I take that as your two-week notice?"

His heart pounded. "Yes," he finally said.

"Alright, then," she replied, and it was like a weight had lifted off his chest. He had put off talking to her about this, but it hadn't been bad at all.

"I can stay longer if you don't find someone to replace me," Theo offered. "I really don't mean to leave you hanging at such a busy time."

Suki waved a hand. "Two weeks is enough time. Hopefully, I'll find someone this week and you can train them a bit before heading out." Theo nodded. "Good. I want you to be happy, Theo, and I'm honored to have been a part of your culinary journey for as long as I have. It's been a joy to see you create."

"That's so kind," he replied, feeling emotional. A lump rose in his throat. "I don't think I've ever expressed just how much I appreciate everything you've done for me, everything you've taught me. Thank you, Suki. Thank you for everything."

"It's been my pleasure." Suki stood, holding out her hand, and Theo shook it. "Alright, now we'd best get back to work."

He nodded, heading out of her office back to the kitchen. He released a long breath, feeling astounded.

Even if he couldn't have Lavinia, it felt good to do *something* to make a change in his life. Something to make himself happy.

# CHAPTER 23

After work at the Rolling Pin Bakery, Theo went to the Baby Dragon Cafe.

It was an hour before the cafe closed, but it was moderately full. There were a few people there alone with their baby dragons; one woman sat on a lounge chair with a cup of tea, her blue azula baby dragon sitting in her lap. Then there was an old couple with a garneta baby dragon asleep in a little bed between their feet under the table. The little draggo reminded him of Biter, and he smiled to himself thinking of the little angel.

Theo went up to the counter, ordering an iced oat chai and sitting down while he waited for Saphira. He had texted her to let her know he had put in his two weeks' notice at the bakery and to ask if she was still looking for a managerial assistant. She had responded with a capitalized "YES" and three rows of exclamation points; she had then said to swing by the cafe when he was done at the bakery to discuss details.

"Theo, hey!" Saphira said, coming out from the kitchen. She twisted her hair back and out of her face, securing it with a clip. A few tendrils slipped out, framing her face, and she blew air up her face. "Sorry, was just going over something with one of the new hires. Let's go sit outside!"

She came out from behind the counter, and Theo followed her to the door leading to the garden. There were a few patrons at tables there and a bunch of baby dragons playing around the hedges or rolling in the grass. Theo spotted Sparky, and once the dragon saw Saphira, his purple eyes lit up. He bounced over, nuzzling his face against Saphira's chest, and Saphira smiled, holding the baby dragon's face.

"Hello my golu-molu," she said. Theo petted Sparky's black scales with his free hand, and Sparky closed his eyes, smiling in contentment.

They walked over to a free table, sitting down, and Sparky followed, sitting down next to Saphira. She absent-mindedly stroked his head. While the weather was chillier, it was sunny out, not yet too cold.

"I'm so glad you wanted to meet," Saphira said. "How are you feeling about putting in your two weeks? I know that's a big step!"

"It is," Theo agreed, "but I'm feeling pretty good about it."

"Wonderful! It's something I am excited about, as it means I get you all to myself." Saphira clasped her hands together and, sensing his rider's happiness, Sparky flapped his wings, bouncing in place. Saphira calmed herself then. "At least, if you'd like to work with me. I know I still need to tell you what such a role would entail and provide you with a formal offer."

"Yes, I'd love to work with you," Theo affirmed.

"Perfect! It would be a full-time, hybrid position, and you can choose your hours with what's convenient to you. Aidan is still finalizing the numbers, but I can give you a quick rundown on what I'm thinking," Saphira said, delving into his starting salary, benefits, and other perks.

It was comparable to what he was making at the Rolling Pin, which was a relief. He had a minimum salary needed to cover his costs, and if Saphira's offer was lower than that, he had considered having to pick up a second job—luckily, that wouldn't be necessary.

"How does that sound?" she asked.

"That sounds great," Theo replied, nodding.

"Perfect—now, for the work." Saphira scooted her chair closer, lowering her voice. Sparky huddled in closer, too.

"This is top secret," Saphira said, "but the main reason I need a managerial assistant is because I want to expand the cafe."

"Oh! What are you thinking?" Theo asked. That would be a huge project; for a moment, he felt daunted. Would he be able to do such a thing? He tried not to think about it at the moment, and instead focused on what Saphira was saying.

"You know how I moved out from the apartment upstairs?" Saphira asked, stroking Sparky's head. He shifted until his head was resting on her lap. "I was originally just going to put the apartment on rent, but then I thought, what if I expanded the cafe into the apartment upstairs to make it two stories? The cafe is so busy! I was also thinking of expanding the cafe's hours, to seven to six instead of eight to five."

"That sounds like a good idea," Theo said. The cafe was always busy; more space and longer hours would bring in more revenue.

"I would need you to come up with a proposal to see if

those ideas are worth the investment," she said. "And if so, how long it would take to receive a return on the investment. Plus, with the expanded hours, would we need more staff? Or how would the schedules work for my employees?"

"That's . . . a lot," Theo admitted. He'd surely have his work cut out for him, but the ideas were intriguing, and he didn't find himself dreading the prospect.

Saphira let out a long breath, looking down at Sparky's face in her lap. The baby dragon looked up at her with his big eyes. "I've been considering it for some time, but I'm a bit hopeless with planning that type of stuff. Aiden said he'd help me out when he got the chance, but you know he's busy with his own gardening business, and now we've been wedding planning on top of that." She bit her bottom lip. "So what do you think? Too much?"

"No! I could definitely do that," he said, taking a sip of his iced oat chai. "You know I love the cafe, and coming up with proposals and projections was what I did a lot of in school."

"Perfect!" Saphira let out a breath, relieved. Sparky nuzzled against her stomach, then trotted off to play in the garden with the other baby dragons. She watched them, smiling. "I used to love spending long hours at the cafe, but I've been pulling back more. I can't fathom figuring out this expansion project on my own." She covered her face with her hands. "Don't think that I'm abandoning my career now that I'm engaged!"

"Hey, you're totally fine," Theo said. "You can shift gears. There's nothing wrong with focusing on different things in different phases of your life." As he said the words, he thought of Lavinia saying the exact same thing to him. His chest ached.

Saphira nodded. "No, you're right. I was just feeling kind of guilty since the cafe used to be my baby, but now I have Sparky. And I want to have human babies soon, too." They both laughed.

"I'm happy for you," he said, and he meant it. "But . . . wow."

"No, I know," she said, widening her brown eyes. "It's scary!"

"Very."

"But exciting, too."

He was trying to see that more.

"Anyway," Saphira said. "I'll finalize the numbers and come up with a proper offer, and you can see if it works for you." He nodded, finishing off his iced chai. "Also! I do still want you to make your fusion desserts, if you think you can? Keep the Baby Dragon Bakery alive?"

"Yes, I'd love to," he said.

"Perfect! Because I cannot lose your baking!" She hummed to herself, trying to see if there was anything she was forgetting. "Oh, and the expansion is secret for now, but you can talk about it with Lavinia. I know you guys tell each other everything," she said with a laugh.

His heart sank. *Not everything.*

"This all sounds great," Theo said, focusing. "And if you want, you can send over your business documents before my two weeks are up at the bakery, so I can get a head start on familiarizing myself with the necessary material."

"Okie!" Saphira nodded. "I'll talk it over with Aiden, and he can get all that to you. He has this whole organizational system that I don't want to mess with."

Theo smiled. "You guys are such good partners," he said. "A good couple and good friends."

Saphira gave him a knowing look. "You can have it all, you know," she said. "Friendship and love, in the same person."

Now *why* would she say that to him?

Theo wanted that. He wanted it badly, but he wasn't sure the world wanted to give it to him. He hadn't done anything to deserve it.

With no response, Theo just smiled, and Saphira didn't say anything else. They chatted for a little bit until Saphira had to go back to check in on the cafe, and Theo headed home.

He entered his quiet apartment, sighing. He thought of Lavinia again, and he got her scrunchie from his bedside table, putting it on his wrist. Sitting down on his couch, he played with the scrunchie, watching it stretch and withdraw, but it wasn't enough.

He had wanted to call her all day, ever since the meeting with Suki, but he'd been holding back, unsure of how to proceed, afraid of what he might say.

Defeated, Theo pulled out his phone. Lavinia had texted him earlier to ask how he was doing, but he hadn't replied with many details.

Now, he directly called her. He was selfish; he couldn't last without talking to her.

"Hey," she said, picking up after a few rings. The sound of her voice was an instant relief. He closed his eyes, letting out a breath.

"Hey," he replied. "Sorry I've been so out of it."

"It's okay," she said. Her voice was small.

"How was your day?" he asked.

"It was good," she replied, and as she spoke, her voice seemed to warm. "Thank god it's Friday, so I'm done with classes and internships for the week. I'm taking time off from the cafe tomorrow, too, since I have a big midterm on Monday and I need to spend all weekend studying or I am going to fail miserably."

She sounded anxious.

"Hey, breathe," he said. "Let's take a deep breath."

They breathed together, and she let out a long exhale. "Ugh, you're right. Anyway. How are you doing? Does your face still hurt?"

"Nah, it's okay, now," he said. "I think I was being a big baby about it, anyway." He was a little sheepish to think back on it now.

"Yes, you were being a big baby," she teased. "You're always a big baby."

He snorted. "Right. This from the girl who has shed literal tears over a paper cut."

"Hey! Paper cuts hurt, okay? They go *deep*."

They both laughed, and he settled into the couch, feeling relaxed. Talking with her made his whole life reset, everything falling back into place exactly the way it was meant to.

"I made fried kulfi falooda yesterday," he told her. "It was so good."

"Oh my god, wait, that is genius," she said, gasping. "How do you come up with this stuff? I want some!"

He smiled to himself. "I'll drop some off tomorrow, if you want."

"Yes please!"

"But you have to share."

"No! I'm going to hide it away or Alfie'll eat it all."

He put the phone on speaker and went to the kitchen to make dinner, and he heard her folding laundry in the background.

"I kind of did something today," he said.

"What?" she asked.

As he washed the chicken meat, he gave the play-by-play from his morning meeting with Suki, how stressed he had been, and how, after a slight push from Suki, he had confessed to being unhappy. He explained how Suki had handled the news incredibly well and supported him in handing in his notice.

"See, I knew Suki would be fine!" Lavinia said, and he heard the smile in her voice. "This is huge, and I'm so glad you took this step. I only want you to be happy, too, and I hope this helps!"

"I hope so, too," he said, pulling out a pan. He sauteed onions and garlic, telling Lavinia about his meeting with Saphira, and Saphira's plans for the cafe's expansion.

He felt daunted again as he recounted the details. As he added chopped tomatoes to the pan, he chewed on his lower lip. "I've never worked a business job before," he said, moving the tomatoes around. "And it's been some time since I've been out of school. What if I don't remember how to do anything?"

"Oh, hush!" she said. "You'll figure it out. You're smart."

"Hmm." He added the chicken to the pan, listening as it sizzled.

"You are!" she repeated, as if she could force him to believe it. "What are you making, by the way?"

"Karahi chicken," he replied, and they continued talking as he finished cooking. When the curry was done, he warmed up some naan, then sat down to eat, keeping the phone on as Lavinia stressed about her anatomy midterm coming up.

"It's my hardest class," she said. "There's just too much to memorize!"

They stayed on the phone a little longer, until Lavinia went down to dinner with her family. He brought his plate over to the sink, washing the dirty dishes from dinner, and as he lathered his plate with soapy water, the events of the day truly sank in.

It felt real now, talking it through with Lavinia, and he felt jittery. This was a big step and, while he was excited, he was nervous, too.

It was scary thinking about the future, getting old, and he didn't know what was going to happen or what was best. The only thing he knew for sure, truthfully, was that his future would include Lavinia. It had to.

He couldn't live without her, which meant that he needed to stop all of this yearning. It was making him miserable, and it was affecting his relationship with Lavinia, he knew it was. And that was something he could not allow.

Later at night, while he tried to fall asleep, he tossed and turned in bed. He thought of the kiss he had shared with Lavinia, all of these other moments between them, and it was maddening.

He loved her. He loved her so much that it physically hurt. There was no denying it or running from it.

She was all he thought about, every moment of every day. He wanted to be around her constantly, and it was obvious, so glaringly obvious that he was in love with her. He knew that these feelings had been deep inside him for a long time, taking root and growing, and now he was overcome by them.

And she was with someone else.

He couldn't believe his own stupidity or blindness, how he had never seen the shape of his own feelings, had never seen the depth or strength of them.

Maybe he really didn't deserve her because he couldn't see that the best thing had been right in front of him this whole time.

And now it was too late.

# CHAPTER 24

On Monday, Lavinia went to Theo's immediately after she finished her anatomy midterm.

She had seen him for about two seconds on Saturday, when he had come to drop off the fried kulfi falooda. She had taken time off from the Baby Dragon to study, and when Theo came by, she had only said hello, barring herself in her room after.

She told herself it was because she had too much studying to do, but she knew that the real reason she stayed away was because she still felt too raw from the heated moment they had shared in his bed. While they had talked on the phone, she didn't trust herself to be around him.

But on Monday, her brain was pretty much mush after the anatomy exam, and she didn't have it in her to fight with herself. The second the exam was over, she didn't think; she texted Theo that she was coming and drove over, knowing he would be home from the Rolling Pin by then.

She still had to study for her pharmacology exam on Thursday, but she needed a break. And sweets. She desperately needed sweets.

Which was exactly what she said to Theo when he opened the door.

"You'd better bake me something, or else," she threatened, entering his apartment. She tossed her tote bag on the ground and kicked off her shoes, going to collapse onto his couch before he had even shut the front door after her.

"It's good to see you, too," he said, talking to the air. "No, I'm doing fine, thanks for asking. Please, make yourself comfortable!"

"Oh shut up." She lifted her head to look at him. He snorted. "I am *dying*," she said dramatically. "My blood sugar levels are *dangerously* low. This is not the time for *sarcasm*."

"Your blood sugar levels are probably never low," he replied. "You have a million stores of sugar in there."

She furrowed her brows. "I don't think that's how that works."

He thought about it for a second, then shrugged. "Hey, the last biology class I took was in high school. You should know more than me."

"I would, but my brain is fried," she said, sitting up. She rubbed her temples. "Now, please, sugar!"

He laughed, and she was glad to see the bruises from the football match from last week had mostly faded. He looked much better now, happy to see her.

"Alright, alright," he said, heading to the kitchen. "How about I make you some hot chocolate?"

"Mmm, yes please!" He had a complicated homemade recipe that took forever to make but always came out perfect. She followed him to the kitchen. "Even though it is way too early for hot chocolate."

"Is it?" he asked, grabbing a saucepan out of the drawer. "It's the first week of November."

"Which is too early," she affirmed. She jumped up and sat on the counter perpendicular to where he was working at the stove, and he looked over his shoulder at her. "Hot chocolate is for December through February, duh. There is a system for these things, you know."

"Right, right, of course." He grabbed some things out of the fridge and set them onto the counter.

"However, because today was really cold, we are making an exception," she said. "As long as you have marshmallows."

"Of course I have marshmallows, what do you take me for? An amateur?" He pulled out the bag from a cabinet and threw it at her. She caught it, taking a mini marshmallow out and popping it into her mouth.

"Perfect."

Theo got started on pouring milk, water, and heavy cream into the saucepan, and Lavinia pulled her sweatshirt off, feeling warm in the small kitchen. She was wearing a tank top underneath, her hair pulled up in a ponytail, and felt much better once she had discarded the thicker layer.

"Are you going to share your top-secret recipe with me?" she asked, watching as he broke chocolate bars into the simmering milk. He continued to break the chocolate as he glanced at her over his shoulder, wrinkling his nose at her.

"I told you it's not top secret," he said, "you just never remember it."

"So it's top secret," she said, eating another marshmallow.

"No, it's water, milk, heavy cream, dark chocolate, milk

chocolate, cocoa powder, and sugar," he said. "Nothing complicated."

"That sounds a little complicated." She shrugged. "Anyway, I don't need to know how to make it since you'll always make it for me."

"Yeah, yeah," he said, waving a hand. After adding in all the ingredients, he turned the heat to low and stirred the pot with a spatula. "How was your exam, by the way? Or should I not ask?"

"It was good, I think?" She made a face. "I kind of blacked out by the end."

"That's always a good sign," Theo deadpanned. She snorted.

"How was your second-to-last Monday at the Rolling Pin?" she asked. "Your last day is next Friday, right?"

"Mhm," he replied, stirring the pot with the spatula. She inhaled the sweet scent of melting chocolate. "It was good. Suki's been interviewing candidates to take over for me, and I think she'll have someone finalized by Thursday? Then I'll be training them for a week."

"Ooh." She listened until her phone beeped next to her. She checked the notification; it was her email.

*Oh god.* Results for her anatomy midterm were already in. With multiple choice exams, the results were always in on the same day, but it usually took longer than this. There must not have been a curve to account for. Consternation prickled through her.

Eye twitching, she opened up her school's portal, wanting to rip the bandage off. If she had failed, she'd drown her sorrows in hot chocolate.

Heart beating fast, Lavinia checked her score and . . . she had passed!

Lavinia squealed, her heartbeat racing.

Theo came over, concerned. "What is it?"

"I passed!" Lavinia said, eyes wide. "Ohmygod, I passed!"

"Great!" Theo grinned. "That's amazing!"

They hugged, eye-level, with her sitting up on the counter. She wound her arms around his neck while his arms enveloped her torso.

She lifted her legs up in exhilaration and he stepped between her knees, coming closer.

Before she could stop herself, she wrapped her legs around his waist to hold onto him tighter, and everything shifted, the moment going from thrilled to tense as he buried his face in her neck.

Her tank top suddenly felt incredibly thin, a paltry barrier between them, and it did nothing to cover the bare skin of her arms, her shoulders, her neck.

She shuddered as his lips brushed against her bare skin, gliding over her collar. She wanted his mouth to go lower, for his body to press closer. He made a strangled sound low in his throat.

Desire hummed through her body, making her feel unsteady, which only made her hold him closer. He fell forward, losing his balance, and gripped the edge of the counter with one hand, while his other hand was on her back, his fingers pressing in, holding onto her as if she was his anchor.

She felt his heart pounding against hers, and she breathed in the scent of him, chocolate and sugar; sweet, so sweet she wanted to lick his skin.

Her body pulsed, and his lips parted against her collar, his teeth skimming across her skin. A shiver ran down her spine.

More, she wanted *more*.

Before she could see what else he might do with his mouth, the sound of sizzling filled the air: the hot chocolate boiling over.

Theo swore, pulling away from her. His face was flushed, but she only caught a glimpse of his pink cheeks as he ran to turn the stove off. She hopped off the counter, landing unsteadily on her feet. Her knees felt weak.

"I'm going to go call Mama," she squeaked.

She grabbed her phone from the counter and ran out of his kitchen. She headed for his bedroom, shutting the door behind her.

Lavinia caught a glimpse of herself in the mirror and her mouth fell open. Her cheeks were red, and there was a dazed look in her eyes. "Good god, get it together," she hissed at herself, fanning the air around her face.

She had been right to stay away; she really couldn't be trusted around Theo.

She dialed Beena's number, holding the phone with one hand while she used the other to slap her cheeks, which did nothing for the redness. She switched tactics and started fanning herself, hand waving aggressively in the air.

"Hello, gudiya, are you done with your exam?" Beena asked. "How was it?"

"Hi . . . Yes, and I passed!" she replied.

"Oh, good, I knew you would!" Beena said. "Have you been running? Why are you so out of breath?"

Lavinia's cheeks heated. "No reason," she squeaked.

"Okay," Beena laughed. "Where are you, with Calahan?"

Her mother's words were like a splash of ice water on her face.

"Um, no," she said, swallowing. "I'm with Theo."

"Okay, well, I'll see you later," Beena replied. "Have fun!"

After Beena hung up, Lavinia mentally scolded herself. Why did she keep forgetting about Calahan? That couldn't have been a good thing. But it wasn't her fault that Theo was right there when she got the news, though surely she was responsible for how desperately her body had pulled him closer.

"You do like Calahan," Lavinia reminded herself, looking in the mirror. "And he likes you!" She scolded her reflection.

Why couldn't that be enough? Why did she always want more, more, more?

This was certainly no time for her to be messy. It was the first week of November; she was at winter's doorstep! Her deadline was fast approaching, and she couldn't jeopardize what she had with Calahan now. She would rather be with him than be alone for the rest of her life.

This was how things were supposed to be, she reminded herself—her and Calahan. It might not have been a grand love story, spun out of dreams, but it was better because it was *real*. It was solid. It wasn't heartbreaking and confusing, like the ground would give out under her feet any moment.

"Get it together," she snapped at the mirror.

With a final slap to her cheek, she went back out, to where Theo was pouring a newly made batch of hot chocolate into mugs.

"Marshmallows?" he asked, though he avoided her gaze. Embarrassment pricked at her.

"Yes, please," she replied, trying to sound normal. She grabbed her sweatshirt from the counter, putting it back on, like a layer of armor. Then, she walked over to his couch, sitting down and grabbing the remote. "Let's watch a movie."

"Sure," he replied, coming over with their mugs. He sat down next to her, leaving about a foot gap between them, then handed her a mug of hot chocolate covered with mini marshmallows. There was a spoon in the mug since she liked eating the marshmallows like soup.

He knew her so well, and yet, he didn't know the most obvious thing. Or he did, and he acted like he didn't. Either way, the result was the same.

They weren't together because he didn't *want* them to be together.

Clenching her jaw, she put on a fantasy film, one they had already seen a dozen times and that was familiar. What wasn't familiar was how they each kept to opposite sides of the couch. She felt the distance between them keenly, along with the lack of commentary, and it only furthered her mortification.

After the movie finished, she didn't linger. She needed to get home, away from here.

As Theo walked her to the door, he hesitated. "Lavinia," he said.

"Yes?" She turned back.

He opened his mouth, as if to say something. Emotion shone in his brown eyes, and her breath caught in her throat.

But then he looked pained, seeming to think better of it. He stopped. He dragged a hand through his wavy hair.

"Drive safe," he said.

"Mhm." Her eye twitched.

She left, feeling absolutely unhinged.

If he wanted to say something, he would say it! She was imagining things because she wanted to, and she needed to stop.

## CHAPTER 25

Lavinia was on edge.
She buried herself in preparing for her final midterm for the next few days. The pharmacology midterm was Thursday afternoon and, as such, Wednesday was her last chance to study before the exam. She was currently at the Baby Dragon, where she had taken over an entire table for four for her, her laptop, her textbook, and her printed-out notes.

At home, Lavinia kept getting distracted by Biter, who was bigger now and slept less. It was virtually impossible to get any studying done when there was an adorable baby dragon vying for her attention and affection, which was why she was studying at the cafe. Although there were precious baby dragons at the cafe, too, they were all being looked after by other people. The moment she got home, she would reward herself for all her hard work with an hour of cuddling the draggo.

For now, she needed to study. There were already two empty mugs on the table, and she nursed a third latte, which surely wasn't helping with the nerves coursing through her body, but she needed an emotional support drink and the coffee was keeping her hands warm.

Lavinia was just about to reach for another sip of her maple latte when she heard someone behind her.

"Hey."

Lavinia jolted, turning to see Theo. He gave her a funny look as she clutched her heart. He glanced at the table, at the empty mugs, then picked up her latte. "Maybe lighten up on the caffeine, yeah?"

Lavinia narrowed her eyes at him, and he took a sip of her latte, sitting down across from her. There was a streak of flour across his cheek, and he was wearing a maroon utility shirt with dark jeans, his brown hair mussed.

Seeing him sent a shiver down her spine as she recalled his lips brushing against her bare collarbone. Her eye twitched, and she mentally scolded herself. He closed her laptop screen.

"Give me my coffee back," she said, reaching for it. He held it up, away from her. "What are you doing here, anyway? Don't you have work?"

"It is in fact after four," he said. He worked from seven to four at the Rolling Pin. "And since I put in my two weeks' notice, I don't stay a second later."

"Love that for you," she said, shifting her focus back to her notes. She put her glasses back on. "Now, sh."

"Alright, alright." Theo pulled his laptop out of his backpack, and she raised a brow. "Saph sent over some of the business files, so I'm going to look through them." He pushed her notes out of the way, making room. She couldn't help it; she smiled fondly at him.

"Look at us, doing work together," she said. "I feel like we're in high school again."

He arched a brow. "That was just me writing all your English essays for you while you drank both our coffees."

"Hey!" She made an outraged sound. "Don't act like I didn't do your chemistry homework! It was a mutually beneficial relationship."

He laughed, and they got back to work, until five o'clock, when the cafe was closing. Theo got up and stretched his arms.

"Come on," he said, closing his laptop. "Let's go before they have to kick us out."

"But I need to study." She pouted. Theo began gathering her things together, putting them in her bag.

"You need a break, and I'm hungry," he said, picking up her tote along with his backpack. "Come on, let's get pizza."

She acquiesced, standing. "Fine. But only because I love pizza."

"Who doesn't?" He put his hands on her shoulders, steering her toward the door. They headed out onto Main Street.

The sun hadn't set yet, but it would soon. She couldn't believe how much quicker the sun was setting these days; the days were getting so short, winter arriving soon. A pinprick of unease pierced her chest as she thought of her relationship deadline, though she had nothing to worry about, she told herself.

Things were good with Calahan, and they would stay that way as long . . . as Lavinia behaved herself.

They made it to the pizza place, entering the restaurant, where a few other patrons were seated at round wooden tables and dark red leather booths located along the walls. The restaurant had warm lighting, and there were additional fairy lights hanging across the roof, wound around wreaths and greenery. Places were already getting festive for the upcoming holiday season; she smiled at the sight.

They sat down across from each other in a booth, and when the server came around, Theo ordered for them while Lavinia took out the notes from her bag.

"Stop." Theo grabbed the papers from her hand.

"Give me!" she cried.

"Give your eyes some rest for ten minutes!" he said, putting the papers down beside him. "You can have them back after you eat."

"Fiiine." She blew out her cheeks, taking off her glasses. She folded them and set them aside. "How were the cafe files? Do you think the expansion project will work out?"

"I do," he replied, as a waiter brought over their sodas. "It'll take some finessing to ensure we're optimizing the funds to execute the project while still generating profit and minimizing our costs."

"I have no idea what any of that means, but love that for you," Lavinia said with a laugh. Theo laughed, too.

He began to describe to her what he was thinking about for the project's proposal, and in that time, their food came: garlic knots, and a gooey pizza, half of the pie covered with onions and spinach, while the other half was covered with jalapeños and pineapple. She had long since stopped being disgusted by Theo's pizza order.

They ate, and the break—along with the delicious food—helped clear her mind. Theo wiped his hands on a napkin. "Come on," he said, pulling up her notes. "I'll quiz you."

"Wait, I have flashcards," she said, fishing them out of her tote bag. She passed the stack over to him. "The different colors are different sections."

"Alright," Theo said, sliding the plate of garlic knots his way. There were still eight left. "You get a garlic knot for every ten questions you answer correctly."

She snorted. "You can't bribe me with garlic knots!"

"Absolutely can. Now tell me, which of the following processes are . . ."

Turns out, garlic knots were a great incentive.

They stayed there for a while, even after the garlic knots were finished off between the two of them, and their sodas went lukewarm. At the table next to them, there was a group of six old ladies there for a post book-club meeting dinner. Lavinia smiled as the ladies all chatted and laughed, clearly getting tipsy after their many glasses of wine.

One of the old ladies got up, grabbing another's hand, and they started dancing between their table and Lavinia's. The other ladies joined in, and then one of the old ladies grabbed the server, who did not look a day older than sixteen. He was all gangly limbs and wide eyes.

"Hey, kid, can you play a song with a beat?" the lady asked.

"Uh . . ." The kid nodded, running off to the front counter.

A few seconds later, the speakers blasted with a quick song, and the old ladies cheered. They started dancing, turning the little pizza place into their personal club. Lavinia met Theo's eyes. They burst out laughing.

"Come on," he said, getting up. He offered her his hand, and she took it. They got up, walking two steps over to the crowd of women dancing.

"Ladies, mind if we join in?" Theo asked. One of the old ladies lowered her massive reading glasses, checking Theo out.

"Oh, honey, we don't mind at all," she said, winking. Lavinia was trying very hard not to die of laughter as Theo's cheeks flushed pink.

Then, Theo leaned in close to her, and she inhaled his scent. He always smelled like dough and sugar, sweet and warm. She wanted to take a bite out of him.

He whispered in her ear, "I've still got it."

She threw her head back and laughed, hitting his chest with her hand. He gave her a crooked grin then started dancing, and she joined in, dancing with these people she didn't know, but it didn't matter, not if she had Theo with her.

More than a few of the old ladies were crowding Theo, vying for his attention, which made Lavinia laugh harder, but Theo had spent more than enough evenings dancing with Beena, so he was used to it. He gave each of them particular interest, taking turns to spin them around, being the perfect gentleman until he ended up back with her.

"Is it finally my turn?" she asked.

"It's always your turn," he said. He took her hand and twirled her. She felt giddy. They both danced, bouncing up and down, hyper and obnoxious, but it was the most fun she'd had all week.

Theo picked her up off her feet and spun her around. She shrieked, laughing, the room spinning with lights.

Until Theo abruptly set her down. She looked over her shoulder, and Calahan was there. Embarrassment shot through her.

Calahan looked surprised but, more so, confused. She had told him earlier in the week that she would be studying for her last midterm so she wouldn't be able to make any plans; he was probably wondering what the hell she was doing here with Theo.

Guilt pierced through her, along with apprehension.

"Cal, hi!" she said, going over. She swallowed, trying to smile. "I was just having a study break."

"Hey," he said, voice tight. "Just picking up."

Calahan looked over her shoulder at Theo, then back at Lavinia, a muscle ticking in his jaw. Lavinia awkwardly shuffled on her feet, unsure what to say.

But then Calahan shook his head, giving her a smile. "Good luck with studying," he said, stepping forward to kiss her cheek. He grabbed his order and headed out, not looking back.

Lavinia watched him go, feeling unsettled.

The next morning, while Lavinia was walking to the library, she received a text from Calahan, wishing her luck on her midterm that afternoon.

**Thanks!!** She sent back, glad that things were fine between them. She had been worried he was angry with her—and rightfully so, if she was being honest—but she was happy that he wasn't.

Her screen lit up with another message: **Do you want to meet after?**

**Sure!** She replied. Maybe they could grab lunch or something.

At the library, Lavinia finished up a final review of her notes, then went to take her midterm. It was difficult. Once she had submitted it, she was exhausted but glad that it was over.

She texted Calahan to let him know she was done as she exited the classroom hall, and he texted back telling her he would meet her there. A few minutes later, he appeared in the lobby, though he wasn't carrying his bag or coat or anything.

"Hey," she said, trying to smile even as anxiety spiked through her. Something was off.

"Hey," he said, walking over. He pulled her over to the side. "So, I've been thinking about this for some time now, and I wanted to say—it's been really fun hanging out this past month, but I think we might be better off as friends, if that's okay?"

Lavinia blinked, shock pouring over her.

"It's been really fun," he repeated, adjusting his glasses, "but I'm looking for something more serious."

"Right," she managed to say. "O-Of course."

"I do really like you," he said, a wrinkle appearing between his brows, "but I don't know if you like me like that? In all this time, you've never come over or invited me over, and we've never met each other's families or friends . . . you know what I mean?" He released a breath.

He was right, and she did understand his point. They hadn't moved forward or developed their relationship. She had just been so preoccupied. They hadn't even slept together; to be honest, sex hadn't even crossed her mind, which she realized in itself was a red flag.

Guilt rippled through her. She felt awful to have wasted Calahan's time.

"Friends?" Calahan asked.

"Friends," she agreed, unable to form any coherent sentence. He gave her a small smile.

"I'll see you at work on Saturday, then," he said. She nodded. The air between them was awkward. Calahan went to leave, but then paused, turning back. "I don't know if I should say this, but I think you and Theo should be together."

Shock poured over her like a bucket of ice water. What could she say to that?

"I'll see you later," Calahan said, holding up a hand in a wave. Then, he was gone.

She stood there, feeling numb. They had only been together for a little over a month so—as far as break-ups went—it shouldn't have been anything world-shattering, but it was the first week of November. Winter was a mere few weeks away, and she would never meet her deadline now.

Dismay swept through her as she walked to her car. Her eyes filled up with tears, her chest constricting with panic. "You're fine," she told herself, hysterically blinking the tears away. "You're fine."

She got back to her car, trying not to cry. But as she sat down in the driver's seat, enveloped in silence, worry set in. If she hadn't been able to make it work with Calahan, who was perfect, she wouldn't be able to make it work with anyone. The fault was in her.

A long life alone stretched ahead of her; she wouldn't have what her parents had. She wouldn't have a partnership, a marriage, a family. She would be alone.

The feeling was only made worse by Calahan's comment about her and Theo.

She wanted that! She wanted that more than anything, but Theo didn't. If he did, he would have made it happen. He didn't want her.

Lavinia started her car, driving home, feeling more and more unraveled as the minutes passed. She pressed a hand against her chest, trying to comfort her bruised and battered heart.

This whole time she had been heartbroken by Theo's

rejection, but she had been trying to convince herself that it was for the best. To move on with Calahan—but even *he* could see what a mess she was.

Her feelings for Theo were not going away. If anything, they were getting worse. After that kiss, after everything this past month. She had tried distracting herself from it with Calahan, but now there was nothing left to distract herself with.

She had to face the truth.

When she arrived home, she ran straight up to her room, closing the door. Heart hammering, she reached into the drawer of her vanity. She pulled out Theo's cologne, spraying it in the air.

The scent hit her, and she started crying as the realization sank in.

She was in love with her best friend.

And everyone knew but him.

# CHAPTER 26

Being an adult was ridiculous because she had gotten broken up with and was having a severe spiral and yet she still had to go to class the next day. Lavinia was barely holding it together by a thread, and things only got worse.

She had told Beena and Garrett about the breakup that night after class, something she always hated to do because her parents were always so upset on her behalf, which only made it all feel worse.

Then came Saturday, when she had to go to work with her ex, a fact that she probably should have thought about before starting this whole thing with him. When she arrived at the Baby Dragon Cafe on Saturday morning, Calahan was already there, taking down the chairs from the tables.

Her heart hammered when she saw him, and she stopped in her tracks by the front door, skin prickling. He paused, looking over at her then away, body language tense. Awkward tension hung between them.

"Hey," she said, and goodness, why was her voice so loud? She lowered it an octave. "Good morning." And now her voice was too quiet. "Good morning," she repeated, hoping her voice was normal.

"G'morning," Calahan replied, giving her a small smile, and seeing that eased some of her nerves. She walked to the counter, setting down her purse and coat before going to take down chairs from the other tables.

She glanced over at Calahan, wondering if she should say something or not. She didn't want things to be tense between them when they'd still be working together. As she continued preparing the cafe, she nibbled on her lower lip.

"All done with midterms?" Calahan asked, when they had both finished with the chairs. She nodded, and they both walked over to the counter.

"Yes, thankfully," she replied, getting the lighter to light the candles on the tables. "Though you probably have loads of grading to do, now."

"Yeah," he said, turning in the direction of the kitchen, "but it shouldn't be too terrible."

"Well, good luck," she said, turning toward the tables.

"Thanks." With a small smile, he went into the kitchen, and she released a breath. That wasn't too bad.

Calahan was being mature about the whole thing, and while things were a little awkward throughout the day, it wasn't too horrible. He was such a great guy—a fact she kept returning to, even later that night when she was home.

She had taken Calahan for granted, and he deserved much better than what she had been giving him. And while she knew Calahan would be okay, she was even more devastated for herself.

On Sunday, she stayed in bed all day, reminiscing as she

went through her phone and looked at all their old photos. She looked happy. Why couldn't it have been enough?

After wallowing for a few hours, she deleted all the adorable pictures of her and Calahan, then their texts. Once that was done and she'd had a nice cry, she texted Genevieve and Saphira her puffy face with the caption **"Me after getting broken up with"** to tell them the news.

Their responses came immediately in the group chat, asking if she wanted to video-call or hang out.

**Yes, please,** she texted them, **but don't mention the breakup or I will start crying.**

**Of course. Should we come over?** Genevieve asked.

**Or do you want to come to mine?** Saphira offered.

**Let's meet at Saph's,** Lavinia replied.

**Okay! Come whenever!**

Lavinia forced herself to get out of bed, washing her face and changing out of the sweats she had been in for more than twenty-four hours. She stopped by the living room to let her parents know she was going out.

Her parents were cuddling on the sofa, talking. Lavinia tried very hard not to give them a dirty look, biting back the words, *Rub it in, why don't you!*

"Have a nice time, pumpkin," Garrett said, though she didn't miss the pity in his or Beena's eyes.

"Mhm." She headed out, driving over to Saphira's. Lavinia stood in front of the cottage and knocked on the door. A moment later, Genevieve answered, clad in black leggings and an oversized black long-sleeved T-shirt.

"Come in," Genevieve said, giving Lavinia a hug.

"Lav, you're here!" Saphira called from the kitchen. Her

hands were covered in mittens as she pulled something from the oven, and the rest of her was in a cute loungewear set. "Give me one second." Saphira pulled out a tray of bubbling macaroni and cheese and set it on the counter beside a dish of mashed potatoes, buttery corn, and a roasted chicken.

"Ohmygod, what is all of this?" Lavinia asked, taking in the spread.

"I just threw it together!" Saphira said, waving a hand. "And the only really impressive part is the chicken, which Aiden made because we need, and I quote, 'protein.'" She used air-quotes.

"I brought face masks and ice-cream," Genevieve added.

"Let's make plates and sit down on the couches," Saphira said, handing out plates.

Lavinia already felt better just from the prospect of a hearty meal and the girls' company. After plating the food, they sat down on the couches, sharing blankets. They chatted as they ate, Ginny telling them random anecdotes about her many cousins, while Saphira talked about wedding planning.

"We're going to finalize a dress in the next month or so," Saphira said. "Cecilia and I have narrowed down a final six." Cecilia was Aiden's mother, and it made Lavinia's heart swell to see Saphira so embraced by her new family.

"Six?" Lavinia repeated, eyes wide.

"It was two dozen before that, so trust me, narrowing it down that much was a real effort," Saphira said. "Though it's been fun playing dress-up! And the gowns are gooorgeous."

Genevieve snorted. "Mother is treating Saphira like her little doll."

"I don't mind it," Saphira said, smiling. "It's kind of nice. It reminds me of Nani-Ma." Saphira's grandmother had passed away a few years ago, and Lavinia was glad Saphira was receiving motherly affection.

"I can't wait to see you in basalta purple," Lavinia said, excited by the prospect.

They continued talking about Saphira's wedding plans, putting on sheet masks which made them laugh from the sheer fact that they *couldn't* laugh or the sheet mask would slip and slide off. When the masks were off and their faces were all shiny, they watched some absurd reality TV show that had them cackling with laughter while eating tubs of ice-cream.

It was a good night and, at the end of it, Lavinia was feeling much better, much more like herself. As long as she wasn't thinking about boys or her failings at love, she was completely fine.

The girls walked her to the door when it was time to leave, since she still had her internship and class tomorrow and needed to get some sleep.

She hugged Genevieve, then Saphira. "Thanks for tonight," she said.

Saphira hugged her tight. "Of course. Love you."

Just then, Aiden was passing by with a glass of water from the kitchen, and Lavinia waved at him. He had been hiding out all night to give them privacy, which he didn't seem to have minded.

"Hey Aiden," she said.

"Hey, Lavinia," Aiden said, smiling. "Sorry about you and Cal."

The girls froze.

And Lavinia burst into tears.

Saphira and Genevieve whirled on Aiden, Saphira with her hands up and Genevieve with daggers in her eyes.

"Aiden," Saphira said. "I told you not to mention it!"

Genevieve was a little less delicate. "ARE YOU STUPID?" she cried.

Aiden's eyes went wide, his face turning beet red. "I'm so sorry," he said, hiding behind his glass of water while he made a run for it, disappearing back into their bedroom.

"I'm sorry, Lav," Saphira said, frowning.

"Boys are stupid," Genevieve added. They both gave her another hug, and Lavinia sniffled.

"It's okay," she said, hugging them back as she wiped her eyes.

"Do you want to talk about it?" Saphira asked, rubbing Lavinia's back.

Lavinia pulled away, facing them. "It's fine, I can't get into it right now."

What would she even say? I ruined a good thing by being in love with my best friend who doesn't feel the same way? It was too embarrassing, and she didn't want their pity.

"Okay." Saphira gave Lavinia another hug. "Get home safe."

"Text us when you get there," Genevieve said, squeezing Lavinia's arm.

"I will," Lavinia said. She left, and as soon as Saphira shut the door behind her, Lavinia heard Saphira and Genevieve yelling at Aiden, which made her laugh a little bit, though she was still down about how things were.

Tears filled her eyes again, and she wiped them away, driving home.

The person she really wanted to talk to about all of this was Theo, but she hadn't told him, and she didn't plan to. He would want all the details, and she couldn't hide the truth from him or he would worry.

So she said nothing.

## CHAPTER 27

On Monday at the Animal Hospital, Dr. Quan pulled Lavinia aside after a patient meeting. She had been out of it all morning, so unlike her usual self, and even Dr. Quan had noticed.

"Are you feeling well?" he asked, eyes concerned.

Where Lavinia would usually automatically reply with a reassuring smile and an "Of course!", today she hesitated. Dr. Quan nodded, understanding.

"Why don't you take it easy and do some paperwork in the office?" Dr. Quan suggested.

"Mhm." Head hanging, she went to the office and spent the rest of the day doing little tasks until the day was over. Then, she went to class, and most of the week passed in a dull gray.

She barely replied to Theo's messages—just enough that he wouldn't worry and ask her what was wrong. She did not answer his calls. She couldn't hear his voice.

This was all his fault, in a way, but she couldn't even blame him entirely when she knew, mostly, the fault was all her own.

Love wasn't meant for her. She wouldn't have what her

parents had. She wouldn't get the grand romance she'd always dreamed of. And there was an acute grief with that realization, the loss of that hope.

She focused on school. After class on Friday, she was in the library studying when Theo texted her: **I heard cal broke up with you, I'm sorry.**

**Who told you???** She sent the text just as she realized. Her mother.

**Beena told me since you weren't answering my calls.**

Lavinia's eye twitched; she needed to have a word with her mother. She texted back: **It's fine.**

His response was immediate: **Do you wanna hang out? Watch a movie? Should I bake you brownies? Anything I can do to make you happy?**

*Yes*, she wanted to reply. *You can fall in love with me. That will make me happy.*

She didn't respond. She couldn't deal with him at the moment, she was too miserable.

But she couldn't avoid Theo. The next day, while she was at work at the Baby Dragon, he came in, and her heart all but crashed at the sight of him. Lavinia stalked up to him, her chest hurting.

"Hey—" he started, but she cut him off.

"Can you go?" she asked. She couldn't deal with him, not now and especially not in front of Calahan, who was in the kitchen at the moment.

Theo's face wrinkled with confusion. "Lav, what . . .?"

"Please," she said, voice low and defeated.

Theo swallowed. "Okay," he said.

He turned around and left, but she knew that wouldn't be

the end of it. She would need to face him eventually, to tell him what was going on, but she had no idea how to, and she didn't want to.

It hurt too much.

That evening after work, Lavinia was in the living room with Biter, throwing the baby dragon into the air and watching as her little red wings flapped before Lavinia caught her again. The little draggo was significantly helping Lavinia's mood—until she heard a car door shut outside. She shot up, already knowing who it would be. Heart beating fast, she ran to the front of the house, peeking out the window, and sure enough, it was Theo.

"Daddy, watch Biter!" Lavinia called, setting the baby dragon down. She sprinted up the stairs, going to Alfie's room, where he was sitting on the floor, building a model airplane.

"I'm going to sleep," she said, trying to sound normal. "Make sure no one wakes me up."

Alfie didn't look up. "'kay," he said.

"Alf," she repeated, tone warning. "I mean it."

He gave her a weird look. "Okay, okay."

"Thanks."

Knocking sounded downstairs, and Lavinia hurried to her room, making it there just as Beena opened the front door.

Lavinia closed her bedroom door, getting into bed.

"Lavinia!" Beena called from downstairs, and Lavinia screwed her eyes shut. "Lavinia, Theo's here!"

A few moments later, Lavinia heard someone coming up the stairs, and she tried to slow her breathing, to make it truly look like she was asleep. Alfie had better stop Theo from coming in; she was counting on him.

"Lavinia's sleeping," she heard Alfie say outside her bedroom door, and she mentally cheered for her little brother. "She said to make sure no one wakes her up."

"I don't think she meant me," Theo replied. It was quiet.

Alfie knew that, for Lavinia, Theo was always the exception.

"Oh, yeah," Alfie said. She heard him skip away. *For god's sake.*

Light knocking sounded on her door. "Lavinia?" Theo's voice. Under the blanket, Lavinia pressed a hand against her chest, curling into a ball against her extra pillows.

The door opened. "Lavinia," Theo whispered. "Are you awake?"

Her heart pounded. She hoped he didn't come any closer, or she was going to have a breakdown.

"Lavinia?" he asked again.

The room was silent.

He let out a long breath, then went, closing the door behind him, and she sighed. Her face broke, tears welling in her eyes, and she squeezed her eyes shut. The tears fell out, and Lavinia cried until she finally did fall asleep.

She woke up about an hour later to the noise of them eating dinner downstairs. She could hear that Theo was still here; he must have been waiting to see if she would wake up to eat, and now she had to skip dinner because she was avoiding him.

Lavinia groaned, reaching over to rummage through her side table drawer. She found some candy and half a granola bar, which she ate, throwing the wrappers onto the top of her side table.

It was another hour before Theo finally left, but by then she was too tired to go downstairs to find food, and she knew her parents would interrogate her about not waking up when Theo was here, so she stayed in bed, pouting. She should have brought Biter up here with her for company.

Lavinia fell back asleep, then woke up a few hours later to the sound of tapping. She thought at first that it might have been one of the tree branches bumping against the side of the house, but it was coming from a different direction than where the trees were.

She looked at her door, but the sound wasn't coming from there either.

Then she realized. *Her window.*

She got out of bed, heart hammering. It was the middle of the night now, and she felt like she was hallucinating as she pushed aside her curtains to find Theo perched outside her window.

"Are you insane?" she hissed, sliding her window open.

But she couldn't help the jolt of joy that ran through her to see him, which only made her angrier. Her stupid, stubborn heart, like a weed that kept growing no matter how many times she had pulled it out.

Theo was hanging off a ladder outside her window, dressed in a flannel shirt and dark jeans. His brown eyes were vivid.

Wind tousled his hair. A chill came in through the window, and she shivered in her pajama shorts and cropped sweatshirt.

"Let me in," he said. Who was he, coming in here and ordering her about?

"And what if I don't?" she asked, crossing her arms over her chest.

Hurt flashed over his face. "Why are you avoiding me?"

Lavinia wanted to pull her hair out. She groaned and

moved aside. Theo slipped into her room, shutting the window behind him.

"Lavinia, talk to me," he said. "What did I do? Why are you angry with me? Are you okay?"

The truth was she wasn't okay; she hadn't been since that first night, at Aiden and Saphira's engagement party.

She had spent all this time burying her feelings for Theo, but they wouldn't be buried. They were bursting out of her now.

She whirled on him, unable to bear it any longer.

"You're my person!" she cried. "But you'll never be what I want you to be. I'll never be what you are to me." The words ripped out of her, leaving her chest feeling hollow.

His eyes were wide. "I don't understand," he said. God, he could be so *stupid*.

"I'm in love with you!" she snapped. "Now go away!"

## CHAPTER 28

His mouth hung agape as he stared at her with wide eyes. She was breathing heavily, reeling from what she had said.

It felt good to have finally told him the truth, but it felt terrible, too.

Her eyes welled up with tears, and she made an irritated sound, turning away from him. She pressed a hand to her chest, trying to stop the pain.

He grabbed her arm, pulling her toward him.

"Wha—"

Before she could ask, he crushed his lips to hers.

She gasped, utterly shocked, but recovered a second later, kissing him back. The kiss was rough, built up out of frustration, and his lips moved against hers desperately. He kissed her hard enough to make her head spin. She felt weak in the knees, and she swayed.

He pulled back, still holding her face in his hands. He met her gaze, eyes dark.

"Do you mean it?" His voice was breathless.

"What?" she asked, utterly confused.

"Do you mean what you said?" he asked, voice breaking as if he couldn't dare to hope. "You're in love with me?"

"Of course I mean it," she replied, heart hammering, and his eyes welled up with tears. "What is it?"

"Lavinia, I'm in love with you," he said. "I have been this whole time; I probably have been my whole life. I just never realized it, or never allowed myself to be because I was afraid of ruining our friendship, of losing you." He swallowed. "And then you were with Calahan, and I was trying to be supportive, but it was killing me, it was actually killing me."

He broke off, catching his breath. "You really mean it?" he asked again, eyes awed.

"Yes, I mean it," she repeated. "I'm in love with you. I have been for a while, but I thought you were rejecting me that night at the engagement party, so I tried not to feel it, but I failed. Obviously. I failed miserably."

She laughed, and he laughed, too, surprised and delighted. His eyes still shone with unshed tears.

"Why didn't you say anything?" Lavinia asked, hitting his chest. "I thought I was losing my mind!"

"I didn't know how!" Theo replied, baffled. "I really thought that you were happy with Calahan, and I just want you to be happy, Lavinia, that's all I want."

"I'm happy, now." She reached for his hand, and he smiled.

"My heart beats for you," he said, bringing her hand to his heart. She felt it beating hard and fast against her palm. "Only for you."

He leaned down and kissed her again, and she rose up onto her tiptoes. She wound her arms around his neck and his hands settled on her waist, holding her tight, bringing her closer to him.

Desire made her limbs loosen, and she walked backwards, bringing him with her until the back of her knees bumped against her bed. She fell back, pulling him over her. The heavy weight of his body settled over hers, and an electric current ran through her, sharp and strong.

She felt the burning impression of his hands on her bare skin as he lifted her top up, and she raised her arms, letting him pull it off. She gasped against the cold air, but she was soon enveloped by the warmth of his body as he kissed her again. Her body ached, and she knotted her hands into his thick hair, pulling.

He nipped at her bottom lip, then her jaw, and she threw her head back, heat pouring through her.

"I can't believe we were wasting so much time being stupid when we could have been doing this instead," she said, undoing the buttons of his shirt.

He pulled back, a smile to his lips. "Not to worry," he said, kissing her throat. "We've got loads of time now."

She laughed, fumbling with the rest of the buttons before she pushed his flannel shirt off his arms. He threw it to the side. "I'm stealing that," she informed him.

"Take whatever you want from me," he said, kissing her again, smiling against her mouth.

His skin was so warm, and her hands explored every inch of him, every contour and dip. They had known each other for years, but she had never known him like this, and she was hungry for him, for every inch.

Her hands moved lower on his stomach, and he kissed her harder, movements frantic. The bare skin of his chest burned against hers, his fingers pressing into her skin.

Heat zipped down her spine. She couldn't get close enough. She wanted more.

She reached for his belt, and he slowed, pulling back to look at her eyes. His pupils were blown wide. "Are you sure?" he asked, voice ragged. He was having difficulty speaking.

"Yes," she breathed. "Lock the door."

He did, then was back in a second, before she could even miss the warmth of his body. He kissed her again, and she bit his lower lip. He made a strangled sound.

She pulled back, looking into his dark eyes.

"We have to be quiet," she whispered, trying not to laugh. "My parents."

"Please don't bring up your parents right now," he begged, but he was trying not to laugh, too, and they both failed, giggling.

"This is ridiculous," she said. "It's like we're teenagers sneaking around and not adults."

"It's good we aren't teenagers," he said, hands dancing across her skin. "I'm way more experienced now."

He gave her a wicked grin, slipping one of his hands under her shorts. Her sharp intake of breath filled the room, and he covered her mouth with his other hand, silencing her. Desire pulsed through her, making her dizzy.

"Do try and be quiet," he said, eyes gleaming with mischief.

She bit his finger, and his lips tilted. He moved his hand from her mouth to cup her face, turning her head to bare her throat.

He kissed her neck, and she swallowed the moan rising in her throat, twining her hands in his hair as he moved his fingers.

And then he showed her just what he had meant about being more experienced now: first with his hand, and then, finally, they peeled off the rest of their clothes, and he pushed inside of her.

She bit hard on her bottom lip, trying not to cry out, her entire body pulled taut as they moved together, their eyes locked. She had never felt more in sync with anybody. They were as one person, completely, entirely.

Pleasure mounted inside of her. It felt like stars colliding, burning together to become something brighter, something new, until white sparks poured over her and she was overcome with pure bliss. She had never felt more alive.

After, they both lay flat on their backs, catching their breath. She turned her head to look over at him, and he did, too.

At the same time, they both grinned. They turned onto their sides, holding each other's hands. He kissed her palm, and delight spread through her.

They already had a million memories together, but she knew this would be the one she would return to again and again.

## CHAPTER 29

The next day was Sunday, which was good, since they had time off from work and the whole day to spend together.

When Theo woke up beside Lavinia, in her bed, his first thought was that surely he was dreaming. But then Lavinia turned onto her side, hitting him in the chest with her flailing arm, and the contact was enough to let him know he was, in fact, awake.

Theo smiled, holding her cold hand, blowing air to warm it. The rest of her was huddled under the blanket, and he put a hand on her waist, gently shaking her awake.

It was still early, and she groaned, rousing. He was afraid she would regret what they had done last night, but when her eyes opened and saw him, she only giggled, pleased.

He smiled. "Should we get up before your parents?" he asked. "Finding us naked in your bedroom might not be the best way to break the news."

"Right," she said. "And what are we, exactly?"

Her tone was teasing, but her brown eyes were serious and worried. Fondness spread across his chest. He smiled.

"Hmm, let's see," he said, pretending to think. "We're best friends, and now lovers." Her face lit up. "In simpler terms, can I be your boyfriend?"

"Hm." Now she pretended to think, trying not to smile. "You might have to convince me. What are some perks I can expect out of being your girlfriend?"

"Why don't I show you?" he said, pushing her flat onto her back.

That distracted them for another half-hour, and after, she stretched like a cat in sunlight, content. "Alright," she acquiesced. "You can be my boyfriend. So long as you keep that up."

He smirked. "Oh, I intend to." He kissed her cheek. "Now come on, we should get up."

"You go shower first," she said. "I need some time before I can stand."

He laughed. "I'm obsessed with you," he said, giving her another kiss.

"Oh, trust me, I know," she said.

Thank god her bathroom was attached to her room and he didn't have to worry about running into her little brother. Theo showered, then came out in a towel, picking his discarded clothes up off the floor, until he searched for his shirt, unable to find it.

"Hey, Lav, have you seen—" He looked up to find Lavinia holding his flannel shirt in her hands.

"I told you I was stealing this," she said, slipping it on. She gave him a wicked smile.

"Mhm. And what, exactly, am I supposed to wear?" he asked. He picked up her cropped sweatshirt, holding it up. "Think this will do?" She burst out laughing.

"I love that look for you," she said, getting out of bed. As she tried to sneak past him, he locked an arm around her waist, pulling her against him.

"Oh no you don't," he said. "I need this back."

He kissed her neck as he unbuttoned the shirt. She snaked a hand into his wet hair, tilting her face to kiss him on the lips, humming.

"Fine," she said, tugging his hair. "But I want it back later."

"Alright, alright, promise," he said.

She slid the flannel shirt off, and he stared at her bare body, his jaw going slack. She gave him a wicked grin, then ran to the bathroom, closing the door behind her.

He heard the shower turn on and had half a mind to join her in there, but knew they needed to go before her parents woke up. Theo got dressed, and Lavinia came out a little while later, getting dressed as well.

After she had thrown on a sweater dress and tights, she brushed her hair then applied lotion. He sat on her bed and watched her, relishing these little moments, still astounded that he was here at all. When she was ready, she opened the drawer of her vanity and pulled something out, showing it to him.

A familiar bottle.

"Is that my cologne?" he asked, walking up to her as she sprayed her wrist. She rubbed her wrists together, pressing them against her neck.

"You left it here the day of the engagement party," she said. "I know I should have given it back, but . . ." She trailed off, shrugging. He put his arms around her, hugging her from behind, and inhaled the scent. She smelled like him.

His chest tightened. "I love you," he said, kissing her cheek.

He had never believed in things like fate or being written in the stars before, but now, there was no doubt in his mind that there were invisible strings at work. How else could he have gotten so lucky to have her in his life? It was nothing short of a miracle.

"I love you, too," she said, tilting back to kiss him. "Now let's go."

Lavinia opened her bedroom door, pausing; the house was quiet. It was Sunday morning, so her parents were sleeping in, which was good. They tiptoed downstairs, careful not to make any noise.

When they got downstairs, Lavinia headed for the kitchen to get some water and he followed, both of them moving quietly. Until they stopped altogether at the entrance.

Alfie was at the counter, eating chocolatey cereal in his pajamas, which were decorated with footballs. Biter was on his shoulder, her little paws holding onto his head. They both looked over at Lavinia and Theo.

Alfie gave them a conspicuous look. "What's Theo doing here?" he asked. Theo's heartbeat quickened.

"Um . . ." Lavinia blinked, glancing at Theo before looking back at her little brother. "Theo and I just had a little sleepover."

"WHAT?" Alfie was outraged. Theo froze, panic rising. At Alfie's tone, Biter growled, narrowing her red eyes at Theo.

"Sh!" Lavinia hissed, not that her brother cared. He was too busy being utterly betrayed.

"Why didn't you tell me?" he asked. Oh. *That* was what he was upset about. "I would have joined you."

Theo pressed his lips together, trying very hard not to laugh at the serious expression on Alfie's face. Ah, the innocence of an eleven-year-old.

"It was a PG-13 sleepover," Lavinia muttered.

"More like R," Theo whispered into her neck, and she elbowed him.

Alfie stared at them, waiting for a response. Even Biter seemed to be waiting; the little draggo was mimicking Alfie's emotions.

"It was a *secret* sleepover," Lavinia said. Alfie crossed his arms, pouting. Biter rested her face on top of Alfie's messy hair, also pouting. Theo's heart melted.

"We'll invite you next time," Theo said, trying to be nice.

"We absolutely will not," Lavinia mouthed at him, and he pinched her side. She squealed.

Alfie gave them a look. "You guys are being weird."

Lavinia walked over to him, holding his face in her hands. "Alf, promise you won't tell Mama and Daddy," she said. "Please? Pretty please?" She scratched Biter's chin, and the baby dragon flapped her wings happily.

Alfie thought about it. "Fine. But only if Theo plays football with me." Lavinia pinched his cheeks, then dropped her hands from his face.

"You got it," Theo said, giving Alfie a thumbs-up.

A shrewd expression crossed the kid's face. "*Today*," Alfie added.

"Done."

"*And*—"

"Oh for god's sake, Alfie," Lavinia said.

"*And*," he repeated, giving Lavinia an arch look. "I get to choose the movie."

"Fine." Lavinia snorted. "Now, remember, shhh." She put a finger to her lip, and Alfie mimicked the act.

Biter watched them, confused, bringing a paw up to her mouth, as well. Lavinia chuckled. She smushed Biter's cheeks, kissing her, then gave Alfie a kiss goodbye, as well.

They put their shoes on and left, and the minute they made it outside, they both started giggling. It was such a silly, unserious situation, but it was so exactly *them*.

As they walked to Theo's car, Theo held Lavinia's hand, and she swung their arms like they were teenagers. It was so sweet being with her that it made his teeth ache, but he didn't mind at all. He'd always loved sugar, and so did she.

They made it to his car, getting in, and he couldn't stop smiling. They had been up late last night, and it was early now, but he didn't feel tired; he had never been more awake. He wouldn't want to miss even a second of this.

This past week had been so confusing because Lavinia had been avoiding him. It had made him miserable because he'd missed her—and then, last night, there had been the shock of that angry confession.

He had never even considered Lavinia loving him as a possibility, because he wasn't like her—he couldn't just go after things with confidence. He had grown up with parents who wanted him not to cause a fuss, and he had thought saying anything to Lavinia while she was dating someone else would be *very* fussy indeed, so he had stayed quiet and wasted all this time.

But they were together now, and he wouldn't waste a moment more of it.

As he drove, he kept one hand on the wheel and the other

on her lap, where her hand was entwined with his. She was holding his hand with both of hers, her cold fingers dancing on his.

"Are you hungry?" he asked, heading for town.

"Ohmygod, yes," she said. "Starving. I didn't even eat dinner last night."

Theo nodded, driving to Main Street. It was still pretty early, so they got a parking spot easily, then walked over to the Baby Dragon Cafe, which had just opened and was still empty and quiet at this time. It reminded him of those mornings he used to drop off bakery deliveries really early, before the cafe even opened.

They ordered, then sat down at one of the tables by the exposed stone wall. Lavinia leaned her chin on her hands, and he leaned forward across the table, wanting to be close to her. Under the table, their feet tapped against each other.

A little while later, a server came with their food: lattes and bagel breakfast sandwiches, as well as slices of a pumpkin olive oil loaf. They dug in, the food particularly hitting the spot since they were so famished.

"I'll be back here tomorrow," Theo said, looking around. A middle-aged man had entered with his opala baby dragon, who was jumping around, happily taking advantage of the mostly empty cafe as his owner ordered coffee at the counter.

"Oh my god, yes, your first day!" Lavinia said, eyes wide. She scooted her chair closer, expression hyper-focused. "How was your last day at the Rolling Pin on Friday? Were there tears?"

He snorted, breaking off a piece of the pumpkin loaf. "No tears, though it was a bit nostalgic," he admitted. "I spent the last few days training the new hire, which you would have known if you weren't avoiding me." He gave her a pointed look, and she kicked him.

"Now is not the time for jabs," she said, biting into her breakfast bagel. "Start at the beginning. We need to catch up!"

"Alright, alright," he said. He wasn't angry with her; he was just glad to be here. He told her about the new hire, who was a nice girl fresh out of culinary school. She was a quick learner, so training her hadn't been difficult, and his last few days at the Rolling Pin had been nice (when he hadn't been worrying over the situation with Lavinia).

"Then, on Friday, an hour before leaving," he continued, sipping his latte, "Suki brought out a special cake she'd made just for me. It was a pear cake spiced with cardamom and layered with this honey buttercream, then topped with thinly sliced poached pears. It was *divine*."

"Ohmygod, that sounds amazing!" Lavinia said, mouth wide. "Why didn't you save me a slice?"

"I did!" he replied. "I brought it over on Saturday."

She looked sheepish. "Oops."

"Your parents and Alfie finished it off."

"Boo."

"Anyway, now tomorrow's my first day, and I'm going to see what kind of schedule I do with working at the cafe or at home, but I know that I'll be coming into the cafe in the morning to make items for the Baby Dragon Bakery," Theo said, finishing off his breakfast bagel.

Before, he would bake large batches of his fusion recipes two to three times a week, but now, since he was working for the cafe, he could make smaller batches every day. As he considered coming in to the cafe every day, he realized something else.

He'd be working with Calahan.

"What's Calahan's schedule at the cafe?" Theo asked, nervous. "Do you think it'll be weird?" He paused. "Also, you didn't even tell me about the breakup or what happened!"

While he was her boyfriend, he was her best friend first, and he wanted to know all the details.

"Oh yeah." Lavinia sipped her latte, sheepish. "We broke up because of you."

Theo blinked. "Me?"

"Kind of?" She winced. "After my last midterm last week, he messaged to ask if we could meet. He said we'd be better off as friends since he was looking for something more serious and our relationship hadn't really developed. Which was fair; I don't think my heart was really in it because . . . well, my heart belongs to you." Theo melted at that. He reached over and held her hand, squeezing. "I think Calahan knew that, and he told me that he thought you and I should be together."

Theo felt a little guilty about that. Calahan really was a great guy.

"And to answer your question: he works here Tuesday and Saturday, and no, I don't think it'll be weird with you working at the cafe," Lavinia told him, entwining their fingers. "I mean, he's been fine with me, and I'm his actual ex. He's such a decent guy I'm sure he'll just be happy that we're happy. Though we probably shouldn't be too obnoxious about it."

Theo brought her hand up and kissed her palm. "I'll try." She smiled, splaying her fingers against his cheek, and they moved on to talking about other things as they finished the rest of their food and coffees.

By then, the cafe was much busier, and they watched the

adorable baby dragons for a bit before heading out on Main Street, where they ambled aimlessly, not really doing anything, just being together, which was everything.

It was colder, and she huddled against his side. He loved having her tucked against him. She was perfectly bite-sized. He wanted to stick her in his pocket and carry her around everywhere, keep her with him always.

As they were walking later in the afternoon, Lavinia's phone rang.

"Yes, Alfie," she said, picking up. They slowed their walking, stopping by a bench. "Yes, Theo remembers he has to play football with you." She rolled her eyes at Theo. He sat down, and she stood in front of him, her hand playing with his. "Yes . . . Okay . . . Alright, alright, we're coming home in a little while." She hung up, shaking her head and laughing. "We'd better get back before that kid snitches."

He nodded. "Next sleepover is at my place."

"Good plan," she agreed. "Can't wait."

Theo pulled her onto his lap, bringing her in for a kiss. She smiled against his mouth.

Eventually, they made it back to his car, and he drove them home, where, as promised, he played football with Alfie out in the yard. Lavinia helped Beena with dinner, and when it was ready, they all sat and ate together, gathered round the table.

The Williamses were the family that Theo had never had, and the feeling was more pronounced now. He felt as if he and Lavinia were closer than ever.

After dinner, Alfie did in fact choose the movie, and they all watched. Biter snuggled in Lavinia's lap, and Lavinia snuggled against Theo.

About halfway through the movie, Biter fell asleep on Lavinia, and Lavinia fell asleep on Theo's chest; she really was tired from last night. He loved the weight of her cuddling against him, a strand of hair falling over her cheek. He tucked her hair over her ear, not behind it.

Her ears always got cold when she was asleep. Whenever they watched rom-coms and there were scenes of the guy putting the girl's hair behind her ear, Lavinia would always hold hers. "Mine get so cold at night!" she'd say. "I would never want a guy to do that!"

When the movie finished, Alfie went up to his room to get ready for bed, and Lavinia was still asleep. Beena put Biter in the bassinet, which was getting a little small for the baby dragon now, then went to the kitchen to make green tea for herself. Garrett followed her. Theo slipped out from under Lavinia, putting a pillow under her so she'd still be comfortable.

Heart beating fast, he went to the kitchen as Beena poured boiling water into two mugs from the kettle.

"Heading home?" Beena asked, smiling. Garrett stood beside her, arm around Beena's shoulder.

"Um, yes, but there was something I wanted to tell you."

"Everything okay?" Garrett asked.

Theo took a deep breath, bracing himself. He knew that Beena and Garrett weren't his parents; they wouldn't be automatically negative or disappointed, but still.

"Yes," Theo breathed. "I just—I want to say . . . I'm in love with your daughter."

Garrett and Beena looked surprised. They exchanged a glance.

"I wanted to tell you myself," he said. "And I hope you're pleased."

"Of course we are!" Garrett said, coming over to give him a hug. Theo released a breath, relieved, but when he looked at Beena, he saw concern on her face. It was there and gone in a flash; then, she was smiling, giving him a hug as well.

"This is wonderful," Beena said, kissing his cheek. Theo smiled.

"That was what I wanted to say," he said, a little awkward. "Also, thanks for dinner."

"Of course," Beena said. Lavinia came into the kitchen, then, stretching.

"Are you leaving?" she asked Theo. He nodded, and she rose on her tiptoes to kiss him goodbye. Then, she noticed her parents. "Oops."

Theo laughed. "Don't worry, I told them."

"Told them what?" Alfie asked, coming into the kitchen as well, this time in his pajamas.

"Theo and Lavinia are dating," Garrett said, smiling proudly.

"I knew that already," Alfie said, unbothered. "They even had a sleepover last night."

"Alfie!" Lavinia cried, mortified. She pinched his side, and Alfie screeched.

"Aaaaand that's my cue to leave," Theo said, smiling sheepishly, though her parents only looked amused.

He headed out and went home. When he arrived, his apartment was so quiet and empty after spending last night and the day with Lavinia. He missed her already.

He would tell her to come over tomorrow, and the prospect brightened his mood. He got to tidying up the apartment, but when he was done with that, he decided to do a deep clean. He even emptied out one of his drawers for her since he knew she'd bring over a million things.

He spotted her scrunchie and put it in the empty drawer, smiling to himself.

He hadn't even known being this happy was a possibility!

Now, he just needed to make sure he didn't ruin anything.

# CHAPTER 30

Everything was perfect.

It was exactly how Lavinia had always dreamed it would be. She had her person, and she knew that this was it.

She felt stable, like all those years of struggling and wondering and waiting had been leading up to this, and it was worth it; it was worth anything to finally be with him. This must have been what Beena had felt like when she was Lavinia's age, when she met Garrett.

It excited Lavinia, the prospect of all that was to come, of spending the rest of her life with Theo. Of eventually getting engaged and married and having kids of their own, and a million more moments and memories, each of them splendid and wonderful and perfect. She was getting ahead of herself, but she didn't care. Everything would be easy.

Everything *was* easy.

She and Theo were at the Starshine Valley fall festival now, which ran for two weekends every November. It was set up in a field in the middle of Starshine Valley, easily accessible for the different areas of the valley: Bayview, where the chimeras resided; the Pines, where the griffins were; the Heights, for the phoenixes; and of course, the Hills, for the dragons.

It was Sunday afternoon, and they had been together for two weeks now, yet it still felt as exciting as that very first day; at the same time, it felt as if they'd been together forever, for as long as they'd known each other.

Theo put his arm around Lavinia's shoulder, and she twined her hand in his. They walked past chimeras roasting corn with their fire, while dragons flew high overhead. A live band played music in the background as children laughed and screamed, running around. There were tents set up with different stations: a best pie competition, judging for the prettiest phoenix, pumpkin carving, s'mores making, apple-bobbing, and fresh apple cider. There were some carnival rides, as well as games like cornhole or a potato-sack race, and then also rides on the mythical creatures.

"Should we go for a griffin ride?" Lavinia asked, pointing to the stall. Griffins had the bodies of lions but the heads and wings of eagles, as well as two eagle claws and two lion paws. She had interacted with a few baby griffins at the Animal Hospital, and they were much gentler than baby dragons and less skittish than baby chimeras.

Adult griffins were sharp, yet gentle, which made them ideal for a recreational ride at a festival such as this. Though griffins were fewer in number than dragons or chimeras, they were not as prized.

"Sure," Theo said, letting her lead the way.

They waited in line, then sat on a griffin when it was their turn. Griffins were smaller than full-sized dragons, but they could still carry two adults. Theo settled in behind Lavinia, his arms around her, and then the griffin kicked off.

Lavinia squealed with delight as wind blew against her face. The griffin made a slow turn over the festival grounds, soaring calmly in the air. The view was gorgeous, the autumn colors glittering like jewels in the sunlight. Theo leaned his chin on Lavinia's shoulder, and she turned her cheek to kiss him.

When the ride was done, they dismounted, then went over to the games. They played ring-toss, doing best out of five, the both of them tied until the last round, when Lavinia won.

"Yes!" she said, jumping up and twirling. "I win!"

Theo looked at her fondly. "I think really it's me who's won," he said, kissing her cheek.

"That was so cheesy." She laughed.

"Just a little." He winked. "Come on," he said, taking her hands. They were cold, and he rubbed them together in his, warming them. He kissed her fingers. "Let's go home."

It was a fun day, and at the end of it, they ended up back at his place with take-out. They mostly hung out at his apartment for privacy's sake and because she wanted him all to herself. She was insatiable for him; she had been all this time, and now he was finally hers. She could have him whenever she wanted.

Unfortunately, they were both busy with work and her with school, so they didn't get as much time together as she wanted, but every chance she got, she stayed the night. She was getting less sleep than ever, but she didn't mind, not one bit.

In his apartment after dinner, they were making out in the kitchen, the dirty dishes forgotten as Theo hoisted her up. She wrapped her legs around his waist, her arms around his neck, and he walked them out of the kitchen. She pulled back, looking around.

"The view is pretty nice from up here," Lavinia joked.

"Sure is," he said, but he was looking at her.

She laughed, running her hands through his hair. She loved his hair. She wrapped his curls around her fingers, tugging, and he nipped at her jaw, kissing her throat as he walked her up against the wall, body flush against hers.

Heat poured through her as he pressed against her, and she brought his mouth back to hers, slipping her tongue inside. Desire hummed through her body, and she made a desperate sound deep in her throat.

He dropped her back to her feet, going to his knees. He kissed her stomach, then pulled down her clothes. Her blood pounded as he lifted one of her legs, hooking her knee over his shoulder. She gasped, holding onto his hair, devastating pleasure pouring through her.

Almost every day was like that: full of fun and heat and tenderness; so achingly sweet.

She liked doing things to bother him like sticking her cold hands against his neck or stealing his favorite flannel tops. She loved annoying him. She loved being her most obnoxious, insufferable self around him without having to worry if he would still like her or not.

It was liberating. She didn't need to pretend anything: to be mature or serious or toned down. She could be silly because that was how she had always been around him; he knew her.

He knew her completely. There was nothing to worry about. She felt utterly loved.

Everything was lovely for a few weeks.

It was so perfect that it made her feel afraid. She needed everything to stay exactly as it was, which gave her anxiety. She was scared, too, that he would get tired of her, the way other guys seemed to.

And the anxiety must have been bad enough because one night, after dinner, Beena knocked on Lavinia's door. Lavinia was sitting at her desk, doing homework, and when she looked at the door, Beena was waiting.

"Can I come in?" she asked.

"Mhm," Lavinia replied, taking her glasses off and setting them on her desk. Beena came over and sat on the bed. Lavinia swiveled her desk chair so she was facing her mother.

"Is everything okay?" Beena asked. "You've seemed a bit tense these last few days."

Lavinia nibbled on her lower lip. "Um, yeah," she said. "Everything's fine."

"Okay," Beena said, giving Lavinia a smile. "Everything's good with Theo?"

"Mhm!" Lavinia said, replying too quickly and giving herself away. Beena nodded. She stood, coming over to stroke Lavinia's hair.

"Well, don't put too much pressure on yourself, okay?" she said. "What you and Theo have is really special. Don't let things ever get sour between you two, okay? It's good to explore if you could be romantic partners, but if it isn't working, there's nothing wrong with being friends."

"Do you think we're better off as just friends?" Lavinia asked, voice high.

"No, honey, I'm not saying that," Beena said. "All I am saying is to be careful, okay?"

Lavinia swallowed. "Okay."

Apprehension coursed through her.

# CHAPTER 31

Everything was going so well. Theo had Lavinia, and he had started working for Saphira as her business manager. He spent his days at the cafe or at his apartment, going through the documents and running numbers, putting together a proposal.

He also baked for the cafe, trying out new recipes, like a mango lassi mousse, or sticking to Baby Dragon Bakery favorites, like elaichi buns. It was fun working at the cafe again—Lavinia had been right about Calahan; he was perfectly cordial—and he loved working with Saphira.

The first day of work, he had a purple bruise on his throat that Saphira pointed out, and he had replied, "Courtesy of Lavinia."

Saphira had almost spat her chai out in his face. Her mouth fell open with shock. "Oh my god," she said. "Are you two finally together?"

Theo's cheeks felt warm. He ran a hand through his hair, nodding.

"FINALLY!" she cheered. She came over and gave him a smothering hug. "I love this."

"Saph," he choked, and she eased up, giggling as she went back to her seat.

"I need to beat up Lavinia for not telling me," Saphira said, "but I love this."

"I mean, it's still new," he said. "It's only been a day."

But Theo had practically told every person he knew, and random strangers, too. He wanted to tell the whole world about him and Lavinia, he was so jubilant, and that joy didn't fade as the weeks went on. If anything, he only grew more attached to her.

Theo often adopted other personas when impressing girls. He acted differently, trying to be more cool and aloof; but it wasn't like that with Lavinia. With her, he could be himself.

Growing up, Theo never knew who he was because his family never liked who he was, so he always tried on different hats, trying to gain their approval (not that it ever worked). But with Lavinia, he felt like his truest self. He liked himself best when he was with her.

Whenever they were apart, he thought of her, like he was doing now at the cafe. It was almost time for him to head out, and he pushed his laptop back, pulling out his phone. He gave Lavinia a call, and when she picked up, just the sound of her voice sent a bolt of joy through him.

"What are you doing later today?" he asked, leaning back in his seat.

"Hmm, studying, studying, and maybe if I'm free, some more studying," she replied. "I'm going to my last class right now."

"Think you have time in your busy schedule for me to come over?" he asked.

"You know, my mom was saying that you should come over for dinner sometime this week," Lavinia said. "She was complaining that I was hogging you! And I was like, well, yes, Mama, he is in fact *my* boyfriend? And then I got yelled at. I think she misses you."

Theo laughed. "I miss Beena, too," he said.

"Wow, so now I have to compete with my *mother* for your affections?" she joked. He snorted.

"Dinner would be great," he said. "I'll see you later."

"Okay, sounds good. Now I really do have to study," she warned.

She wasn't kidding. When he went over later, she was up in her room and only came down to give him a quick kiss hello before running back up the stairs. Theo walked over to the family room, where Beena and Garrett were on the couch, sharing a blanket as they did a crossword puzzle together.

Alfie was on the floor, playing with Biter, who was the size of a small dog now, no longer tiny. She spent most of her hours awake now, and he could see how mischievous she was getting, red eyes sparkly and alert.

"Hiya," Theo said, entering the room.

"Hey, honey," Beena said. Garrett gave Theo a smile, and Theo went to sit with Alfie on the carpet. Biter jumped over to him, crawling up his chest, and he hugged her. "Hi, angel."

"Lavinia said that no one can bother her until at least seven," Alfie informed Theo. "But that's okay since I know you don't want to hang out with her anyway."

He hung out with Alfie and Lavinia's parents until seven, when Lavinia came down for dinner. He was pretty much dying to see her by then, even though they had seen each other this morning at his apartment before they had both left for work.

He shot up, going to hug her, not even caring as her parents dramatically aww'd at the display of affection.

"You guys are too cute," Beena said, getting up. She walked past them to the kitchen, squeezing both of their arms.

After dinner, Lavinia disappeared back to her room, but this time Theo followed, closing the door behind him.

When he entered, she was already wearing her glasses and sitting on her bed with her laptop in front of her, jotting something down onto a flashcard. Instrumental music played in the background, and he went over, sitting down next to her.

"What playlist are you listening to today?" he asked, looking over her shoulder. She opened the music tab to check.

"A moody year at your elite boarding school," she said, switching the tab back to her class notes. He brushed her open hair aside, kissing her neck.

"And where's the playlist titled 'my best friend is about to kiss me senseless'?" he asked.

She laughed, turning to him with an arched brow. "Is he?"

"If you give him the chance," he replied, pulling her in for a searing kiss. She kissed him back, smiling against his mouth before pulling back.

She glanced at the clock, then took off her glasses before turning back to him. "You can distract me for twenty minutes," she said, "and then I really have to study."

"Mhm, sure," he said, pulling her onto his lap.

Theo was happy, and when he was happy, he got stupid.

Home alone that evening, as Lavinia studied at her own place, he called Amaya, wanting to tell his parents about all the big changes going on in his life. For some reason, he thought they would be happy for him. That—finally—they might be proud.

But when he told his mother the news about his latest job, she was only confused.

"You're working where?" she asked.

"The Baby Dragon Cafe," he repeated, joy already fading. "As a managerial assistant."

"You're an assistant at a cafe?" she said, tone disdainful. Theo's heart sank. This was a bad idea, but it was too late, now. He got up off the couch, pacing around his apartment.

"I'm not, like, a barista," he said, feeling embarrassed. "I'm helping the owner oversee a possible expansion project. I'm managing the business side of things. You know, making use of that business degree?"

As Theo said the words to his mother now, he wondered why he ever felt proud of himself for his new job. It was nothing to be proud of. He could see that, now.

"Oh," Amaya said. "Well, that's nice, dear." Her voice was blank. He felt small. Awkward silence hung between them, before his mother cleared her throat. "What else is new?" she asked.

"Um." He paused. "Lavinia and I are going out."

Maybe Amaya would be pleased by that; his parents had always been impressed by Lavinia, at least, since she always did well at school.

"Lavinia?" Amaya repeated. There was something in her tone of voice that made Theo's blood run cold. *Why was she so surprised?* "And you?"

"Yes, Lavinia and me," Theo said. "Why?"

"Nothing," Amaya replied. "I just wouldn't have expected..." She trailed off, and the unspoken words hung over him.

He opened his mouth to ask his mother what she meant, but then stopped himself. He wasn't sure he wanted to know the answer.

"Anyway, do come visit soon," Amaya said. "It's been so long since we've seen you. Your father was asking about you, as well."

"Okay," Theo replied, voice quiet. They chatted for a few minutes more, and then he hung up.

All in all, the conversation made him feel like absolute shit. He continued pacing around his apartment, wondering if he had tricked Lavinia into being with him somehow. He didn't know what she saw in him.

He was trying to be positive, to be full of light, the way Lavinia was, but it was hard. It felt like he was playing a long con. He didn't like it.

She was the easiest person in the world to love. Who wouldn't love her? But just because he loved her, did he deserve her?

She deserved a fairy-tale love story, with a knight or a prince or a lord, because she was just like the heroines of the romance movies she loved, beautiful and funny and clever, with such a big heart, and so full of life.

But there was nothing special about him. His own parents couldn't be bothered with him, which must have meant that, fundamentally, there was something wrong with him.

It was a stroke of pure luck that Lavinia had been his best friend for all these years and her family liked him, but being a friend was one thing and being a partner was another.

Guilt stabbed at him, and no matter how he tried to ignore it, the feeling wouldn't go away.

# CHAPTER 32

Because Theo hadn't visited home for a few months, his mother kept calling, and Lavinia suggested that perhaps he should go for a visit.

"Just for a little while," Lavinia said. "And I can go with you! For moral support."

She hadn't seen his parents in years, probably not since high school. She didn't like them because they always made Theo upset and because they didn't appreciate Theo, which was unfathomable to her. But she knew that Theo didn't want to cut them off entirely, and if he kept putting off a meeting, he'd only get more agitated every time his mother called.

"I don't know," Theo said, rubbing a hand over his face.

It was late at night, and they were sitting on the couch in his apartment. She was wearing one of his flannel shirts and a pair of his socks. Her legs were draped over his lap. She had a drawer of things at his place, but she still liked stealing his clothes.

He was wearing fleece shorts and nothing else. He absentmindedly drummed his fingers over her bare legs.

"I do have to visit, though," he said.

"So I'll go with you!" she replied.

He frowned. "It's going to be miserable."

"So we'll be miserable together."

That made him smile, though he still hesitated. Finally, he sighed. "Alright. But don't say I didn't warn you."

So, the next weekend, at the end of November, she got ready at her place and he picked her up. When she got in his car, she noticed that he looked different. He was wearing a sweater and slacks, his hair combed neatly. She resisted the urge to run her hands through his hair and ruin it.

"You look nice," she said, reaching over to kiss his cheek. He gave her a tense smile.

"You do, too," he said. He squeezed her thigh. She was wearing a sweater dress and little heels, her hair pulled back in a fishtail braid that Beena had done for her. "Ready?"

"Let's go," she said.

He drove her to his parents' place, the house he'd grown up in. It was strange coming back here after so many years, but it must have been stranger still for Theo. All those memories.

She thought back to the day he had fallen from the apple tree; all that blood, all those tears. She shuddered, holding Theo's arm tighter as they made it to the front door. Theo took in a deep breath, then knocked on the door.

A moment later, the front door opened to reveal Amaya, Theo's mother.

"Theo, hello!" she said, smiling. "And you must be Lavinia. Come in."

She was a thin woman with warm brown skin, and she ushered them in. Her outfit was simple and elegant, a midi skirt and turtleneck sweater. Lavinia saw, when she entered the house, that it was similarly decorated in a clean and sophisticated fashion.

"Hey," Theo said. Amaya squeezed his arm.

"Thank you for having us," Lavinia said, wondering if she should hug Amaya or not. Probably not, since she hadn't even hugged her own son.

"Of course," Amaya said, taking their coats. "It's been so long."

She led them into the house, and Theo's father, Rishi, appeared.

"Theo," he said, shaking Theo's hand. It was jarring for Lavinia to see; she was so used to Theo hugging her parents hello, yet his own parents were so cold. Rishi shook Lavinia's hand next, then said, "Come, let's eat."

He led them to the dining room, the sound of their shoes clicking on the tile floors. Amaya returned after putting away their coats. The table was already set, the food in closed dishes. Amaya must have set the food out just before they arrived because—when she lifted the lids—steam rose from the dishes.

It was a good thing she and Theo had been on time. Lavinia had prepared for tonight to be different than what she was used to at her own home, but that didn't stop the experience from being unsettling.

"Please, begin," Amaya said, gesturing to Lavinia. She nodded, plating rice and a beef curry onto her plate, which she thought was an interesting choice. Theo didn't like beef curries; Beena never made them if she knew Theo was coming over.

After Lavinia had served herself, the others took their helpings as well. Theo's plate hardly had any food on it, and

Lavinia waited for Amaya to scold him, urging him to take more the way Beena and Garrett did, but Amaya was silent.

"Water?" Rishi asked Lavinia, holding up the crystal pitcher.

"Yes, please," she replied, holding out her glass.

He poured her water, then asked, "Tell me, what do you do?"

"I'm in veterinary school," Lavinia said.

Rishi's eyes brightened at that. "A wonderful profession," he said. "Quite competitive, too, from what I hear. You must be terribly clever."

Lavinia didn't know how to respond to that. "Oh, uh, thank you," she said, smiling.

They ate dinner, and it was worse than she had expected, though she did have low expectations to begin with. His parents were normal, polite and nice, even, but they were just so quiet.

She could hear the clattering of the utensils against the plates, and every little noise was amplified. It made her want to be quiet, too. She felt awkward. The room was almost stifling.

Worse, Theo was so drawn into himself. She hadn't seen him like that, not for a long time, not since they were kids. It reminded her of the first day she had visited him after his knee injury, how depressed he had been.

It was horrible to see him like this again, as if he was bracing himself for blows. She didn't realize it would be like this, or she would have never suggested coming.

Amaya and Rishi didn't seem to care about Theo much. They asked Lavinia questions about her work at the Animal Hospital, what courses she was taking for her veterinary degree, but she could tell it was because they were impressed by her career path.

"You've got such a good head on your shoulders," Amaya

said. "You could teach Theo a thing or two." She smiled as if she was teasing, but Lavinia did not think she was.

"I don't think Theo needs any tips from me," Lavinia replied, her smile tight. "He does well on his own."

Rishi chuckled, as if she was being silly, and Lavinia's eye twitched. She tried not to show that she was upset or angry, but the emotions simmered inside of her. Clenching her jaw, she took a long sip of water, hoping to cool down.

She wanted to tuck Theo into her pocket and steal away with him, keep him safe forever. She didn't say anything to his parents because she knew it would only hurt Theo. He did love them, in a way, and—in the end—they were his parents. It was why they were here at all.

Luckily, they all finished dinner soon thereafter. Amaya went to get dessert, and Lavinia set down her napkin. "Where's the bathroom?" she asked, needing a breather.

"Across from the stairs," Rishi told her. "I left the light on, so it should be easy to find."

She nodded and excused herself, trying to take light steps because her footsteps sounded so loud in his big, empty house. She made it to the bathroom, closing the door behind her.

Looking in the mirror, she released a long breath. "Good lord," she muttered to herself. She had brought her phone with her and checked the time now. It had only been forty-five minutes, but it felt like hours had passed.

Feeling unsettled, she texted her mom. Beena knew what Theo's parents were like, and Lavinia needed to discuss this with *someone*. Beena replied back and they texted a bit, though they'd have a full debrief later. Right now, Lavinia needed to get back; she didn't want Theo to think she'd abandoned him.

She washed her hands, dried them, then headed back out, a smile ready on her face when she entered the dining room. As she sat back down beside Theo, she noticed that he was deadly silent, staring at his plate with blank eyes.

Her smile dimmed. She wondered if his parents had said something while she was in the bathroom, but she couldn't ask right now.

Amaya brought out the dessert, a fruit trifle that they ate in silence, and once that was done, Theo stood.

"Thanks for dinner," he said, giving his parents a tight smile.

Lavinia stood as well. "Yes, thank you so much," she said. "Everything was lovely."

"Thank you for coming," Amaya said, smiling at both of them. Rishi walked them to the door while Amaya grabbed their coats.

Theo and Lavinia slipped their coats on, then headed out; once they were outside, Lavinia released a long breath, glad that it was over. They walked to his car, the night chilly. Lavinia huddled close to Theo, holding his arm.

"Did they say something to you?" she asked. He shook his head.

He was being startlingly quiet, and it hurt her to see him like this. She didn't understand how his parents couldn't see how remarkable their son was.

In the fantasy shows and movies that Theo liked, there was always a character who was pure of heart and good, a shining light against evil, and Lavinia thought that Theo embodied that perfectly.

She loved him so much, and she had for so long, it was hard to discern when that love shifted to develop into something deeper than just friendship. He was so easy to love, she didn't understand how his parents didn't love him—but that was a fault in them, not him.

They reached his car, and before Theo could go around to the driver's seat, she held him back.

"I love you," she said, rising onto her tiptoes to kiss his cheek.

"I love you, too," he whispered, gathering her into his arms. She hugged him. He held onto her tight, and she heard the sound of his ragged breath. He was trembling, and her heart broke.

After a little while, he pulled back and gave her a weak smile. It didn't quite reach his eyes, and she saw that he had retreated somewhere she couldn't follow. She didn't know what to say.

He opened the car door for her. She got in, and then he did as well, driving her back to her place.

"Do you want to come in?" she asked. He shook his head, staring ahead. Her heart sank. "Okay, get some rest."

She knew he just needed some time, and then he would be fine.

But things weren't fine.

The entire week, he was quiet and distant, not just as her lover but as her friend. He was moving farther and farther away from her, disappearing like a fading echo. They hardly touched or talked, which was devastating, especially after those days being entwined in every way.

*Maybe he needs more time*, she told herself.

But the next weekend, he still wasn't doing any better, and suddenly, she was scared.

She could see that he was unhappy, and she didn't think it was just the meeting with his parents that had caused it, because that was a week ago, now. She thought about what Beena had said, about not letting things between them go sour. How there was nothing wrong with being just friends.

It felt like there was something going on that Theo was too afraid to tell her.

Dread curdled her stomach as the possibility entered her mind: Was he unhappy with *her*?

# CHAPTER 33

Theo knew it was a bad idea to see his family.

It went as badly as he had expected, but it was worse because Lavinia was there to witness it. Surely now she saw how much he didn't deserve her.

It was over a week ago, but Theo couldn't get his father's voice out of his head. During the dinner, when Lavinia had gone to the bathroom, Rishi had turned to Theo, curious.

"Lavinia is such a lovely girl, so accomplished and clever, what is she doing—" Rishi started, but broke off as Amaya touched his hand. Theo already knew what Rishi would have said.

*What is she doing with* you?

He had asked himself that question dozens of times during the past week, the words playing on a loop in his head. Theo didn't deserve her, and Lavinia would realize that soon. More and more, he felt like he had tricked her into being with him, and the thought made him sick.

He needed to be a worthy partner. Lavinia wanted a perfect relationship, like the one her parents had. She looked up to them, held them as her standard, and he did, too, but could he be that perfect? He knew that Lavinia was, already, she always had been, but *him?*

He heard his father's voice: *What is she doing with* you?

Theo felt himself growing distant, not like himself, but he didn't know how to stop. He knew he should have been over it by then, and usually his parents' comments didn't bother him for so long, but this was different. This had to do with Lavinia.

The insecurity was eating at him, and he couldn't bring it up to her, as if once he brought it up to her, she, too, would ask the same question: *What* am *I doing with you?*

So he stayed silent.

He was with Lavinia now at his place. It was Sunday, and he had been quiet all day. He knew he should have been more attentive, but he was still in pain from meeting his parents, and he couldn't manage it.

Lavinia suggested doing a few different things, but he didn't want to, and so they ended up marathon-watching a television show all day. She made her usual commentary, but Theo couldn't find the energy to respond.

He let her choose what to watch, saying he didn't have a preference. He hoped letting her choose would make her happy, but she seemed irritated, silently stewing. He knew he should ask her what was bothering her, but he was afraid she would say: *you.*

For dinner, they ordered pizza, but he had no appetite.

"Don't you want to eat?" Lavinia asked, gesturing to his untouched plate. He set it on the table.

"Maybe later," he said.

He was so in his head that he didn't realize until after the movie was done that Lavinia hadn't eaten, either. Guilt gnawed at him. He wanted to tell her that she should eat. He tried to come up with something to make it up to her for being so lame all day, but she got up before he got the chance.

Taking a deep breath, she stood, and he saw she was frowning. He was just realizing now that she had been quiet for the past hour. She nibbled on her bottom lip, and he could almost hear her thinking. Then, she swallowed and turned to him.

"You're unhappy," she said.

She could always read him so well. He stood, sighing, and she looked up at him with big brown eyes. "Yes," he replied, and her face flashed with pain. "I'm sorry."

"No, don't apologize." She lifted her chin, forcing a smile. "It isn't your fault. I understand."

He let out a breath, relieved. He knew she'd understand; she knew about his difficult relationship with his parents, after all.

"Thank you," he said, running a hand through his hair. "I didn't know how to bring it up—"

"You don't want to be with me, and that's okay," she said. "We should go back to being friends."

Theo's heart stopped, his brain short-circuiting at her words. He thought for sure he had heard her wrong, but then he saw the tears in her eyes.

"What?" he asked, confused. It was taking him some time to digest what she had said, to understand what was happening. Had he fallen asleep? Was this a nightmare? He pinched his arm, but no, he was awake. He was still processing her words as she fled toward the door.

"It's okay, really," she said, voice breaking. She put on her shoes, her back to him. "I have to go."

"Wait!" he cried, grabbing her hand. "What are you saying? Lavinia, what are you doing?" She wouldn't look at him, her cheeks wet with tears.

"We don't work like this," she said, voice defeated as she stared at her shoes. "We should go back to how it was." Her body was shaking.

"Don't do this," he said.

"I'm sorry," she said, and she ran.

Theo went after her, calling her name as she ran down the hallway toward the stairwell, but she didn't stop. He didn't want to force her to talk to him, not when she was so clearly in pain.

Pain that *he* had caused.

She had finally caught on to what a dead weight he was and was swimming free while she still could. The realization made Theo stop in his tracks.

He went back to his apartment, searching for his phone. It was in his bedroom, and he dialed her number.

She didn't pick up.

His stomach turned; he was going to be sick. Tears pricked his eyes, and he tried to blink them away, a strange taste in his mouth.

It was over.

A heavy weight pushed against his sternum, and he gasped for breath. It felt physical in a way he had never experienced, his heart breaking. Like something was pushing and pushing, and his heart was splintering and splintering then . . . *crash!* It shattered.

He fell back onto his bed, trembling, and then he cried. The tears came down fast, and his bedroom blurred.

In the dim white light of his bedside lamp, he curled into a tight ball, utterly alone. He pressed his hands against his chest, as if that could keep the pieces of his heart together, but it did nothing.

Everything hurt.

# CHAPTER 34

Lavinia cried herself to sleep, then slept for hours and hours. She finally woke around one in the afternoon the next day, by which point she had missed most of her classes for the day, but she would worry about that later.

She pried her eyes open. She had been hit by a cab once while crossing the street, but this felt even worse than that—like being hit by a truck. Her body felt embedded in her mattress, as if last night she had slept in softened clay that had hardened come morning.

Lavinia attempted to move, but nothing happened. Perhaps she would be fossilized like this. She could end up in a museum with a tag: "Local Girl Lost Will to Live After Breakup".

She tried to get up a few more times, her limbs stiff, but she couldn't manage beyond pushing up to lean against the headboard. She grabbed her phone from the side table.

Releasing a long breath, Lavinia scrolled through the endless notifications she had, not reading any. She could hear her heartbeat very clearly, like someone was playing the drums right into her ears.

She had done the right thing, she reminded herself. Theo never would have done it; he would have stayed with her and been unhappy, just so he wouldn't have to hurt her feelings, and she loved him too much to allow that to happen.

Staying with him would have meant success for her—she would have met her self-imposed deadline—but she didn't care about any of that if he was miserable. She would rather be alone and dejected herself than see him unhappy.

With a whimper, Lavinia threw herself out of her bed, nearly falling. When she looked back, she half expected a mold to appear where she had lain, but of course, the mattress only held a small indent from where her body had been.

She grabbed her water bottle, downing half of it, then took a deep breath. Tears sprung in her eyes, and she swore, then started crying again. It hurt, all of this hurt. She loved him. Her heart could be so stupidly stubborn.

"Fuck's sake," she muttered, wiping her cheeks, which were starting to feel rough to the touch and not baby smooth as they usually were. She grabbed tissues and cleared her eyes and nose, trying to get it together.

There was no convincing herself she was fine—she wasn't, she absolutely wasn't—but she needed to keep going.

After about three tries, Lavinia made it out of her bedroom. Alfie was at school, while her parents were at work, and Biter was with Famke's caretakers. The entire house was quiet, swirls of dust shifting in the shafts of sunlight.

Lavinia went to the bathroom, and she was afraid to look in the mirror, but it was unavoidable. She caught a glimpse of her own face, and watched as her features broke into a sob once more, like a marble statue, crumbling.

"You're okay," she tried to tell herself, but her voice was rasped from sleep and crying.

"You're okay," she tried again, this time smoothing her dark hair, tucking it behind her ears. Her face was colorless and pale but her eyes were bloody red.

After freshening up, she felt slightly better, but as she went back to her room, tears began rolling down her cheeks again, so consistently that she almost didn't notice them, just like she didn't notice breathing.

She changed out of her pajamas and into something comfortable and dry, and it felt like she was moving through a gel because when she looked at the clock, an hour had passed. She opened her bedroom window, letting in a gust of frigid air.

She took a deep breath, until her lungs stung. Then, she went down to the kitchen. She hadn't eaten anything since lunch yesterday, but she wasn't hungry.

Even so, she knew she should have something, so she warmed up a glass of milk. After drinking the warm milk, she went back to her bedroom, where she saw one of Theo's flannel shirts hanging over her desk chair.

It was like a knife sliced clean through her, tearing at all the careful threads she had used to pull herself together to exist all day.

She began crying again. Feeling horrible, she slipped his flannel shirt on, then curled into bed once again. She just lay there, staring out the window, watching the clouds move and the sky darken as time slipped away.

A little after five o'clock, she heard the front door open downstairs, and dread coursed through her. She would have to face reality. Her family would ask her, and she would have to tell them the truth.

She listened to the sound of Biter's baby dragon babble as her parents and Alfie chatted downstairs, her parents done with work and Alfie done with football practice. Then, she heard footsteps coming up the stairs.

It was Beena; she must have seen the light on in Lavinia's room, and she approached. When she saw Lavinia in bed, she furrowed her brows, confused. Beena was in dark blue scrubs, her hair tied back in a braid. Just the sight of her mother's face made Lavinia want to start crying again. She burrowed deeper into bed.

"What are you doing home?" Beena asked, voice gentle. "Were classes canceled?"

"I didn't go today," Lavinia said, not moving. Her mother came and sat beside her, and Lavinia avoided her gaze.

"What's wrong?" she asked.

Lavinia closed her eyes, not wanting to see Beena's reaction. "Theo and I broke up," she somehow managed to respond, and then her voice broke. She had spent all this time trying not to think of it, but there it was. Her lip trembled, and tears rolled out of her closed eyes. "Please don't ask me about it."

"Okay, gudiya," her mother replied. She sounded calm, which was good. Beena got up and stroked Lavinia's hair. "I'll bring you something to eat."

Beena brought food up a little while later: a steaming bowl of hearty chicken corn soup. Lavinia hardly ate; her stomach hurt too much.

An hour later, Garrett came up to take the tray away, and Lavinia tried to give him a brave smile, failing miserably. He came over and kissed her cheek.

"Get some rest, pumpkin," he whispered.

Hours passed, and Lavinia hardly noticed. She heard the door creak open and sincerely hoped it wasn't her parents wanting to ask her about what had transpired. Luckily, it was only Alfie, in his pajamas. He was holding Biter, who was trying to jump out of his arms.

Alfie came over and deposited Biter on top of Lavinia's stomach, then turned to go to Lavinia's desk. As Lavinia petted the baby dragon's head, Alfie grabbed Lavinia's laptop from her desk and climbed onto her bed, getting under the covers with her. She turned her head, facing him.

"What?" she asked, voice small. He slid deeper into her bed, until they were at eye-level.

"Can we watch a movie?" he asked. Then, he reached under the blanket and she heard him rummaging around in his pockets. He pulled out candy, offering it to her.

Biter's eyes lit up, and she reached a paw out for the brightly wrapped candy, but Alfie tsked at her. "Biter, no," he said. "That's not for you. *This* is for you." He pulled out a chew toy from his other pocket, and Biter latched onto it, nibbling.

"It's a school night," Lavinia whispered. "You'll get in trouble."

He gave her a conspiratorial smile. "Don't tell."

She finally managed a small smile. "Okay," she said, sitting up a little. Alfie popped open her laptop, balancing it between them, and then put on a funny animated movie while Biter played with her toy.

She pressed her freezing feet against his leg, which had long since stopped fazing him, but this time he squealed, making her laugh with his dramatic reaction, which she knew was for her benefit. Biter squealed, too, and Alfie said, "Biter, sh!" Biter hissed at him, swiping at the air with her paw.

"There, there," Lavinia said, scratching Biter's chin. She relaxed, nestling comfortably in Lavinia's lap as they watched the movie. When it was done, she did feel a bit better.

Alfie closed the laptop, looking over at her. "Are you still sad?" he asked.

She nodded, tears welling in her eyes. "Only a little though," she said.

Alfie frowned. "Do you want me to sleep with you?"

She was hardly keeping it together, and she didn't want Alfie to see her at her lowest. She shook her head. "Otherwise Mama will find out about our movie night and she'll yell at us," she said.

"Oh yeah." He giggled.

"But I love you," she said.

"Love you, too." He hugged her tight.

"Take Biter to her bed, too," Lavinia said, and he scooped her up. The baby dragon was sleepy, too, and she yawned, flashing her teeth. Alfie and Biter left, leaving her alone.

Then it was time to sleep. She closed the lights and tried not to ache.

But as she lay there, she thought that this grief would last forever, that it would never go away. It felt like a rock lodged in her ribs, and she would never be able to push it out.

She would just have to carry it with her, wherever she went.

## CHAPTER 35

Lavinia carried on with work and school the next day, but she could hardly make it. It was early December and the days were short and cold.

In the living room that evening, she sat on the couch, hugging a pillow as she watched Biter sleep on a nest of pillows and blankets on the carpet. She tried to remind herself she had done the right thing, but it was hardly any consolation. She was so *sad*.

A few moments later, Beena entered, changed from her work clothes into a sweater and lounge pants. Lavinia was already in her pajamas for the night: fuzzy socks, sweatshorts, and an oversized sweatshirt.

"Hello, darling," Beena said, standing by the entrance of the living room.

"Hi," Lavinia replied, voice quiet. Beena came and sat down on the couch beside her, settling down against the pillows. Lavinia released a long breath, turning to face her mother. "I know, you're going to say I told you so," Lavinia said, laying the pillow flat on her lap. Beena was confused, and Lavinia continued. "You said not to let things get sour between us, and that's what happened. And everything is ruined." Lavinia's eyes welled up with tears.

"Oh, gudiya, nothing is ruined," Beena said, pulling Lavinia toward her. Lavinia sniffled, leaning against her mother's chest as Beena stroked her hair. "Your and Theo's relationship is so much stronger and deeper than all this. You'll get through this rough patch."

"What if we don't, Mama?" She was so scared.

"Sh, I know you will," Beena said. "Have more faith in yourself."

"How can I? When everyone leaves me in the end?" Theo hadn't, but he had *wanted* to, and so she had taken the step she knew he would be too anxious to take on his own.

Beena pulled back, and Lavinia looked up at her mother's furrowed brows. "That's not true," Beena said. "Where is that coming from?"

"It is," Lavinia said. "All my boyfriends have dumped me because they got tired of me. I'm easy to like but difficult to commit to."

Beena thought for a moment. "Think of all the people you love, the people in your life who have been there," she said. "They are committed to you. Saphira and Ginny and Theo—your oldest friend! He's been here through all your phases. We're your family so we're stuck with you, but Theo always *chose* to stay. He actively chose to be there, by your side."

Lavinia hadn't thought of it like that. Deep down, she knew that was true, but she had let her anxiety overwhelm her. What if she had latched onto this idea that she was easy to love but hard to commit to, when she could just choose to let that thought go and not let it affect her?

"It's all such a mess," Lavinia said, her head hurting. She didn't know *what* to think anymore. "I thought I would have it all figured out by now, the way you did."

Beena looked confused. "What do you mean 'the way I did?'"

"You and Daddy met the winter you were twenty-four," Lavinia said.

"Lavinia, you cannot put an arbitrary deadline on yourself!" Beena scolded. "Things happen in their own time. Everyone is different! Just because I met my future husband at a certain age doesn't mean that you must, too! It's much more important to be with the *right* person than to just be with anyone by a certain time. And you cannot compare yourself to me and your father; you can't compare yourself to anyone!"

Everything Beena was saying made perfect sense, and deep down, Lavinia knew these things. They weren't complete revelations. It was just a matter of choosing to believe in them rather than believe in all her anxiety-ridden ideals.

"Your love story is yours, it's unique and wholly specific to you," Beena continued, then paused. "And Theo. I only bring him up because I don't think that your story is over. What matters is that you love him and he loves you."

"Of course I love him," Lavinia said, and a lump rose in her throat. "But Mama, Theo was unhappy. That's why I broke up with him. I knew he would never do it himself, and I didn't want him to feel like he was stuck with me."

Beena was taken aback. "He told you he was unhappy?"

"Yes," Lavinia replied.

"Unhappy with *you*?" Beena clarified.

Lavinia paused. "Well . . ."

Her heartbeat quickened as she realized she had been so upset that day that she had perhaps jumped to a conclusion when she shouldn't have.

"Um," Lavinia said, sitting up. "I need to call Theo."

Beena smiled, kissing Lavinia's cheek. "Good idea."

Lavinia got off the couch, running up to her room for her phone. It was in her tote bag, and she'd left it on silent for the last two days, ignoring Theo even as he called, which she realized now was cowardly.

Trembling, Lavinia called Theo's number. Her hands shook as she held the phone up to her ear, listening as it rang. But he didn't pick up.

Lavinia tried calling again ten minutes later, but again, there was no answer. She was worried he was angry with her—as he should have been—for breaking up with him so callously even when he had asked her not to. She had done so out of fear, but she didn't want to be the type of person who let fear rule her.

She wanted to be brave.

Grabbing her purse, Lavinia ran down the stairs, throwing on her coat and shoes, calling, "I'm going out!" before leaving her house. The wind was frigid. She screeched against the cold on her bare legs, closing the front of her coat as she ran to her car, adrenaline pumping through her.

Getting in, she drove directly to Theo's apartment, heading in and not waiting for the elevator. She ran up the stairs, going straight for his place.

She knocked on the door. "Theo!" she called. "I'm sorry! Theo!"

But there was no response. She put her ear to the door, listening. With a groan, she fished around her purse, searching for the spare key, then let herself in.

The apartment was empty.

She deflated.

She went to his bedroom. Her scrunchie was on top of his bedside table, and she touched a hand to it. She had noticed it the first day she'd been over, when he'd proudly showed her the drawer he'd emptied for her.

"I thought I'd lost this!" she had told him, and he had only smiled.

He had held onto it the entire time, this artifact from her.

She slipped it onto her wrist now, sitting on his bed, which was unmade.

Guilt pumped through her. She had doubted him and his feelings for her, when he had given her no cause to, and she had bolted at the first sign of trouble.

She hoped she could fix things—she knew she could. She *would*. She wouldn't stop until she had.

Lavinia sat and waited for him to return.

## CHAPTER 36

Theo had spent the last two days being miserable, but as he played back their last conversation for the fiftieth time, he finally realized something.

When she had said, "You're unhappy," she had been thinking that he was unhappy with *her*—which was entirely *not* what he had meant! Once he realized that this might have been a misunderstanding, he drove to her house.

He had been calling her for the last two days, but she hadn't picked up, and he figured she might need space, but screw that. He needed to see her.

Theo knocked on the door, and Beena answered.

"Theo, hello," she said, surprised. He hoped she didn't hate him. "Come in," she said, and Theo entered.

"Is Lavinia here?" he asked, looking around.

"She just left," Beena said.

"Ah fuck," Theo said, then winced. "Sorry."

"It's okay," Beena said, taking his arm with her free hand. "Come on, let's have a little chat."

She brought him to the family room, where Biter was

asleep in a nest of blankets. Theo sat down next to Beena on the couch.

"Why don't you tell me what happened?" she asked, eyes warm and patient. Theo gave her a rundown on the disastrous dinner at his parents' place, what they had said, how it had gotten into his head and made him be distant toward Lavinia.

"I know I don't deserve your daughter," Theo said, hanging his head.

"Hey." Beena lifted his chin so he would meet her eyes. "When people tell you that they love you, you have to believe them, or you end up in a situation like this. Has Lavinia ever made you feel like you don't deserve her?"

"No."

"What about me? And Garrett and Alfie. Have we ever made you feel less than?"

He shook his head, eyes welling up with tears.

"Then you just have to believe that we love you, that you *are* loved." She let go of his chin, but he kept her gaze. Her voice softened. "Even if your parents don't love you the way they should, you are still worthy of love and deserving of it."

Tears fell down his cheeks and he let out a shuddering breath, nodding. She was right. He couldn't shoot himself in the foot by letting his insecurities cloud his judgment, especially not if it meant losing Lavinia.

He needed to be brave.

"Understand?" Beena said.

"Yes." He stood, reaching over and kissing her cheek. "Thank you."

"Of course." She smiled, touching his face. "Lavinia left about twenty minutes ago, so you might still catch her at your place."

He nodded, making a run for it. He drove back home, bypassing the elevator and taking the steps two at a time to the fourth floor, heading straight for his apartment, hoping to see her waiting for him by the door.

But she wasn't there. He deflated, depressed. With a sigh, he let himself into the apartment.

And like a dream, she came out of his bedroom.

"Lavinia!" he cried, just as she called his name, and they met in the middle, crashing into each other. She wrapped her arms around his neck and he held her torso tight.

"I'm sorry," she said.

"No, I'm sorry," he said, pulling back to look into her teary eyes. "When you asked if I was unhappy—I wasn't unhappy with you! I could never be unhappy with you. You make me happier than I ever even knew was possible."

She sniffled. "You didn't get tired of me?"

"Tired of you?" He was astounded. "If I was going to get tired of you, it would have happened when we were eight, Lavinia. Since then you've stolen all my favorite flannel shirts, and your hands are always cold, and you make me watch all those romcoms, but no, I could never get tired of you, or any of those things, or any part of you. Take all my clothes—everything of mine is yours! And if your hands are cold, it means I can make it my mission to keep them warm, and I don't really mind those movies, since they teach me how to love you better."

Her lower lip trembled as her eyes welled with tears. "I know I can be stupid and delusional," Lavinia said, and he frowned.

"Lav, what are you saying? You're not stupid, or delusional, don't be mean to yourself, I don't like it!"

"Okay," she said. "Maybe I can get too in my head, sometimes."

"Me, too."

They both laughed, teary-eyed. He cupped her face in his hands and pulled her in for a searing kiss, opening her mouth against his, both of them snatching the other closer.

She pulled back, catching her breath, and he rested his forehead against hers, his heart hammering against his chest.

He looked into her eyes, brushing away the tears on her cheeks with his thumbs. "I know I'm not perfect, but I'm going to try to be better about not letting my insecurities get the better of me," he told her.

"Theo, you are perfect," she said, "you're perfect for me. You're my favorite person in the whole world. I can't live without you."

"I can't live without you either," he said. "I know you believe in fairy tales, and you deserve a prince or a knight in shining armor, and I'll be that for you because our story *is* a fairy tale. We've always been written for each other, since the very beginning, first as friends and now as something more." He kissed her again. "Lavinia, I love you completely and totally, in every way that a person can love. You're my best friend and my lover and my partner and my soul mate and my match—you're the reason I live!"

"Really?" she asked, eyes wide. She reached for his hands, entwining their fingers as she smiled. He smiled back at her.

"Really. Even when I was uncertain about the future, there was one thing I was always certain of when I thought of what was to come, and that was you," he said. She released a long breath, stepping forward to hug him. All the tension left his body as he held her against him, one hand in her hair and the other on her back as her hands slid up his shoulder blades.

"I'm sorry for being scared and running away," she said,

pulling back to look up at him again. "You're everything to me. If I don't have you, I don't have anything. I love you so much. And you're wrong—I don't need a prince, or a knight in shining armor, or a lord. I just need you, my best friend, Theo, exactly as you are, exactly as you've always been. To me, you're enough. You're more than enough, and you always have been."

Then it was his turn to get teary-eyed, though they were both smiling as well as crying. He pulled her in for another kiss, then scooped her up princess-style.

She giggled against his mouth, and he carried her to his room, gently setting her down on the bed. It had only been two days, but he had missed her keenly.

She looked up at him from under dark lashes, pulling him on top of her, and the feel of her body beneath his was a wondrous relief, like finally he was back where he belonged.

Desire spread through him, and he kissed her harder. She made a desperate sound and opened her mouth against his, her hands tugging at his clothes. They undressed each other until they were both bare.

He slipped his tongue into her mouth as they kissed, his hands moving across her skin, feeling every soft curve and contour, tasting every shudder and gasp. She twined her hands into his hair, wrapping the locks around his fingers, their lips fused as he settled over her.

They moved together, holding on as if they would never let each other go again.

# EPILOGUE

The winter came and passed, and in May, the renovations at the Baby Dragon Cafe were finally completed. Saphira hosted a private party the night before the big launch, and she invited the people she loved most: Aiden, Genevieve, Emmeline, Lavinia, and Theo.

Of course, there were dragons in attendance as well: Sparky, along with Genevieve's baby dragon, Fang, who had been hatched in December and was now six months old and quite mischievous.

They sat together on the side now, black-scaled wings folded behind them. Sparky was almost triple the size of Fang, keeping the six-month-old in check as they both sipped draggiatos, the new dragon-specific drink that Saphira had concocted specifically for her reptilian patrons.

They were all upstairs, in the newly renovated second floor of the cafe. One wall was covered in floor-to-ceiling windows, giving them a gorgeous view of the night sky outside Main Street, the thousands of stars glittering above them.

Saphira walked to the front of the cafe, Aiden by her side. Saphira wore a beautiful pink sundress, and as she held up a glass of champagne, Lavinia squeezed Theo's arm, looking up at him with stars in her eyes.

"Before the official opening tomorrow, I'd love to make a toast to all you, my loved ones, for helping out during this period of change," Saphira said. Then, she looked at Theo. "But I'd like to especially thank my managerial assistant, for so flawlessly overseeing this project. The cafe could not have grown without you." She raised her glass. "To Theo."

"To Theo," they all chimed. Theo's cheeks turned pink, and he held a hand to his heart in gratitude, bowing his head.

"Okay, now everyone eat and have fun!" Saphira said, turning to kiss Aiden. He pulled her closer, and Lavinia turned to Theo.

Being with Theo was even better than all the love stories and love songs she adored because this was real—this was hers. Theo was hers.

"I'm so proud of you," she said, going up on to her tiptoes to kiss his cheek. He smiled, and she saw that finally, he was proud of himself, too.

It had taken time and effort, and he had cut off contact with his parents because they only made him feel bad, but now, Theo was much more confident in himself.

"Thank you," he said, kissing the back of her hand. "I'm exhausted, but it's amazing to see the cafe now, after everything. I really did that."

"You did!" She laughed, and he laughed with her.

"I couldn't have made it this far without you," he said, pulling her into his side. She hugged him, leaning against his chest.

Things changed, and would continue to change, but as long as they had each other, there was nothing they couldn't handle.

# ACKNOWLEDGMENTS

Alhamdulillah; that's book seven, which feels a little unreal! Thank you for returning to Starshine Valley with me, and I hope you'll stick around for the next story, too! Emmeline can't wait for the attention to be hers.

This story would not exist without the tireless effort of everyone who worked with me behind the scenes, so thanks are in order. Thank you to my incredible agents, Victoria Marini and Sheyla Knigge. Thank you to my astounding editor, Amy Mae Baxter, who I love working with; let's do a million more books together, thanks! Thank you to Penny Isaac for your incredibly thorough copyedit. Thank you to Anne O'Brien for your wonderful proofread.

Thank you to the entire team at Avon UK for bringing this book to life. Thank you to Emily Langford and Ellie Game for the cover and interior design. Thank you to Alex Cabal for the cover illustration. Thank you to Emily Hall and Jessie Whitehead in Marketing for your work promoting my book. Thank you to Katie Buckley, on the sales team, and the entire team at Harper 360 for getting this work out in the US:

Emily Gerber, Sophia Wilhelm, Jean-Marie Kelly and Angela Thomson.

Thank you to my family: Mama, Baba, Sameer, Zaineb, and Ibraheem. Thank you to my best-friend-cousins: Hamnah, Umaymah, Noor, and Mahum. Thank you to my best friends: Arusa, Isra, Sara, and Justine. I love, love, love you all!

Thank you to early readers, Famke and Zai. Thank you to anyone who's read my work or spread the word; I appreciate it deeply.

Please pray for me. Until next time. xx

# Loved *The Baby Dragon Bakery*? Don't miss this exclusive first look at *The Baby Dragon Bookshop*!

## CHAPTER 1

Snow fell from the sky in thick clumps, blanketing the hills of Starshine Valley. Emmeline Sterling watched from the window as the snowflakes fluttered down, a steady stream of white against the cold and dark night.

Winter was always her favorite season, but there was no time to appreciate the season's beauty now. Taking a deep breath, she returned to her task: she needed to find a needle and thread.

"Aha!" she spoke aloud in the empty bedroom, spotting what she was looking for in the dresser drawer. "There you are." She grabbed the needle and thread in one hand, shutting the drawer with a snap.

Her heels clicked on the marble floors as she exited the bedroom, joining the sounds of the party raging below: the clinking of champagne flutes, the quick melody of music, the laughter and chatter. Wind whistled outside the great Sterling estate, home of Emmeline's only paternal uncle and favorite cousins.

She was here for her youngest cousin, Genevieve, today. Ginny was throwing a combined birthday party for herself and her baby dragon, Fang, who just turned one year old. Only the most enthusiastic threw parties for their baby dragons, and Ginny was enthusiastic indeed.

Emmeline walked down the stairs, back to the party, where Ginny and Fang were attached at the hip, even now; as most of the dragons played outside in the snow, Fang never strayed more than half a foot away from Ginny. His black scales glimmered under the lights, his purple eyes adoring as he looked over at his rider. Dressed in a black velvet jumpsuit, her dark hair pulled back in a neat fishtail braid, Ginny looked at her baby dragon with equal affection.

The party was in the ballroom, which was used for in the winter months, when it was too cold to have parties outside on the grounds. Emmeline weaved her way through the joyous crowd; through the big windows on the end of the ballroom, the snow fell down faster. As Emmeline searched for her aunt, she was stopped by cousins who wanted to say hello and ask her advice on various topics, then she paused to ruffle nieces' and nephews' hair.

She petted baby dragons and evaded uncles' questions and kissed aunts' cheeks, before finally, *finally* making it to the other end of the ballroom, where her aunt was seated at one of the tables, her mood twice as sour as the citrus souffle served for dessert.

"I'm back!" Emmeline said, sitting down on the empty chair beside Auntie Marie, the eldest of the Sterling siblings. She wore a sleeveless navy blue sheath dress with an embroidered shawl around her shoulders, her dark hair pulled up in a neat twist to reveal the pearls on her ears and necklace.

"Darling, there you are," Marie said, clutching her shawl around her arms tighter. She leaned in close, dropping her voice. "Did you find it?"

"Yes, Auntie," Emmeline replied. She held up the needle and thread, and Marie released an exhale. She dropped her shawl from one shoulder, revealing a slight tear in the seam on the dress's shoulder. Emmeline quickly threaded the needle and got to work.

"I will be having *words* with my tailor," Marie fussed, brows crinkled with distress. "I cannot imagine how such a thing could have occurred."

"Don't worry," Emmeline coaxed, fingers moving quickly. "Just a moment and you'll be back on the dancefloor with Grandad."

Emmeline winked, and Marie finally smiled.

"Your grandad needs to share his secrets with the rest of us," Marie said, shaking her head. "I have no idea how his knees haven't given out!"

"All done!" Emmeline said, finishing off the stitch. She pulled a compact mirror from her purse, then opened it for Marie to see.

"Excellent," Marie said, and warmth spread through Emmeline's chest. She stood, offering her aunt her hand.

"Can I get you anything else?" Emmeline asked.

"Get me a coffee, dear," Marie said. "All that tension has given me a headache."

"Of course." Emmeline set off, finding a waiter on the sidelines to bring Marie her coffee. "Decaf, with two creams," she instructed. If Marie had caffeine this late at night, she'd never be able to fall asleep.

The waiter nodded, heading off to complete the order, and Emmeline scanned the room, catching sight of a table full of discarded dishes. She tsked, then stalked over to another member of the staff. "Can you please pick up the dishes from that table?" she asked, pointing it out.

Then, there was a spilled drink, and Emmeline had to make sure that got cleaned up before somebody slipped. All night, she'd been keeping her eyes peeled, and little things kept popping up.

Releasing a sigh, Emmeline rubbed her temples. Luckily, the party was almost over, and with it, the tension of the last few weeks would be over, as well.

When Ginny had asked Emmeline to help with throwing the joint birthday party, of course Emmeline had said yes, even though Ginny's mother, Cecilia, was well-versed in throwing such parties.

"I can't ask my Mum because you know she will just do too much," Ginny had explained.

"Don't worry," Emmeline had replied. "I'll handle it."

She had spent the last few weeks organizing it all, and the party had gone off without a hitch, which was to be expected. Emmeline Sterling never failed. Things always went flawlessly according to plan, and everyone had complimented her all evening for such a job well done.

She was used to the praise, but still it warmed her, and she tried to hold onto that now as her head pounded. Eyes scanning the ballroom, she looked around at her expansive family, taking in the sight of laughing children and couples holding hands, cousins jesting and aunts scheming.

Emmeline smiled to herself. The Sterling clan was big; she had three aunts and one uncle—Edmund, Ginny's father—and then Emmeline's father, Charles, was the youngest of his siblings. The offspring were then divided into two sections: the older ones in their late thirties and early forties who were married with children, and then the younger ones who were all in their mid to late twenties or early thirties.

In the younger section, Aiden was the oldest, then Emmeline, but Aiden was a bit reclusive, so it was Emmeline who took care of everyone and everything. While she did love being there for people, she was growing tired.

She thought of stealing away for a moment, but just as she turned, she caught two of her nephews arguing, little faces turning red. With a sigh, she walked over to them, crouching down to grab hold of both their shoulders.

"Hey, you two," she said, and the five and six-year-olds turned to her.

"He won't play with me!" the younger of the two complained, lip wobbling.

"You keep cheating!" the older one told Emmeline.

It was well past both of their bedtimes.

"Why don't you go find your mothers, hm?" Emmeline suggested. "I think there's hot chocolate."

Both little boys forgot their argument. "With marshmallows?" the younger one asked.

"With marshmallows," Emmeline confirmed, standing up straight again.

"Race you!" the six-year-old said, and then they were off. Emmeline watched as they ran into the crow, past a familiar face.

"Emmeline!" Saphira called, spotting her. She waved, and Emmeline went to where Saphira stood with Aiden. Saphira was one of the newest additions to the Sterling clan, as the massive engagement ring stacked with a diamond wedding band would attest to.

The sweet owner of The Baby Dragon Cafe was dressed in a flowy midi dress in a deep pink color, her wavy black hair styled in a complicated updo—which must have been courtesy of her mother-in-law. Ginny had always been boyish, and Cecilia had long since yearned for a daughter-in-law who would allow Cecilia to dress her up. Saphira had a girly and romantic style and thus happily obliged.

Her dress was accessorized with a stack of gold bangles and a simple nose-pin, both of which she always wore, as well as heels that had since been kicked off, as Saphira was now barefoot.

The couple smiled as she walked over to them.

"I feel like I haven't seen you all night!" Saphira said. One of her arms was around Aiden's waist as she was tucked into his side, but with her free hand, she reached for Emmeline.

"Oh, you know me," Emmeline replied, pulling Saphira out of Aiden's arms and twirling her. Saphira laughed.

"Hey, don't steal my dance partner," Aiden objected, wrapping his arms around his wife from behind. She giggled, leaning back against his chest as she held his bare forearm. The sleeves of his white dress shirt were rolled up.

Without heels, Saphira was average height, considerably shorter than Emmeline, who was around the same height as Aiden when she was wearing heels. While he was an even six-feet tall, Emmeline was two inches shorter, but Saphira was more than half a foot shorter and as such, she fit adorably in Aiden's arms.

Emmeline wrinkled her nose at them fondly. "You two are too cute."

Aiden smiled, while Saphira giggled.

"We're missing Millie tonight," Saphira said. Emmeline felt a slight stab in her chest at the mention of her little sister.

"I miss her, too," Emmeline replied.

She didn't have many close friends of her own—she had never needed any, not with a family as large as hers. She had always had a built in partner-in-crime in her sister, Milicent, who was a year younger than her. Unfortunately, Millie had gotten married a few years ago and moved hours away.

With three children and another on the way, she didn't visit more than a few times a year, and Emmeline sorely missed her, though she was used to the ache of it, now. Sometimes, it almost felt as if this was how it always was, and she was surprised to recall memories in which Millie lived in Starshine Valley. It was strange how when you got used to things changing, it almost felt as if the way things used to be hadn't happened at all.

Looking at Saphira now, Emmeline could barely recall a time in which she didn't know Saphira—the bright soul had quickly become like a close cousin to Emmeline. After all, Emmeline was Aiden's favorite cousin, and he was a very strong contender for being her favorite, as well, his rank only increasing ever since he had gotten together with Saphira, who Emmeline had technically known first, as Saphira sourced her coffee for the Baby Dragon from Emmeline's dragon-roasted coffee company, Inferno.

"She's due any day now, isn't she?" Aiden asked.

"Her babies are *so* cute!" Saphira said. Millie's son, Noah, was four while her daughter, Ira, was two.

"They take after me," Emmeline said proudly, lifting her chin. She and Millie often got confused for twins, and Millie's kids definitely took after their mother.

"You get all the credit then?" Aiden teased.

"Of course!" Emmeline replied. "I'm the one who told her, I said, 'Millie, you *must* marry a man with weak genes because if *my* nieces and nephews don't look like me, I will riot.' And then she did just that."

Saphira and Aiden both laughed. "I guess we need to find a man with weak genes for you," Saphira said.

Emmeline waved a hand. "Don't worry about me."

"Why are we worrying about Emmeline?" a familiar voice asked.

Emmeline turned to see Lavinia Williams join them. She was wearing a forest green dress that hugged her curves, along with platform heels that added a few inches to her short height. A delicate gold necklace hung from her neck; in the center was a small letter T.

The meaning behind the letter stood beside her: her boyfriend, Theo Noon. Tall and lanky, in slim black trousers and a neat white button-down shirt. They were holding mugs of hot chocolate in opposite hands while their other hands were clasped together, fingers entwined.

The pair were childhood best friends but had started dating last year. Lavinia used to work at the Baby Dragon, and Theo worked there as Saphira's business manager, as well as the bakery for the Baby Dragon Bakery, the bakery section of the cafe.

"We're not," Emmeline replied, shifting the focus away from how single she was. "We're more focused on how cute these two are."

"They're still in their honeymoon phase," Lavinia said.

"They've pretty much been in their honeymoon phase since they met," Emmeline replied, earning laughter from the rest of them. Aiden and Saphira didn't even attempt to disagree, they only looked at one another with stars in their eyes, lips turned up into smiles.

"*We* could be in our honeymoon phase, too, you know," Theo said, pinching Lavinia's side. She squealed.

"Stop trying to propose to me!" Lavinia hit his chest. "Not until I graduate in May!"

*What a problem to have*, Emmeline thought wryly, a painful twang reverberating in her chest. Lavinia and Saphira were both younger than her, and it was Ginny's twenty-second birthday, which made Emmeline feel *ancient* at twenty-nine, not at all helped by the fact that she was turning thirty in January with no possibility of a grand romance in sight.

She had only had one serious relationship post-university. Since then, she'd surely had her flirtations and her fun, but there didn't seem to be anybody who could pierce her very soul.

Shaking her head, Emmeline pushed the thought away before it sent her into a spiral. She focused on the conversation at hand.

"How's the ring hunt going?" Saphira asked Lavinia, who made a pensive sound.

"It's going," she said. "They're all just so pretty! I can't narrow down the shape."

Aiden and Theo exchanged a fondly amused glance over the girls' heads. Then the song changed; the chords made Saphira's eyes light up and Emmeline grin. It was one they both adored.

"Sorry, Aiden," Emmeline said, taking Saphira's hand, "but your girl is mine for this one."

She stole Saphira away, and Saphira grabbed Lavinia as she went, the girls walking over to the crowd of dancing partygoers. Across the dance floor, the birthday girl caught sight of them. Her mouth fell open, and she ran over.

"Wait for me!" Ginny cried. The girls opened their little

circle, pulling Ginny in as they danced together, laughing and having fun.

Until Emmeline caught the sight of flames in the corner of her eye.

"Uh oh," Lavinia said, slowing.

Emmeline narrowed her eyes. "Don't worry," she told the girls, catching Ginny's gaze. "I've got it."

With a squeeze of Ginny's hand, Emmeline was off, grabbing two members of the staff as she went. At the scene of the crime was Motu, her brother's baby dragon, who had lit a tablecloth on fire and was now watching the flames with shocked purple eyes.

"Motu!" Emmeline scolded, and the baby dragon immediately looked chagrined, hiding his face behind his wings. She tsked at him. As the staff members put out the fire, Emmeline knew it wasn't the baby who was at fault, but his rider. She scanned the crowd for Haris.

When she spotted him, he was laughing with their cousin Oliver and Emmeline's other brother, Naveed. Both her brothers looked like her, though their skin was a lighter shade of brown. Oliver caught Emmeline's gaze first, and he immediately stopped talking, elbowing Haris apprehensively. Emmeline crossed her arms against her chest as her younger brother followed Oliver's gaze, then swallowed. He slowly walked toward her.

"Uh—Everything okay, Emmy?" Haris asked, giving her a small smile. His dimples made an appearance. He was trying to be cute. She glared.

"You tell me," she said, voice sharp. Motu walked over to Haris, then, the draggo's little head hanging low. Haris was twenty-four and in medical school; he was not doing the best job training his baby dragon, who Emmeline ended up babysitting half the time anyway.

She had told him on a number of occasions not to hatch his egg whilst still in medical school, but had he listened? No. Sometimes, she really hated being right.

Haris had the decency to look embarrassed as he scooped Motu into his arms. Emmeline looked over at the burnt tablecloth the staff members were replacing,

"Look at Fang!" Emmeline scolded, gesturing to Ginny's well-behaved baby dragon calmly bopping her head to the music as she flapped her wings.

Even though Motu and Fang were a month apart—with Motu being the elder—Fang was much more well-trained. While Ginny devoted her time to Fang after graduating from university last May, accelerating Fang's training until he had his first flight at just seven months, whereas Motu had only had his first flight last month, and was still a bit rough around the edges due to Haris being too busy with medical school.

"Sorry," Haris said sheepishly. Emmeline gave him a dirty look. She didn't even need to say anything; the look was enough for her brother to understand how disappointed she was. He hung his head.

She took Motu from him, and the baby dragon came to her willingly, despite how she had scolded his rider. The little draggo knew their family dynamics.

Taking Motu away from the crowd, she went upstairs, where it was much quieter than the party going on in the ballroom. She passed by the living room to another section of the mansion, Motu touched a paw to her cheek, looking up at her with big purple eyes. Her heart softened.

"Your rider needs to be more responsible," she whispered to Motu, smushing his face. Motu flapped his wings. She laughed. "Come on."

She rang for a dragon caretaker to come look after the baby dragon, and a few moments later, one arrived, taking Motu from her. As the caretaker did so, the edge of Motu's wing flapped in her hair, which was twisted back to stay out of her face while she was running around.

The caretaker left with Motu, and Emmeline was alone. In the quiet, she sighed, and as she turned, she caught sight of herself in a gild-framed mirror.

She was wearing an off-the- shoulder dress with dramatic bell sleeves, the gown floor length but with a slit going up one thigh to reveal her strappy jeweled heels. While the outfit was still perfectly in place, her hair was coming undone. She pulled the hairpin out, and her hair cascaded down, falling to her hips. It was glossy and pitch-black, cut in long layers.

She shook her hair out, meeting her gaze in the reflection. Her kajal was a little smudged and her blood-red lipstick had faded, but she still looked immaculate. Rolling her shoulders, she adjusted her elaborate gold nose ring, her only jewelry, then headed back to the party.

And that was where she saw Luke Hayward.

Her enemy.

Emmeline stopped in her tracks before the living room, her heartbeat jumping violently. He was the only one up here, though he hadn't seemed to notice her just yet. Leaning against the wall, he was entranced with the view from the wide windows, watching the snow fall fast.

He was dressed in an all black suit, sans a tie, his black

dress shirt open at the collar to reveal the chains on his brown-skinned neck. It wasn't the only jewelry he wore; rings covered almost every finger, and there was an earring looping in one ear. His signature look.

For a moment, Emmeline thought she was hallucinating. She really must have been tired. She took a step forward, looking closer. There was no way he was here.

But then he must have heard her, and he turned. His dark eyes fell upon her and the devilish tilt of his lips sent sparks down her spine, informing her that he was in fact very much real.

"Hayward," she snapped, stalking over. He pushed off the wall easily, straightening. Emmeline had always been tall, and she was used to being one of the tallest in the room, especially with her high heels, but he was still taller, easily clearing six-foot-two. Another reason to hate him.

"Sterling," he said easily, eyes lighting with amusement.

Irritation burst through her as she stood before him. She didn't understand—what was he doing here? She had sent out the invites; she knew for certain he wasn't invited. He was not part of any of the Drakkon circles. He was a chimera-owner and lived in Bayview, down by the lake. Starshine Valley was divided into sections, and everyone tended to stay in their own part.

Except for him. He was always trying to poach her business. While her coffee was dragon-roasted, his was chimera-roasted. His business, Tempest, rivaled her. She had started her business straight out of university seven years ago and he had started his business about two years later, all but stealing her idea, though he applied it to chimeras.

He was a ruthless businessman—successful, gorgeous, and heartless.

She knew he was trouble from the first time she had heard about him, when she was a senior in college and Millie was a junior claiming to be in love.

"What are you doing here?" she asked.

"Maybe the birthday girl invited me," Luke replied, running a hand through his long black hair. A frisson of heat shot through her, but she promptly ignored it as a fierce protectiveness came over her.

She stepped toward him, poking his chest with a finger.

"Stay away from her," she snapped. "You've already broken one little sister's heart."

He cocked his head to the side, regarding her. His dark eyes were like charcoal, simmering with heat just beneath the surface, and his gaze pierced through her. "You got your revenge for that in kind, if I recall."

She feels a stab of guilt at that—though there was no reason for her to. Emmeline was not the kind of person who had regrets.

Luke's gaze dropped down to where her finger was still on his chest. He bit the air by her hand, and she snatched her hand as the sound of his teeth clamping shut sounded.

He looked up and met her horrified expression with a wolfish smile. Her pulse quickened, blood pounding through her veins like the beating of a drum.

She was about to do something drastic when she heard a voice say, "Ah, Luke, there you are."

If you loved *The Baby Dragon Bakery*, you can go back to where it all began with *The Baby Dragon Cafe*!

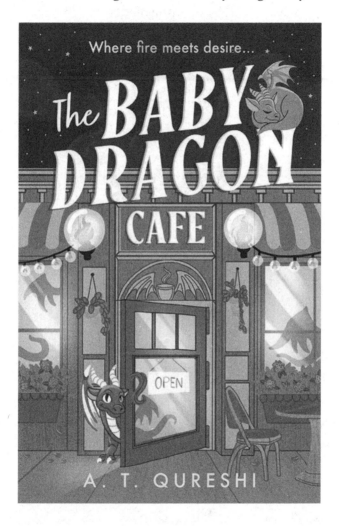

And in 2026 *The Baby Dragon Bookshop* will be opening its doors!

**COMING SOON**

# The BABY DRAGON BOOKSHOP

A. T. QURESHI